THE
WAVE

KRISTEN CRUSOE

Red Door

Published by RedDoor
www.reddoorpress.co.uk

ISBN 978-1-913062-50-7

A CIP catalogue record for this book is available from the British Library.

Cover design: Patrick Knowles
www.patrickknowlesdesign.com

Typesetting: Jen Parker, Fuzzy Flamingo
www.fuzzyflamingo.co.uk

Printed and bound in Denmark by Nørhaven

To my father, B. Dalton Crusoe, for everything

Prologue

The wave began in the Southern Ocean. Steep and intense, it toppled over and over until it escaped, became a swell, and traveled across the world, its fetch long and powerful. Wind and tide carried it north. The Coriolis effect pushed it back down towards the equator until it found its way into a small, quiet cove in the Pacific Northwest.

A young boy, dressed in a red superhero T-shirt and blue shorts, squatted beside a tide pool, his gaze focused on a snail edging towards a sea anemone. The boy watched as the anemone's tentacles swirled and reached out, as though tempting the snail to come into its embrace. The boy wanted to warn the snail, to reach into the pool of cold, clear water and save it. But his mommy had warned him not to touch the sea creatures because they might sting. He looked down the beach where she was lying on a towel, her head lowered, eyes on the book lying in front of her. He knew she couldn't see him but he always tried to do what she told him. So, he watched, concentrating on the snail's progress.

'Hurry little snail,' he said out loud. 'Turn around, come to me, you're getting too close to the creature.'

He could hear his father's voice. He sounded happy now, not like earlier this morning with Mommy. He was talking on his phone, walking away towards the caves at the far end of the cove. Seagulls cried out in excitement, skimming the waterline, gathering the feast left by the low tide. The gentle hymn of waves as they rolled onto the beach beyond soothed him. He never saw it coming, that one wave. A sneaker wave it was called. A swell that began in the Southern Ocean, traveled across the continent, landed on a beach in the North Pacific, and drew all it met back out to sea on its retreat.

PART ONE

Chapter 1

Clair

Dr Clair Mercer, after poisoning her husband, overdosed on vodka and sleeping pills, and then stumbled into the Pacific Ocean to drown. A man, fishing off the rocks nearby, saw her and called 911. Soon coast-guard helicopters, emergency ambulances, and police cars occupied the quiet cove. Noise, lights, and hands pressing down on her chest brought stark recognition of her reality.

Oh, God, she inwardly cried, *I'm alive*. A deep sadness, a longing for before. If only they would leave her the hell alone.

'Give her another amp of epi,' a male voice called out.

'Clear,' a female voice commanded.

'What's the story here?' A different male voice asked. 'Paramedics reported a cold-water immersion, near drowning, out at Seal Cove. What happened? Did she fall off the rocks? Swept off?'

Another voice – female, clipped, urgent: 'Fisherman reported seeing her walk right into the water. Called 911. Tried to reach her but couldn't. Coast-guard cutter was out doing training runs, so they were quick on the scene. Name's Clair Mercer according to the driver's license in her wallet. She left her purse containing ID, an empty bottle of Ambien, and empty vodka bottle on the beach. Looks like she meant to kill herself. She got bashed up against the rocks pretty bad but that kept her from being swept out to sea on the rip tide.'

'What's her core temp? Get that warming blanket going.'

Soon all the voices and words merged into one sound. She didn't want to let go of before, the feel of the ocean, cold at first then warm, welcoming. Where her boy had last been. She wanted to be with him. He had been so close, his energy translucent, hovering in the blue light just beyond reach. The lights above burned her eyes, sticky with salt. Tears formed and ran down her cheeks, spilling into the corners of her mouth, tasting like the ocean she had just been wrenched from. And what about Adam? What had happened to him? Was he alive? What if she really had killed him? A wave of dread so powerful that it made her retch, washed over her.

'She's vomiting,' a voice called out. 'Get me suction, now.'

Through her distorted vision, she could make out several faces, male, female, dressed in different colored scrubs. Off to the edge of the crowd around her body was a face like an angel. *Maybe I am dead,* she thought. Hair the color of light, pale and glimmering. Their eyes met for a second, then darkness covered her again. A cold she could not have imagined gripped her. Strong, like a force beyond this world. She was carried down, sight coming back now. Not sight with her eyes, but a primordial way of seeing through the lost eye. Light beamed through the pulsating waves, wrapping her in music. Unlike any music she had ever heard. Not horns, or strings. Percussion and bells. Her ears exploded, the sound rushing in to fill every neuron in her brain. The music cocooned her, lifting her up and tossing her into space. Crystals scattered, infinitesimal sparkles cascading all around her. Voices chanting ancient hymns drew her deeper and deeper, and then, a sudden jolt.

'Give her point five ketamine. Get her intubated, she's crashing!'

* * *

Time, misshapen, passed. Days, weeks, minutes, she didn't know. Transferred to the intensive care unit, Clair Mercer shunted between sedation and wakeful agitation until sleep, so deep it felt like dying again, consumed her. Soft voices, shoes sliding on linoleum floors, smells of bleach, alcohol, and plastic filled the space around her.

'Clair, good morning. My name is Elaine. I'm your nurse today. You're in the intensive care unit. You've been here for two days, on a ventilator. That's the tube you feel in your throat. You were in an accident, in the water. You're much better now. Clair, please, open your eyes. We're going to remove the tube this morning.'

Clair recognized the voice, felt a warm hand on her arm. She gagged, coughed, feeling the tube in her throat being removed, soft hands moving her gently from side to side, a warm cloth wiping her face, arms, hands. Surrendering to the light filtering in through the curtains across the room, she could almost imagine she was home, in her own bed, except for the beep, beep, beeping of the monitors tracking her every heartbeat and breath. She could see through the glass door at the end of her bed. Bodies moving quickly, the squeaking of rubber-soled shoes mixing with light laughter and early morning conversation.

A sudden swish, the curtain pulled across a metal rod, and

a figure emerged from the shadow. A woman, short, sturdy, with a stethoscope draped around her neck walked up to Clair's bedside, took her hand at the wrist, feeling her pulse. Watching the monitor as she did, she quickly glanced down at Clair.

'Ah, good morning. I see you're awake. I'm Dr Hawk. How are you feeling? Any pain, shortness of breath?'

Looking up at the doctor's smiling face, Clair felt comforted. But it didn't last. Awakening brought remembering. Waves of grief, loss, and terror washed over her. *Did I really kill my husband? Do they know? Am I going to jail?* A moan, cry, animal-like in its intensity escaped her throat. Curling into her side, drawing her knees up, holding her face in her hands, she cried, 'No, no, this can't be, please don't let it be.' Over and over, this litany of sorrow rocked her back and forth in the bed.

Another woman stepped quietly into the room. Tall, slender, with white blonde hair, she sat in a chair beside Clair's bed. Nodding at the doctor, she said, 'I'll sit with her now.'

'Hello Clair, my name is Dr. Juliette Taylor, but please, call me Jet. I'm a psychologist and I will be working with you. Once you're able to leave the ICU, we'll transfer you to our psychiatric unit, where you will be safe. How does that sound?'

Looking away, her eyes searching for an escape outside the window, Clair saw an airplane soaring past towards the small airport near the sea.

'Do I have a choice?' she asked, watching the plane disappear into the marine layer, as it circled for a landing.

'Clair, you are on a Hospital Hold, which means that we can keep you for treatment, for up to five business days. This sounds harsh, I know, but it is so that we can perform an evaluation, to determine if you continue to be a danger to yourself, or anyone else. So, no, you don't have a choice about coming to the psychiatric unit, but you do have a choice in how you engage with us there, to help yourself get better.'

Jet stood, looked at Dr. Hawk.

'Thank you, Jet. She's medically cleared so she can go anytime,' Dr Hawk said, walking back out into the busy ICU. 'What a terrible tragedy.'

***

Clair sat frozen in place, feeling like her body hovered a few feet away. If she glanced out of the corner of her eye, she thought she might catch a glimpse of herself, unraveling like a spool of yarn across the blue-carpeted floor. She looked up at the face of the woman sitting across the narrow rectangular room, lined with chairs in fabrics made to sustain hard wear and tear from humans under immense stress. They were close. Clair shifted in her seat, turning her body away. She wrapped her arms around herself, then folded her hands into her lap.

'I don't know where to begin,' she said, chewing the inside of her cheek.

'Start from the beginning,' Jet said, a half-smile on her face.

'But which beginning?' Clair asked.

Gazing out of the window at the bright spring morning, a testament to the futility of her rage, her fury, she felt a burning in her core like an ember deep inside, searing her heart. She wanted wind, lashing rain, deluge, and flood. Thunder, lightning. Anything other than this quiet room, with its pale, ivory walls and this woman who radiated such kindness and compassion. How had she gotten here, to this place? This was not supposed to happen. She was supposed to be dead, washed out to sea. And him, he was supposed to be dead too – a long, painful dying that would remind him of what he had done. Over and over with each rasping breath. She was not supposed to live, to be locked up, being helped when she knew she was helpless.

Still she sat, eyes vacant, staring at a marine painting on the wall over Jet's head. A scene that was meant to bring a sense of joy, peace. For Clair, it brought only horror. She sank deeper into silence. Sounds of the psychiatric unit broke into the stillness. Breakfast was being carted away. The paper plates and plastic utensils, Thermoses of coffee, still caffeinated at this time of day, and other detritus of mealtime for twenty or more patients, all struggling to fit into a normal routine. First breakfast, then hygiene, then morning group. Clair refused it all. She hadn't eaten in two days, taking only sips of water. Refusing medications. Speaking in short staccato responses to questions. Yes. No, I don't know. I don't care. She had been served with a notice of involuntary commitment. Offered an attorney. A hearing was scheduled, to determine competency to stand trial for the attempted murder of her husband. They said she had to talk, to tell her story. It would help her. Still she remained silent, until now. Something about this woman, Jet, opened her up. Clair thought she knew her from before. But couldn't remember. That hair, white blonde, wrapping around a heart-shaped face; dark eyebrows and eyes deep blue and discerning. A large yellow dog sat on its haunches in the corner. Jet had introduced her as Maggie, a therapy dog. She locked eyes with the dog, then feeling such unconditional kindness emanating from her, looked away. It was all just too much. This being alive.

Clair's breath came ragged, remnants of the endotracheal tube causing throat constriction. With gaze cast down at the floor, words trickled out, a whisper on exhalation.

'I waited for the wave, the one that would take me to Devon, my son. I wanted it to locate me, to find me. I was sending out a GPS signal. I knew from physics that energy is never destroyed, it just changes. Every atom, molecule that made up my boy still exists, right. He's still out there.'

She looked up at Jet, her eyes glistening, challenging. Dark brown hair, limp and tangled, fell around her angular face. She pushed it back, then let her hands fall back into her lap.

'Sometimes I can feel him, his hand in mine, his breath, sweet and soft, on my cheek, like when he used to lay his head on my shoulder when we read together.' Clair leaned forward, wrapping her arms around her body.

'I had to get rid of the blockage, the barrier to reconnect with my son,' she said. 'I watched, waited for that special wave, the seventh one, the biggest one, to take me out. To join him. I remembered reading a book, *Papillon*, where a man waited for the best wave to help him escape his prison island. That's what I was doing – but not escaping from, going to. Going to my Devon.'

'But why kill your husband, Clair?' Jet asked.

'I couldn't live. Couldn't see a life ahead for me and it was because of him. Adam was the obstacle. I wanted him to see it coming, to feel the fear, to be sorry for once in his wretched life. To feel blame, pain, anything besides his own fucking needs and pleasures.'

She spat the words, gripping the chair arm, pressing back, resisting an explosion of movement. This room was so small and her grief so big, she wondered how she could contain it.

Her gaze shifted back to the painting.

'When I got home from work…' she stopped, caught her breath, shuddered. Her hands – long slender fingers, chipped nails – gripped her knees, drawing them to her chest. 'Or what used to be work,' she went on, bringing her eyes back to Jet. 'He was on the deck, laughing into his phone. His hair was getting long, curling up at the edge of his collar. I used to love to play with it when it got like that, curling it around my fingers as we sat and talked. Or maybe I just imagined that too. Like I imagined so many other things, like him ever truly loving me or Devon.'

Clair stood up, walked over to the window, looked out onto the third floor parking lot, almost empty at this time of day. Her body, still bruised in places, moved slowly, carefully, like an old person. An ambulance passed by, without lights or sirens. A bad sign, she thought. No life, no need to hurry. She turned back to look at Jet, lifting her head ever so slightly. A sad smile twitching at the corner of her mouth.

'I really had no choice,' she said. 'I knew I had to die, and I couldn't let him live on, as though nothing had happened. So, yeah, I had some pills left over, from when Devon was, well, from when he disappeared. Lots of them really. I didn't want to be numb, after. I wanted to feel everything. And then, nothing. But, Adam first. I went into the kitchen; saw he was drinking his good Scotch. She must be special, I remember thinking. I ground up the pills, mixed them in. It wasn't enough. So, yeah, I crushed some more, made a cheese spread I knew he loved, spread the drugs on some bread. Cheesy bread he called it. Sprinkled it with paprika to cover any white powder or funny taste. I thought about how the food would slow down digestion, take longer. I mixed him another drink. Added some of his blood pressure pills to that. Decided that would be OK, it would give me time, and draw out his suffering, his knowing he was dying.'

Clair stopped talking, walked back to her chair. 'Well, that didn't work out for me either,' she said. 'I failed at dying. Failed at killing. And failed at saving my son.'

The room held the silence while Clair sat, legs crossed. Tremulous fingers brushed against the chair arm, jagged nails catching in the worn fabric. She looked down at her hands.

'I used to play cello,' she said with a short laugh, looking up at Jet. 'Now look at them.'

'We can get you an emery board, Clair,' Jet said. 'You can tidy up your nails, wash your hair, get freshened up. You'll feel better. But, let's continue for a bit longer, if you're OK? Tell me about your life before.'

Clair nodded, resting her hands in her lap.

'Once upon a time, I was happy. Or if not happy, content. My life was the way I wanted it, orderly, neat, like an equal equation. And it was enough. Before that day, that party, an invitation to hell, when my order dissembled into disorder, all my carefully constructed equations tumbled, unequal and insolvable.'

She began pacing the room, circling the narrow oval table in the center. Finally, abandoning resistance, she folded into the chair. Her gaze drifted back up to the painting, fixed on a scene drawn by her mind's eye; a recollection she had resisted for so long. Clair remembered.

Chapter 2

Clair five years earlier

The invitation sat on the kitchen counter, propped against a bowl of green apples. Looking at it she remembered a still life painting from the Dutch Renaissance she had seen in the Rijksmuseum in Amsterdam several years ago. Apples, wine bottle, blue ceramic vase with yellow dahlias. The promise of a quiet, simple, orderly life; day blending into week, into month, without disruption appealed to her. But this scene was different. Here was that note that had been crumpled up then smoothed out again, beckoning her attention. She stared hard at it while she poured another glass of the deep red.

It had been a long day. Overwrought graduate students, faculty with too much time on their hands and not enough imagination, constantly bombarded her quiet office space with questions and complaints. She didn't want to go to the dinner party at the dean's. As a member of the search committee for the new college president, it was an expectation, a duty. Still, she resented it. Why she had agreed to be on the search committee, she didn't know. A moment of weakness? She was tenured so they couldn't hold it against her. She had never engaged in social niceties. So why now? No time to speculate, she chided herself, upending her glass, swallowing the last of the wine. The phone chimed an incoming call.

'Hello,' she said, her annoyance audible. It was so seldom her phone rang.

'Clair, are you coming tonight? This is Claudia, by the way. In case, you know, you don't recognize my voice.'

Standing at the kitchen sink, looking out at the late fall garden, the last of the roses tilted upwards, straining for remnants of fading sunlight, she grimaced. She turned away, resisting the urge to go out there, stand still in the light, repelling the coming dark and inevitable evening that lay ahead.

'Yes, I'm coming. Why? I mean, why do you want to know?'

'Just seeing if you would like to walk to the dean's with me. I'm just a few blocks over. I can be at your place in fifteen minutes?'

Clair thought at once that this was a plan to make sure she went. Phillip must have put Claudia up to it. Fight, flight, or freeze battled for primacy. Freeze won. More than anything she wanted a way out of this evening. Looking longingly at the half-empty bottle of Burgundy, at her couch and the book lying on the table, a paperweight holding it open to the last page she'd been reading, she sighed heavily, shoulders drawing back in an effort to steel herself.

'All right then. I'll meet you in front.'

She didn't want Claudia, or anyone from the faculty, coming into her home, this sanctuary she had created for herself. When she closed the door, she could breathe. Be herself without artifice. No one visited or called, from work. The few people closest to her were fellow members of the string quartet

13

she played cello with. But even they didn't visit her at home, or socialize outside of practice and performances. And that was how she wanted it.

Clair poured another glass of wine, and carried it with her upstairs, to her bedroom. Throwing open the closet door, she scanned her meager options. Black pant suit, or navy? Long black dress, or gray? Clothes had never been important to her. She wore what she considered her uniform: dark suits with a white or pastel-colored button-down shirt. When she was lecturing in front of students she wanted them to focus only on what she was saying, not what she was wearing, or not wearing in the case of some of her female colleagues. Hair pulled back into a severe knot at the bottom of her crown, glasses, and only a blush of lip gloss, she was the picture of serious. Even her car, an older model dark blue Volvo wagon, spoke of her staidness.

There was one dress pushed to the back of the closet, a long emerald green slender sheath, with a deep, square neckline. Jodie, her sister-in-law, the one family member who refused to accept her efforts to estrange them, who consistently emailed, sent funny cards, odd gifts from around the world, wherever she and Ben – Clair's older brother – happened to be working, had sent it to her from Thailand last Christmas. Both were members of Médecins Sans Frontières, Doctors Without Borders: he a pediatric trauma surgeon, she an obstetrician. Jodie had said the green would bring out the sparkle in her hazel eyes and the gold highlights in her brown hair. Eyes and hair that she had always considered dull brown. As she slipped on the green dress, enjoying the feel of the silky fabric against her skin, she ruminated on this invitation and the event ahead.

She couldn't believe that the dean would be so certain she wouldn't come as to send an escort. Was her presence so important? She was a well-known author, scholar, and yes, even to her own eyes, brilliant mathematician. Maybe she was needed to show off this side of Dalton College. Previously known mainly for its arts and letters, the science and math departments had become the biggest draw in the last few years, bringing in more money in tuition and grants than all the other departments combined.

Eyeing herself in the mirror over her dresser, she added a floral silk scarf, lightly draping it across her chest, leaving a hint of pale, smooth skin between the scarf's edge and the crêpe neckline of the dress. Placing a pair of gold hoops in her ears, she considered letting her hair down but decided not to. It remained in its cloistered bun. She chose a pair of low black flats, not wanting to add to her height; at five foot ten she found she often towered over her co-workers, even most of the men in the math and science departments. It was growing cooler in the evenings so she tossed a dove gray cashmere sweater across her shoulders.

'I'm a showpiece. Best dress the part then,' she said aloud to herself in the mirror, before turning and heading downstairs and out the door to meet Claudia.

* * *

He was the first thing she heard and the first person she noticed when they walked into the already crowded room. Standing a head above the cluster of people pressed around him, his voice boomed over the background sound of soft Brazilian jazz, cutlery, crystal, and bodies shuffling around a small space. A burst of laughter followed his words, whatever he had said amusing to the group. He brushed his prematurely silver hair back from his face and glanced around the room, his eyes finding hers. She was standing at the entranceway, waiting for Claudia to hand her coat to a young woman, a graduate student most likely, serving as hostess. Clair held his gaze, something stirring deep inside her belly. Heat moving up causing her face to flush, she was helpless to stop it. She turned abruptly to the hostess, reaching beyond Claudia, and almost throwing her sweater at the girl. Breathing in deeply, she took a moment to reclaim her equanimity. *Good God*, she thought, *what was that?* When she turned back around, he was there, at her side, glass of champagne in his hand. She could feel his breath on her neck. A head taller, he stood close enough to almost touch, his body heat tangible.

'I know you, but I don't,' he said, leaning towards her so that she caught a light scent of citrus and patchouli.

Clair felt the room collapse into just him, standing close to her, his heat causing the tiny hairs on her arms to quiver. She focused on taking the glass of champagne, sipping, and swallowing.

She smiled, hating that she had to look up. It made her feel somehow infantile. She turned slightly to the side, scanning the room, her breath beginning to find a pattern again. One long exhale and she was ready to engage in the glib sort of conversation she remembered these faculty events requiring.

'I'm Clair Mercer, Science and Math. And you are?' She knew who he was, but she didn't want to give that away.

'Adam, Adam Gage, Theatrics.'

She liked his voice, low, deep, a fine baritone, she thought.

'I know, yes, I have seen you on campus, usually surrounded by a group of students.'

'Yes, well, goes with the territory. They all feel like this is their one big chance, to get a start, a leg up. It is only college but, for so many, it's a chance.'

She expected him to be glib, sarcastic, demeaning even, but he wasn't. He seemed to care about these students and their high hopes.

'And what about you? Did you have your chance?' she asked, looking sideways, not directly at him, but holding him in her space.

'Now, that's a story for another time. Can we have another time?' he asked, his eyes, serious, contrasting with the smile on his face.

'Yes,' she said, wanting to end the back and forth. 'I would like that.'

He didn't leave her side the rest of the evening. And she remained with him, drinking more than she should, reeling under his attention. Adam Gage, head of the drama department, and with a reputation for attraction and seduction. Never with students, she had heard, but certainly with faculty, and with women from town who he directed in local theater productions. And now, here she was, caught up in his web, enticed, enthralled, and allowing it all to come to her. Claudia, a constant presence, circling and touching his arm in passing, made Clair wonder if perhaps she had been or was, one of these women. But she didn't linger on the question. She surrendered to the attention and the feeling of sensuality it brought her.

After the party, he walked her home, the streets empty, dry leaves blowing along the sidewalk. The air was cold, brisk, smelling of fir. She huddled inside his long, dark wool coat, his arm around her, holding her tightly to his side. He reached up and untied her hair, saying, 'Let it loose, feel the wind in your hair, in your veins.'

She turned to look at him, and he stopped walking, pulled her into his body, kissed her lips, cold and sweet. She kissed him back. When they arrived at her door, he entered, without a word and without hesitation, they began undressing in the hall, moving slowly and awkwardly toward the stairs, up the stairs, into the bedroom, onto the bed and into rapture. She didn't know what had happened, she didn't care. She felt herself opening, flowing, and feeling moved from deep within, unbounded and complete.

In the morning, he placed his palm against her bare belly. 'I hope there's nothing in here,' he said, with a slight smile.

She met his gaze, amazed he was still there, in her bed. And now this. Unthought of.

Then she did think. Blinking away the brightness of the possibility, her mind leaping to a reality never before considered, she said, 'I'll have it of course, if there is.'

Chapter 3

Clair Present

Clair looked at Jet, the memory of that morning fresh as a wound. 'And I did,' she said quietly, hands clasping together as in prayer.

'That's enough for today, Clair, you did well,' Jet said, standing and laying a hand on Clair's shoulder. 'I think we made a good start.'

Start on what? Clair wondered. *My recovery? Conviction? Imprisonment after this hospitalization? Just what is starting? And for there to be a start, what has ended?* She sat still, jumbled thoughts roiling in her mind, words and images tossed like pebbles caught in the white water as it merged with the sand. Adam eating the cheese toast, her driving to the cove, the water, cold, clean, healing. Oh, to be back in that space and time where everything made sense.

'Are you OK? Can you find your way back to your room?' Jet asked.

Clair, jolted from her reverie, nodded, rose from the chair, hands pressing down on the chair arms, feeling her way, bone against muscle against flesh.

'I'll be OK,' she said, voice tremulous.

'I believe you will too, Clair,' Jet said. 'But we have a lot more work to do. Will you join group today? I think it will help you.'

'Maybe,' Clair whispered.

'Well, that's better than no.' Jet opened the door, allowing Clair to pass through.

Patients, bleary eyed from medications and too much sleep, stood with backs against the wall, waiting to be told what to do, where to go. One woman was running on a treadmill set up in a corner of the hallway, the rhythm of her footfalls creating a downbeat to the sounds of morning.

Clair caught the eye of a young man, his head lifted, mouth moving silently. Rather than being repelled by these fractured souls, she felt a closeness, a kinship. Having broken a universal taboo, the taking of another's life, even though she failed, she had earned her place in this purgatory. She walked past patients and a few staff standing sentinel, into the community room where morning group was held, and found a seat in a corner, next to a long, wide window overlooking a wooded area. A residual smell of microwave popcorn from last night's movie activity and old coffee from breakfast sitting in urns on a side table lingered in the still air.

Sun streamed in and, like a cat, she curled into the chair, wrapping her arms around her legs, eyes finding a spot on the horizon to fix upon. A patch of green, a meadow at the top of the woods, two deer grazing. Letting her body warm in the gentle heat, her thoughts settled there, with the deer. For a moment, she allowed herself to drift towards that meadow in the woods. Then a sound, harsh and wrenching, brought her back.

The woman sitting opposite Clair was crying. Big, gulping breaths, head held between hands, chipped nails, red polish creating patterns like blood splatter. Her hair hung in lank strands between long, slender fingers, dark roots showing through yellow. Clair felt that the woman consumed all the air in the small space, already dank with body odor, sweat, dirty feet, and fear.

'Barbara, do you need to take a break?' Jet asked.

Clair marveled at how calm her voice was, without showing any of the frustration or annoyance she must be feeling. *Well, she is the therapist,* Clair thought. *Of course, she doesn't show her true self in these group sessions. Or, in our private ones either,* she considered. Clair wondered about Jet, about what she was really like. *Maybe in another world, another time, we could have been friends.*

'No,' Barbara murmured, getting hold of herself. She shook her head, making her body rock like a dog shaking off water. 'I'm OK, I'll be OK.'

Sitting, observing, Clair watched as the patients opened themselves up, baffled at their sheer lack of restraint. First Barbara, depressed. Then Rick, manic, speech like a firecracker barrage. Gabe over in the corner, hearing inner voices, tuning out everyone else's. Three new admits overnight. Two young women, one with gauze dressings around her wrists, and an older man, eyes vacant and scared. It took a lot to get admitted to this locked unit, Clair knew. Back before, she had a couple of grad students end up here for treatment of depression. And now, here she was. A danger to herself and others. Well, one other.

Jet continued going around the room, for morning check-in. Each person had to rate their emotional and physical well-being on a zero to five scale. And the confidentiality statements, the respect for others, and on and on. Clair had heard it every morning for the past five days now, since joining morning group, sitting quietly, not sharing, not disrupting, just getting through it, waiting. For what, she wasn't sure.

When Clair's turn came, she passed. She had nothing to say to these people. In her misery, she couldn't abide with those who only thought they knew what pain was. How she envied Gabe, living in his own world, where nothing could reach him. Sure, he had demons, but he could medicate them away. Or not, but at least he couldn't love, not really. Unable to feel love, he couldn't feel loss. *And Barbara, what a waste,* Clair mused. *She has it all, or had it all before she threw it away. If only, I could go back,* she thought. *To before. To before I had anything.*

She brought her attention back to the group. Jet was talking about something called 'radical acceptance'. It was a way of making peace with themselves when they couldn't control the events in their lives. It isn't about condoning what has happened to us, to derail our lives and land us in a psych unit, but about accepting that it happened and move on. Move into a future that can be different from the past. The key, she said is to focus on this one moment, and then the next, and so on and not think too far ahead. Clair thought about this, about how she might use this information to get out of here. To finish what she had started and failed at. This time, she wouldn't try and cover it up as anything but what it was, a revenge killing. She could accept that. She began to feel something besides despair, anaesthetized, frozen. A stirring inside her belly, a quickening of heart, breath, so much like the first time she felt Devon. A thing so small she almost didn't notice. Hope.

She thought back to that morning, just six months ago, spring break. To before, when the worst thing had seemed to be his obsession with his latest romance. He loved all the shine and glitter of those early days, when everything was possible. She remembered how it had been for her. Oh, the waves of intense emotion that vibrated through her. Seismic shifts from elation to despair, all based on the sound of his voice, his touch, a look. She pitied the woman on the other end of his attentions, his current lover.

It was supposed to be a day off for them. A special family day. A day to reboot, to establish new patterns. Even one small change, just being able to enjoy a day away at the coast, might create better, happier ways of being together for them back home. It was possible, she knew that from her teaching. The butterfly effect. Small, iterative changes could have magnificent effects in all sorts of things, so why not in their relationship? Looking back, she saw that there had been such a change, but horrific in all ways. And still, the pain moves through her, looking for purchase. He had been anxious to leave. His anxiety became her anxiety. Oh, if only, if only. Remembering. She had been in the kitchen, packing a picnic lunch, bread, fruit, cheese, wine, all laid out on the blue-patterned tile table. She moved a vase of yellow daffodils, their blossoms lifted to greet the early morning light filtering in through the open window, to one side making room to lay out special snacks for Devon. Goldfish, fruit roll-ups, juice drinks. She had to be careful about his sugar intake but still, it was a holiday. She was so intent on her task she didn't hear Adam come in.

'Can we hurry it up a bit? I want to get back before dark,' Adam had said, his voice registering his annoyance.

He stood in the doorway, dressed in his weekend attire of soft, fitted jeans and plaid flannel shirt. She felt frazzled, still in her nightgown and robe, hair spilling out of a messy bun.

23

She turned to him, trying hard not to react with anger but failing. She felt her stomach clench, heart begin to beat faster, harder.

'I'm trying. You could help, you know.'

Adam shrugged, taking a cup out of the cupboard over her head. She could smell his aftershave, a scent that reminded her of their early times together, causing a frisson of sadness along with a fleeting speck of hope that, maybe today, they could reignite some of that connection.

'He only wants you. And besides, I have to make a few phone calls,' he said, pouring coffee into his cup from the French press warming on the stovetop.

'Again, really? I thought today was going to be our day away from all of this. From work, from well, everything,' Clair said, her voice rising, giving her emotions away. She hated that and took a deep inhale to try and calm down.

'It is, but I just have to make this one call. Something I need to arrange for later,' he said, coffee in one hand, phone in the other. He set the coffee down to open the door leading out to the deck.

'One call, or a few? That could take an hour or more?'

'Just the one, really, it won't take long,' he said, picking up his cup and elbowing the door open.

'OK, I'll get him going, but can you at least pack the car?' she said, hating that she sounded like she was pleading, but unable to stop herself.

'I don't know what to bring. How the hell should I know? You're his mother. You do all this. I just show up and look like I'm a dad, but we both know who runs this family,' he said, staring down at his phone.

'And whose fault is that? Where have you been the past

four years? At work. At school. With your precious students who, oh yes, need you so much.'

Her hands gripped the edge of the sink. She wanted to grab the phone away from him and throw it across the kitchen. But she didn't. The morning was reeling away from her expectations of a happy outing.

'You're a teacher,' he said, looking at her. 'You know how it is. How can you, of all people, who works until one or two in the morning, accuse me of caring too much about my students?'

'I work till all hours because I can't work until he's asleep. Unlike you, I can't just go and do whatever I want when I want. Or haven't you noticed over the past years; our son is different.'

'Oh yes, believe me, I know, and if I forget for even one millisecond, you remind me.'

She turned back to the counter, began packing their lunch again. Her chest and shoulders slumped, like a deflated balloon. Wanting to rescue any hope for a good day, she exhaled, retreating from the argument.

'Can we just let it go for a day?' she said, her back to him. 'Can we act like a normal happy family, for just today?'

'Yes, yes, lay everything you want to take out here. I'll load up the car. I'm just going to the deck for a moment,' he said, pushing the door open wider with his hip, half in and half out.

'The deck? Why out there?' she turned around again, her face showing her disbelief. 'Can't you make your call here? I won't listen to your precious conversation.'

'It's not that, it's all the clatter and banging around once he gets up. I need some quiet time.'

Waving a hand at him, she said, 'Go then, get it done. This thing that's so important on this, the one day during our entire spring break we are spending time together as a family. Maybe then you can be with us, not with… well, with whomever it is you have to be with right now. Just go.'

Looking back, now, here in this place, with all that had happened, why didn't she just go without him? Jet's voice called her back to the room. They wrapped up by checking out, reciting their numbers again. When her time came, she said four and a half. She knew Jet would want to hear this, to know that this work had helped, and that she was improving. What she really wanted to say was zero. The memory of that final morning, so pathetic in its mundaneness, in its predictability, so lowly. Devon, he was like the sun. He shone so bright but all Adam, and yes, maybe by that time she too, could see was the shadow of the perfect child they had expected. And so, they mired themselves in their prosaic worlds of work, argument, loneliness, and heartache.

* * *

After group, it was time for therapeutic activities. She had been working hard to fit in to the milieu of the unit. Getting up, dressing in the blue scrubs that came without even a string tie around the waist to hold them up. Anything that could be used to strangle, choke, cut off blood was censored. Contraband they called it. She ate, exercised, and participated in group activities. One day, they were creating a group collage from magazine pictures. They would find a picture that looked like how they felt that day. At first, she had found a photo of a canyon, empty of all but shadow, cut in two by millions of years of wear, its river so far removed it no longer seemed to exist. This was how she felt, empty and dredged. But, instead of cutting that one out, she chose a picture of a valley, with sheep grazing on green hillsides, a red barn sheltering daffodils and crocuses. This was the opposite of how she felt, and this was what she shared. It gave her a sense of power, of control. She could find an equation that fit here. She just had to first figure out the numbers. Having a future to look forward to – being 'future-oriented' was how they put it. This was essential in not being suicidal. She did have a future she was looking forward to – a future where she would die. And maybe this time, he would too.

Annie, the recreation therapist, was rounding, looking at the different pictures patients were gluing to the large sheet of white paper. She stood behind Clair, leaning over, resting a hand on the back of her chair.

'That is really lovely, Clair. Does this remind you of any place in your life or is it something you look ahead to?' she asked.

'It does remind me of an area I used to pass on my way from home to the coast. Yeah, I hadn't thought about that, but it does. It always brought me a sense of peace and hope.'

'That's good. I'm glad to hear that you are able to connect with those feelings again.'

Annie walked on, looking over another patient's shoulder. Clair remembered the day, the drive to the coast, that morning. There was that red barn. Devon had called out to look at the lambs. To look at the baby sheep. The memory of that joyful expectation – his belief in her, that she would keep him safe, that his world was a place of wonder and delight, not one where a monster wave could come out of nowhere and sweep you away from all you knew and loved – brought tears, shame, and she bolted, knocking over her chair.

She walked quickly to her room, private now without a

roommate, and curled into a ball, clasping her pillow against her aching chest. She lay there for several minutes, rocking herself, tiny moans escaping from deep inside. Linda, the psychiatric aide checked on her. Clair waved her away. Once the emotional avalanche had passed, she sat up. *I have to get out of here,* she thought. *I just have to get out.*

Clair looked out the window and saw Jet coming across the parking lot, a man walking with her. Small, slender, black hair. He wore a suit with a white shirt, thin, dark tie. Clair felt a churning in her gut. Jet had said there might be an interview soon, because of the attempt on Adam. *Oh God,* she thought. *Is he coming for me?*

Chapter 4

Clair

It was the first time Clair had been off the locked unit since she was first admitted. Jet's office was in the hallway along with several staff offices and a clinical pharmacy. It felt strange to see and hear normal people going about their day to day jobs, talking about the coming weekend, plans for kids' ball games, shopping trips to Eugene, and those simple activities that make up a life. Her legs felt shaky, steps uncertain as she followed Jet through the door into a square room, with floor to ceiling windows looking out towards the mountains to the east. A marine layer caressed the tops of Douglas firs, spruce, and scattered redwoods that lay a deep green covering over the land. A clearing, where fir and spruce forests had been cut down, stood out like a wound. It made her sad to see this, and then she remembered why she was here. Looking to her right, she saw him; the detective. Her heart contracted; her mouth suddenly dry. She pressed her lips together to keep from crying out. Jet motioned for her to sit on a chair, next to a small wooden table holding a vase of holly, her back to the window.

'Clair, this is Detective James Santiago, of the Harbor Police Department. He's here to ask you some questions about what happened. Do you feel up to talking with him? It's up to you. You can refuse, and you can also request an attorney to be present. I can stay with you, if you like.'

'I'm OK,' she said softly. 'I can talk.'

'Do you want to have an attorney present, Clair?' the detective asked.

He was polite but official. His voice held a slight accent. She noticed a neat mustache over his small, bow-shaped mouth. He stroked it lightly from time to time. Old acne scars covered his cheeks like moon craters seen from the earth. His eyes were the deepest blue. She felt she might fall into those eyes and disappear. Was this part of his technique, to throw his suspects off guard? She shook herself clear of any notions he might be kind or caring.

'No, but I would like for Jet, uh, Dr Taylor to stay.'

'I'm going to record this,' he said, and it wasn't a question.

He pulled a small camcorder out of his satchel, sitting it on the edge of the windowsill. Clair felt naked and cold. Jet noticed her shiver and offered her a blanket from the couch on the other side of the room. Clair had been in sessions with Jet many times over the past several days. It had always felt safe. It didn't feel safe today, not with Santiago here.

Clair sat, her hands folded neatly in her lap, and waited. Jet and the detective sat either side of the table Jet used as a desk. Bare except for a computer and a photo of Jet and a young woman who looked just like her. A graduation shot, black gowns and caps with purple tassels tilted to the left. Both smiling broadly, their arms around each other, free arms waving at someone in the distance.

It was time now. The story was advancing, and she couldn't do anything to stop it. Each remembering, each telling, invoked memories, or were they imaginings? She didn't know.

This man, this detective, Santiago, the way he looked at her, with such empathy. Where did he get that? And yet, he had the power to stop all of this and just send her to prison. They were giving her a chance. But a chance for what? Life, she didn't want. Freedom, that terrified her. Absolution, impossible.

A click sounded from the small camcorder set up on the windowsill.

'Detective James Santiago, Harbor Police Department. Dr Juliette Taylor is also present. It is Thursday, September 27, 2018. We are at Harbor Hospital in the office of Dr Juliette Taylor. I am interviewing Clair Mercer on the events of September 20, 2018.'

'I know now I was psychotic. I must have known it then, but I couldn't stop it. Couldn't stop myself.' Clair spoke directly into the camera, as though it was a person. Her hands busied themselves rolling up her scrub top into a tight knot at her waist, then letting go, again and again as she spoke.

'After I, you know, mixed his drink, dumped the powder from the pills into the drink and mixed the rest into the cheese mixture. I made him the cheese toast, gave them to him. He didn't even say thank you. He just kept talking on the phone. I watched him take that first sip, afraid he would taste something strange. But it was his good Scotch. He didn't notice. He took a big bite of his toast. I remember some of the cheese stuck to his bottom lip. It made him look sad, old. Well, after, and I thought he was dying, dead, I got my bag, made sure I had what I needed, and walked out to my car. I remember how bright the sun was. The late summer haze from the cooling ocean drifted across the coastal range scattering rainbows across the horizon. I saw them as a sign, like a bridge, you know, from here to there.'

She looked up at Jet, hoping that somehow, magically, through this telling, this moment of joyful recognition of beauty, somehow the terrible events of that day could be erased. Like the tsunami tide, a surge so powerful that it could take it all away. Seeing only assent in Jet's gaze, she dropped her own, staring at the silvery threads woven into the deep indigo carpet at her feet. Then at her feet, wearing the blue booties the hospital provided for the psych patients. This jolted her back to the reality that was now. The tide was surging back in.

'I got in my car. Began the drive to the coast, to the beach where, you know, where I lost him, my boy. It was about a thirty-minute drive, maybe more, depending on traffic. This was a Friday afternoon so yeah, lots of people heading to the coast, slowing down the 101. Escaping the valley heat. But it was OK. I wasn't in a hurry. I was just on my way. I had finished my business at the house. Adam was done. And I was going to join Devon. To become part of that watery sanctuary that had enfolded him. To immerse my atoms and molecules with his.'

Clair was shaking her head, pleading with her eyes, spreading her hands towards Jet and Santiago, beseeching them to understand.

'I was on the river road, just before the turn off, when I saw his car for the first time. That damn new black Mercedes he insisted on, saying he had to maintain a certain image for his students, his public. How could it be him? I disbelieved my eyes, but at the same time I questioned why I hadn't taken his keys with me. Is this his ghost, coming to haunt me already? I just drove on, faster.'

'Take a breath, Clair,' Jet coached. 'Take a minute, we have time.' Jet reached across the table, touched Clair's forearm. 'Are you OK? We can stop and do this later.'

'No, I want to get it over with,' she said, shuddering. 'Please.'

Santiago nodded.

'I turned onto the coast road. It was still so bright. The western sun was shining in my eyes, blinding me. But he was there. In my rearview mirror. He would gain on me, then withdraw, like a shadow. Even the wind, the trees colluded in his stalking, throwing leaves and debris in my path. I drove so fast, but my older car was no match for his machine. He stayed with me. I slowed down through the village of Seven Devils. Then rushed to the turn off where I parked to walk down to the beach. I felt sure I had lost him. He must have died again on the way, crashed his car. I hurried down the trail. It was getting dark now, but I could still see the path. Each root, remembering how Devon had skipped and leaped over them on that day, before. I made it to the cove. I felt so safe now. I had made it. Then I heard a car door slam. Sound carries, you know, close to the water. I froze.'

Clair sat rooted in the memory, her hands tight fists. She felt her nails pressing into her soft palms, bringing her back to the present.

'When nothing happened, when his ghost didn't come, I sat down on a rock, at the far end of the cove. I could see a fisherman making his way across the rocks on the other end, but he wasn't looking my way. At least I didn't think so.' She sighed, letting her hands release, rubbing them briskly against her upper arms.

'I had brought a bottle of vodka with me, and the pills. I sat there on the beach, waiting for the tide to come in. I waited, waited, then noticed it wasn't coming in, it was going out. I remember feeling woozy and nauseous. The sound of waves pulling me forward was irresistible. I knew it was now or never. I began walking into the water. Cold, so cold. My breath caught. All I could think about was Devon, what he must have felt, that shock.' She looked up at Jet, her eyes reddened, wet.

'I was told he would have lost consciousness at once, that the shock, the hypothermia would have been like a salve. That he wouldn't have had time to be afraid.' Tears flowed down her face. A gasp, and she crumbled into herself, hugging her arms around her middle.

'I just wanted to be with him,' Clair explained. 'It had been six months since he left. He left in March, such an unkind month. The great whites come through then. The orcas. It was too dangerous for him. I had to find him. And I was so close, I knew it. A water spirit had come to take me to him. I could feel him there, drawing me in. I could hear the song of the sea, hear the voices. Don't you believe me?'

Clair broke down, sobbing. Her head hung on her chest, too weak to lift her hands to support herself. Slowly, she melted, head resting on the edge of the desk, back and shoulders heaving.

Through her tears she heard Santiago speaking, saying something about the interview ending. Jet had walked around the table, sat beside her. Clair could feel her presence. She could hear Jet and the man talking, voices coming from far away. A door shut. She couldn't, wouldn't open her eyes. Her failures, as a mother, a wife, even as a teacher, a role she couldn't find her way back to after Devon, all came crashing down, an avalanche of feeling. She had held back the dam for so long.

She began to hear soft music, a drumming sound, muffled, like the first time she had heard Devon's heartbeat on the ultrasound monitor. Like when she'd been in the water. Will that sound be a part of her for ever, she wondered? The swish, swish of fluid moving through her body, their connection. She realized she was lying on the floor, curled into a pile of bolsters and cushions Jet placed around her office. Hugging one of the cushions to her chest, she allowed visions to come. She could sense Jet in the room, could hear paper crinkling, computer keys tapping. She felt a warm breath from the ventilation fan, heard its rumble. Sinking deeper and deeper into the carpet, the cushions, she drifted. Back, and further back. To another beginning, the one that cracked open the fragile mold that had been her life.

Chapter 5

Clair

She knew right away, noticing a hunger unlike any she had ever felt, gnawing at her insides. Her breasts tingled, nipples dimpled and erect. Then the morning nausea, which only strong black coffee seemed to help. They hadn't seen each other since the party. Since their night of sex. Not up close. She had seen him across campus, as usual, surrounded by a cluster of students. He had called, left messages. Written her poems sent to her college email. He was taken, he had said. Is it possible to fall in love after only a few hours? She was his Sylvia. His altar. Would she meet him for a drink? Dinner? They must go see the new play at the Theater on the Bay. She hadn't responded yet. She wasn't sure how she felt.

The proof was sitting there, on the vanity counter. The urine test kit. No guessing with Xs or Os. Just the word 'pregnant' in bold black letters.

It couldn't be, she thought. Forty-one-year-old single women do not get pregnant after just one time. That is for teenagers. But there it was, staring her in the face. She stood up, walked into her bedroom. She looked around. Her world, so carefully arranged, so dear to her after the chaos that had been her life growing up. Nothing here was uncertain, unpredictable. Except for this speck of life growing inside her.

Clair sat on the side of her bed, the rich blue duvet yielding to her weight. She rubbed her hand against its silk. Sighing, she dialed a number into her phone. She hadn't talked to her brother Ben in weeks, maybe longer. It was really his wife, Jodie, she wanted to talk to. They were on service in Yemen. She wasn't sure what time it was there, but she called anyway. A moment of hesitancy hit her. Her problem, although huge to her, was small when she thought about the people whose lives Ben and Jodie were helping. She almost didn't call, but then, she wanted to talk with them anyway. It had been too long. And she did need Jodie's advice. Ben, although understanding and kind, could sometimes revert to behaving like their father, and be judgmental. He would retract once it was pointed out to him, but often, that was his learned response. One she didn't want to encounter right now.

The call went to voicemail. Jodie was probably in the birthing tent. A short, generic message letting Jodie know she was OK and they would talk later. She sat there for a few more moments, until hunger pulled her downstairs. A toasted bagel, scrambled egg, coffee, then a race to the toilet. Shakily getting dressed, a plastic baggy of dry crackers tucked into her tote bag, she left for class. She placed the phone in her jacket pocket on vibrate so she wouldn't miss Jodie's call. The seminar was with her graduate advisees, and they wouldn't object to her stepping out. They might even enjoy it, she thought.

She had just launched them into a discussion on the meaning of infinity from a mathematical perspective when she felt the vibration against her hip. She heard it buzzing, humming like an annoying insect and she couldn't make it stop. She felt a hand, gently rocking her shoulder.

'Clair, wake up. You're dreaming.'

Jet's voice was out of place here in her classroom. Who? What? Her mind cast about for focus. Then slowly, like a diver following air bubbles to the surface, she rose to awareness. Lamenting inwardly, not wanting to lose that fragile connection to the first, pristine knowledge of Devon beginning to grow inside her, she turned away from Jet's voice, burying her head deeper in the cushions. She lay there for what seemed like hours. Her back hurt. Her hip hurt where her weight pressed into the carpeted floor. She was thirsty and had to pee. Sensing Jet beside her, she slowly turned onto her back, staring up at the white ceiling. A string of overhead fluorescent lights, turned off, crossed the space, reminding her of her classroom, of the students, of the call. Of her dream. Of the beginning and the end, and now, of this. She rolled onto her side, pushing herself up into a cross-legged sitting position, elbows on her thighs, head in her hands.

'That seemed like a powerful dream, Clair, I hated waking you, but you were beginning to shake. Are you OK? Can we talk about it?' Jet asked.

'I was dreaming of the day I had proof of my pregnancy,' Clair said, looking forward. 'I was waiting for a call back from Jodie, my sister-in-law. I had been teaching and turned my phone to vibrate. When the call came, I couldn't get it to answer. You woke me up. Now I'm back. And it's gone again. That's all I can remember.'

Jet sat down opposite her, also in crossed-legged position. She tucked a flat cushion under her bottom, settling in. 'I didn't know you had a sister-in-law. I didn't know you had a brother,' she said. 'Where are they?'

'Yeah, they're in Yemen now,' Clair explained. 'Working

as doctors in one of the refugee camps. I love them, especially Jodie, my sister. More like a sister than an in-law. Ben, well, he has a lot of our father in him and it does come out under stress. Jodie helps him. That's why he joined the mission, to get away from home and be as different from Dad as he could be.'

'Tell me more about that, Clair. You've never talked about your family, your upbringing.'

'Why?' Clair asked. 'What has that got to do with this?' she waved her hands around the room, as though her current universe existed only of this room, herself, sitting on this carpet, wearing the blue scrubs. And this woman, her confessor.

'Everything has to do with everything,' Jet said. 'We won't know until we know.'

Clair laughed. 'That reminds me of the lesson I handed my class on that day – the day I was dreaming about. Infinity. OK, I'll talk. But I need to get up first, use the bathroom, get a drink. Is that OK?'

'Sure. You can use the bathroom here, in my office. I'll get you a water.'

Returning, Clair re-settled on a chair, her tolerance for proximity spent. A bottle of water sat on the table at her side.

'Where to begin?' she wondered out loud. 'I know, start from the beginning.'

Jet smiled at her, nodding.

'Not much to tell really. It is a common variety of the American narrative we call family life. Too much money, leisure, expectations. Our father was cold, indifferent, and completely lost at home. An eminent neurosurgeon, at ease with a scalpel in his hand, speaking medical lingo, he mostly showed up for family dinners, endured them with disdain, and then escaped to his home office. Mother was the social one, always one big event after another. If she was home, she was either drunk, high, or well on her way. Our father had hoped Ben would follow him into neurosurgery. Didn't expect anything from me. Ben left home as soon as he graduated from high school. Moved across the country. Became a surgeon yes, but not neuro. He was four years older than me, which left me alone in that house of horrors through high school. I left too – in my mind. I became lost in numbers. The beauty of equations. Math. Something that made sense and wouldn't leave me, let me down. Something I was good at. Like Ben, as soon as I could, I left.'

Clair reached for her water, taking a sip, cocking her head slightly to the left. 'Are you sure you want to hear this? It isn't very interesting,' she said, frowning.

'Yes, I do,' Jet replied. 'It's important for me to understand more about you, and the choices you have made. It helps me help you.'

'OK, well, for me, college was a balm. A place where I existed and excelled. Ben met Jodie. They married. She found out about me and dragged him here, where I was in college, at Christmas to meet me on campus. We had the best time, hiking in the forests along the coast. Eating clam chowder at Moe's. Hunkering down into our tent, eyes burning from the campfire smoke. Jodie and I bonded. Her strong black female persona captured me like it had Ben, and we became a little family. She said she became a birth doctor to help women experience the miracle of childbirth without trauma. I knew she would be the one to help me work through my own questions. And she did.'

'And, do they know you're here? Do they know what happened?' Jet asked.

'God no!' Clair shuddered. 'They're deep inside the danger

zone in Yemen still. I don't want them to know. I don't want them to have any more fear or worry in their lives.'

'But what if you had died, Clair? How would they have felt? Wouldn't that have caused them pain, grief?' Jet asked, with kindness in her voice.

Clair's face fell, her eyes tearing up. 'Yes, but at the time, you know, I wasn't thinking about anyone else. I was just wanting my own pain to end.'

'And now, Clair, how do you feel about being alive?' Jet asked quietly.

'I don't know,' Clair said. 'At this very moment, sitting here with you, maybe I can be alive.'

'OK, then, I'll take that for now,' Jet said, smiling. 'Let's go see what's for dinner.'

'Jet, what's going to happen? You know, with Detective Santiago?'

'Oh, he'll be back. He's not finished with us.'

Chapter 6

Adam

A tapping on the door, half shut against curious gazes and noise from the busy medical unit, brought Adam out of his reverie. He had been looking out the window of his third-floor room, over tree tops, towards the sea. Heavy clouds moved in from the north, signaling a cooling off of what had been a late summer heatwave. The night had been long, noisy, his intravenous drip pump alarming at what seemed like minute to minute intervals. Codes were called through the long hours of the night. His patient safety assistant, a young man with long braids flowing down his back, explained their names to him. Code Blue was for sudden death from heart or respiratory failure; Code Silver meant a patient or visitor had turned violent; Code Amber was for a child abduction, usually from the maternity ward. He wondered about those people for whom the codes had been called? Did they make it? Looking towards the door, he saw Claudia hesitating at the opening, holding a small bag and coffee from the hospital café.

'Come in,' Adam called to her, easing himself up in the bed. He felt foolish sitting there in the thin, faded hospital gown.

He smoothed his hair down as best he could, grimacing as he caught a hint of his breath, stale and tasting of old, undigested food. Rubbing his eyes, his face, feeling the stubble, he did his best to find a smile, as the old Adam might have done. He didn't feel like that man anymore. Humbled, brought down by a love or hate so strong it almost killed him, felt almost like a re-birthing. To what, he wasn't sure.

'Thought you might like a cup of real coffee, and a bagel,' she said, walking over and setting the containers on the over-bed tray. 'How are you feeling?'

'Like shit. And I probably smell as good too so keep your distance,' he said, half-jokingly, but also not wanting her there.

She had probably saved his life. Thinking back to that afternoon, how if Claudia hadn't dropped by to talk about the upcoming production of their senior class play, *Emma*, he would not be here now. The front door had been left wide open. Claudia had walked in, through the living room, and into the kitchen, finding him, calling 911, saving his life.

'Claudia, thank you for what you did. I really don't know what to say.'

'Nothing to say, Adam. What in God's name was Clair thinking?'

'I don't know. I'm going to visit her, talk to her. Try and find out. I think she just snapped. We had been getting better, after, you know, Devon, and then, this.' He looked down at his body as though it were a wrecked car.

'Adam, be careful. She's crazy. She might try to hurt you again.'

'I don't think so. And anyway, I talked to the therapist, a Dr Taylor. She said it might be good for me to see Clair, let her see I'm alive, and OK. The staff on the psych unit will be sure I'm safe. They monitor everything on camera. And will stand by.'

Claudia stood quickly, the metal chair scraping against the linoleum.

'And why would you care, Adam, after what she did? I'm the one who saved you,' Claudia said, leaning forward, hands resting on the bedside table.

'Because she's my wife, Claudia. And I have to find out why she wanted me dead.'

A nurse bustled in, smiling and fresh faced. Claudia stepped aside.

'Good morning, I'm Amanda, your nurse today. How are you feeling, Mr Gage? Ready to get this needle out and go home?' she asked, reaching for his left hand, removing the dressing over the insertion site.

'Really, I'm being discharged?' he asked, his face lighting up.

'Yep, we have your marching orders. It will take me a while to go through and get everything ready. You'll have a few prescriptions to take home. But you should be out of here in an hour or so.'

'Is it OK if I leave my room, go down to the psychiatric unit? My wife is there. I want to visit her.'

'Let me give them a call, make sure it's OK. I'll be right back, let you know.'

* * *

Adam stood in front of the door, his hand frozen in mid-air. A sign, CAUTION! ELOPEMENT RISK HIGH taped to the outside of the small glass window insert. He wondered if it was meant for Clair. A metal intercom instructed visitors to press the button. He did. A woman, identifying herself as Sandra, unit secretary, asked for his name and the name of the patient he was visiting. He felt naked and vulnerable standing there, wearing the same clothes he had been found in, lying on his kitchen floor, unconscious, two days ago. Claudia's question came back to him. So why was he here now, coming to Clair, like a supplicant? Seeking what? Absolution? He had done nothing wrong. She was the one who had tried to poison him. Jamming his hands deep into his pockets to stop their trembling he leaned forward, into the metal disk.

'Adam Gage, here to visit Clair Mercer, my wife,' he said, his voice tenuous, uncertain. He felt eyes on him, and looking up, saw the security camera mounted on the ceiling above his head. Glancing around nervously, he breathed a sigh of relief when he saw there were no other staff or patients down the hall. He didn't want to be seen or recognized.

'Wait. I need to find out if we have this person here on the unit,' Tonya said.

'What? I know she's there. What do you mean? She's under hold orders. My nurse just called to check it would be OK for me to visit.'

'Sir, you have to wait. 'I'll be right back.'

Adam looked around. The hallway behind him was empty. Feeling weak, he leaned against the side of the door. What would he say to Clair? Maybe she wouldn't see him. What would he do then? He had to talk with her, find out why she tried to kill him, and herself. It was crazy. Maybe she really was crazy and now he would add this to his long list of miseries. How had it all gone so wrong?

'Open the door when you hear the click. Wait in the sallyport for the second click. Then you can come through,' a different voice said.

He was met on the other side by a short woman wearing black scrubs. Adam followed her down the hall. Large photographs of local scenic sites covered the walls, along with art work done by patients, he assumed. Positive affirmations were written on every available flat space reminding patients and staff that 'Everything is Temporary' and to 'Be in the Moment'. It was hard to tell staff from patients. Everyone wore scrubs. It seemed patients were uniformly dressed in blue whereas staff wore a variety of colors. And there were the eyes. Patients' flat, restricted gazes held no joy, no eagerness for the next moment. Or in a few cases, eyes were wild, drifting from side to side, looking for what? Adam wondered. A way out or a way in?

They stopped at a door directly across from the nursing station where several men and women sat at computer monitors. Glass walls and locked doors kept them safe and isolated from the outsiders.

He heard his escort speaking through the small opening in the doorway, her head leaning through.

'Clair, you have a visitor. Do you want me to let him in?'

'Who is it?' Adam heard Clair ask.

'Says he's your husband,' Belinda answered with a doubtful tone. Several seconds passed.

'He can come in.'

Adam was surprised at hearing Clair's voice, usually soft, lyrical, but today, hoarse, flat. He stepped inside, half afraid of what he would find.

The room was dark. He could make out her form sitting cross-legged on the twin bed, closest to a set of windows. Curtains were pulled tightly together but a sliver of light pushed its way through, scattering dust mites in the air.

'Clair, you look well,' he said, remaining in the doorway.

'No, I don't and you don't have any right to bullshit me. So, stop. Why are you here?'

Adam walked into the room, sat on the side of the second bed in the small room, resting his elbows on his knees. He leaned slightly forward, his gaze focused, intense.

'Clair, it wasn't my fault. It wasn't your fault. It was a natural disaster. An act of God, if you will. A goddamn sneaker wave took Devon. There are signs up warning people about them everywhere. It happened. Every year it happens. You have to accept this and move on.'

'How dare you even mention him in my presence!' she cried. 'You have no right.'

Adam felt a rush of anger, so strong he had to stand, to move. He walked towards the window, then back to the bed again. He sat, not wanting to hover over her. Taking in a deep breath, exhaling through his mouth, lips pursed, he clenched his fingers, pressing his nails into the soft flesh of his palms.

'He was my son too. I have a right, as much as you.'

'No, you denied yourself that right, after you realized he wasn't your perfect little mini-you. Once you learned about the autism, you disengaged. You know you did – from both of us.'

He did know. And it shamed him.

'Clair, I didn't come here to fight. I came to see you. How are you?'

She looked so bereft sitting there, on the narrow single bed. Her hair, usually well groomed, was oily, hanging down in shards along her thin jawline. He felt an overwhelming ache in his heart, wanting to enfold her, erase all the pain and terror of the past few months. Frozen in place, he held her eyes in his gaze, willing her to answer.

'Oh God, Adam, I am so sorry.' She cried, dropping her head into her hands. I didn't want you to die, not really, well maybe I did at the time. But I had just wanted a way out. You were my way out.'

'I've never had anyone love me enough to want to kill me before,' he said, with a crooked smile.

She looked up at him. 'Love. I can't speak that word with you. I loved you. Devon loved you. And you squandered it, on your affairs, your minor successes. Devon was the only real thing in your life, in my life. Everything else, counterfeit. That's what you lost, Adam, on the beach. You lost your one connection to truth.'

'Clair, you lost it too. Where were you when the wave came and took him? The wave may have been an act of God but we, Clair, you and I, we didn't pay attention. We weren't watching. What were you doing?'

Clair stared at him. This question had been haunting her for the past months. It had driven her crazy.

'You were there, on the beach, like me,' Adam said, looking out the window. 'You were right there, Clair.' He turned back to face her. 'How did you not see the wave?'

'I was looking the other way. I was so angry at you, I stared after you, walking that walk, talking on the phone to your latest girlfriend, and I was watching you. I wasn't watching Devon; you were supposed to be watching Devon,' she hissed the words out. 'Just that one time, it was for you to be a father. And you couldn't. Wouldn't.'

A noise outside the door startled him. He realized they had been loud, and loud voices on the psych unit brought attention. Any disruption in the calm milieu could signal a meltdown, or the need for a safety team intervention. Turning around, he saw a huddle of patients at the door. A tall man, name tag identifying him as Matt RN, was easing his way through them, telling them to go back to their rooms or to the community room.

'Everything OK in here?' he asked, looking at Clair.

She nodded. 'I'm sorry we got so loud. We'll keep it down. Thanks Matt,' she said.

'No problem, but you only have a few minutes left.' Then, looking at Adam, he said, 'Visiting hours are over.'

'What happens now, to you, Clair? The detective, Santiago, came to see me. I'm not pressing charges if you're wondering about that. And, I wasn't talking to a girlfriend. It was Claudia, about the upcoming performance. It was work, it was always work, Clair.'

Adam had walked out into the hall. He looked back at her, face pale and gaunt. She shrugged, looking out the window.

'I was told there will be a hearing. The criminal justice system for the mentally ill runs like a machine. They have five business days to make a decision as to whether or not to take me to a commitment hearing. An examiner met with me, interviewed me, and decided I might be crazy. At least, crazy enough to not be held responsible for what I did, you know, to you. So, I'll have a competency hearing to see if I'm sane enough to stand trial. Today is day four.'

'But I'm not pressing any charges, Clair. I don't blame you for what you did. Why can't they just let it go?' Adam said, waving his hands in the air.

Clair swung her legs off the bed, stood, and walked over to the windows. She turned her head back to look at Adam. He was standing in the doorway, one foot inside the room, the other in the hallway.

'You don't have to press charges, Adam. The DA can do that himself. If I'm not sane, I'll be sent to the state hospital forensic unit to get treated, until I am deemed sane enough to participate in my own defense, as though I have any defense. And you know what, I don't care. I died that day back on the beach.'

* * *

Once back outside, Adam breathed in the fresh air, scented from the tall Douglas fir trees circling the hospital. He felt a jolt of memory, bringing him back to his first time, stepping out of the plane onto Pacific Northwest tarmac. The air, so dense with moisture, the smell of ocean and forest blending together in a way that was captivating. He had come here to interview for a job as director of theater at the small, liberal arts college, tucked away on the coast. Leaving behind his hopes of being a real actor himself, settling on teaching and coaching students, feeding their dreams instead. A regular paycheck and benefits won out over dreams of stardom, he remembered thinking. He beeped the car door, falling into the soft leather seats. Leaning back, resting his head, he closed his eyes. He felt the sting of salt as tears burned, his vision blurring as he remembered Clair the first time they met. And then, when he had found out about the pregnancy, regretting his first reaction.

She had walked into his office on the third floor of the Tioga building, overlooking a small lake. It had been spring, new buds bursting through winter foliage on the rhododendrons. He had been coaching a student, young, female, through an emotional scene. His door had been open, as he always left it when alone with a student. Hearing a knock, he had looked up, startled to see her standing there.

Since their night together, after the party, they hadn't seen much of each other. He had tried, but she had always found reasons why she couldn't meet him for dinner, or a concert. After a few weeks, he had stopped trying. He had enjoyed their time together, brief and passionate as it was. Her keen intelligence and dry humor were so different from his other female friends and lovers. His initial surprise quickly receded and pleasure took its place. But not for long.

'Hi, I'm sorry to interrupt Adam, but I need to talk with you.'

'OK, Ashley, we can finish up this evening, during rehearsal. Nice work today,' he said to the student.

'Come in, Clair. I think this is the first time you've been up here, isn't it?' he asked, motioning for her to come to a setting of chairs around a small, rectangular table in the corner of the room. A large desk, make of Port Orford white cedar held a place of prominence in the other corner. The rest of the room was open space. Except for the walls, which were covered with photographs, posters, and diplomas. Bachelor of Arts, Florida State University. Master of Arts in Theater, Columbia University. PhD Philosophy, Columbia University.

'I'm pregnant,' she had blurted out, continuing to stand in the doorway. She had held her hands over her lower abdomen.

He had stopped in his movement to sit down on one of the chairs. Standing back up, he had walked over to her, gently guiding her inside and shutting the door leading to the hallway.

'Come in, Clair. Please,' he had said. 'Sit down.'

She had walked over to the chairs, sitting on the edge of one. Adam had sat across from her. He had leaned over, taking her hands, icy, the bones small, fragile. He had held them, massaging the tender flesh between her thumb and

51

index finger. She had drawn away, folding her arms around herself.

He had sat back in his chair, crossing one leg over the other.

'Are you saying that it is mine?' he had asked, his head tilted to one side.

'Yes, it is your baby, of course it is. And I'm going to have it. We can have this baby together. We can be a family.'

'I barely know you. You don't know me. I tried but you didn't want anything to do with me after our night together. That is not a family,' he had said.

'We'll learn. I know you felt what I felt. It's just our ages, and our roles here on campus. We are more discreet than others might be. But now, we can be open, share our story. Make a family.'

'I don't want it,' he had said simply, his hands folded in his lap. 'You can get an abortion, can't you? Isn't that the most logical thing to do? I'm old, Clair, and you're old too – to have a baby. It will change everything.'

'I'm healthy, and not too old. I saw a doctor. Everything is fine. I'll be fine and so will this baby. I won't abort. I'm having this baby, Adam, even if I have to do it without you.'

'Well, you'll have to do it that way then. I'm just not interested in being a father. Never have been. If you bring a paternity suit, I'll help with child support, but really, Clair, you won't need it. You make enough money and if this is your choice, then you should pay for it. I'm not trying to be rude here, just realistic. I shouldn't have to pay for what was a single night of pleasure. You're responsible too.'

Clair had stood, pulling her coat tightly around her slender frame. He had tried not to but couldn't stop his eyes moving to her belly, looking for the telltale bump.

'All right, if that is how you want it to be,' she had said. 'I won't ask you for any support, you're right. I won't need it and I really don't want you to feel obligated. If you want to have any sort of relationship with your child, it needs to come from your heart – not any legal relationship.'

He had stood, uncertain what to do. His hands had pushed deeply into his pockets, fingers curling around loose coins, keys, and bits of torn paper.

'I'm pretty sure you'll regret this,' she had said to him, turning to look back as she walked towards his door.

* * *

Over the next few months, as her belly grew and people began talking, it was generally accepted that he was the father. He would interrupt gossip sessions in the faculty lounge, and catch curious glances from faculty and students. He had gone to her office one afternoon, as the summer sun cast shadows along the cobbled sidewalk outside her window. Students, eager for summer break, had been scampering over the quad, a square field of grass and sculptures.

'I made a mistake,' he had said, standing in the doorway. 'I do want to be a part of this. Can you forgive me my stupidity? I don't know what I was thinking – well, I wasn't thinking, I was reacting. Seeing you, here, with my child growing inside, I want to be with you and him, or her. Do we know?'

'No, I don't know. And, Adam, there is no "we",' she had countered. 'You can't just walk in and suddenly become a father. Things take time. I need time to think about this. About what it will mean. I think you're just doing this because you're embarrassed. Peer pressure has gotten to you. Your image of the great man on campus has been distorted.'

'You're somewhat right,' he had said, a sheepish look on his face. 'I know people are talking and that they remember that night, how we were together. And even though we never really dated – do people our age do that? – well, this is a rumor mill. Everyone knows everyone else's stuff and loves to deconstruct every action into finite bits and pieces of intention and consequence. But, Clair, it's really just me seeing you. You're beautiful. You carry yourself like some queen. I've never seen you shine so brightly. Your beauty and strength amaze me. I just want to be a part of your life and our life together.'

He had walked over and lain a hand on her belly. She had let him. It had felt like that first morning after.

'What exactly are you asking, Adam?'

He had dropped down to one knee, rested one hand on her belly, the other on his heart. She had laughed out loud.

'Dr Clair Mercer, esteemed math professor, cellist, and mother-to-be, will you marry me, your ever humble and devoted Adam?'

If only, oh God, he anguished, rubbing his eyes with his hands, if only she had said no. But she hadn't and they had found happiness, even after Devon's shattering diagnosis. *I must get her back,* he cried, lowering his head to the steering wheel. *I will get her back,* he promised himself, sitting up, starting the car, and driving towards home.

Chapter 7

Clair

The mental competency hearing was held in the community room, the only room on the unit large enough to contain all of the people and equipment needed to determine if Clair Mercer was mentally ill, and if she would be able to participate in her own defense. A charge of attempted murder had been brought by the Harbor County district attorney, a bitter man who resented having to come up to the hospital to hold the hearing.

In addition to the DA, there was the judge, his polar opposite, a woman who had a daughter with mental illness and showed generous mercy and compassion, within the legal limits, to persons with psychiatric disorders. Clair's attorney, fresh out of law school and seemingly terrified of the 'mentals' as he called them, had spoken to her briefly. He thought it would be in her best interests to be found not guilty by reason of insanity.

Odors filled the small space, redolent of human body odor, bleaching products, food smells, anxiety and fear. A court reporter, the mental health investigator, numerous witnesses, and staff on the unit sat in plastic folding chairs, looking stiff and uncomfortable. Clair had been allowed to put on street clothes gathered for her from the patient clothes bin. She had showered, washed and combed her hair. She had even applied a little make-up, thanks to Jamie, one of the nursing assistants who kept a stash for her favorite patients.

The proceedings were identical to any courtroom, with the swearing-in of witnesses, wrangling over esoteric legal nuances, chair legs scraping across a linoleum floor as witnesses came and went. Throughout it all, Clair stared out the window, disengaged, and disinterested in the outcome. She realized sitting there that she no longer wanted Adam dead. She had lost her desire for revenge, and now wanted only her own peace. It mattered not where she was physically. Her peace would come to her once she could die and be with Devon. She knew she would find a way. Jail might be easier than a locked psych unit, she considered. Less intense monitoring. Maybe someone would kill her, if she pissed them off enough.

As these thoughts rumbled through her mind, other images began seeping through. She would glance over at Adam. He had been discharged a few days earlier, and was back to his well-groomed, well-dressed self. And seemed to be enjoying his new role as sorrowful but merciful victim.

A few of their friends from the college were there. More his than hers, Clair considered, watching Claudia be sworn in. Clair had always felt like Claudia wanted Adam for herself. So many women did.

'And what was their marriage like, as you remember it?' the district attorney asked Claudia.

'Well, after the initial celebrations, walking across campus holding hands, sitting together at faculty meetings, eating together in the faculty lounge, all under our noses, as though trying to convince themselves they were happy, I did notice that Adam looked unhappy. I felt like he missed his old life.'

'Why did you feel like that? Can you give a specific example?' he prompted.

'It was after one of his play rehearsals, that had gone especially well. The two young students had fallen in love in front of our eyes during the rehearsal, and we were all in love with each other. It was a high moment, a high feeling. We wanted to go out and celebrate. At first Adam was right there with us, gathering up his satchel, his leather jacket, moving about with speed and grace, like the old Adam. Then his phone rang. You could see him deflate. It was Clair, we could hear him talking to her. Telling her that yes, he was wrapping up and would be home soon. But he didn't go home. He came with us. And I do think that is when things changed.'

That night was fresh in Clair's memory as well. Yes, that was the beginning of the change, for her. She had waited for Adam. When he had finally made it home, he had smelt of beer, smoke, and testosterone. She had been eight months pregnant, big and clumsy. Her feet had felt like boulders, and her face was puffy from lack of sleep and an overload of fluid coursing through her veins. She had been told she was at risk from pre-eclampsia and had to be on strict bedrest. They had fought. She remembered throwing a glass figurine of a sea-lion at him. They hadn't been sleeping together for the past month. He had said it was to help her rest but she knew he was repulsed by her size and overall slovenliness.

'And what else do you remember? Was she ever violent?' the DA asked.

'Well, after that night we did see more of Adam. In fact, he seemed to live at the theatre, often sleeping in his office. I never saw her be violent but then, I didn't see her very much at all. She took a leave of absence during the final weeks of her pregnancy and stayed home after that, to be with the boy, since he was ill. I knew she had been teaching online, and Adam said she was beginning to talk about returning to her classes on campus, right before her son died.'

Clair stood, her chair clattering as it was pushed forcefully behind her.

'You don't know that! No one knows. He is not dead, Claudia. You have no right to say that. We don't know where he is, but we don't know he is dead,' Clair cried.

The security guards rushed over to restrain her, fearful she might lunge at the witness. Clair held her arms up in a submissive gesture, finding her chair and sitting back down. The judge scolded her, admonishing her to remain quiet, seated, or she would be escorted back to her room.

'Are you all right, Dr Parker?' the DA asked Claudia. 'Do you need a break?'

'No, I'm fine,' she said, glancing at Clair. 'I'm sorry, Clair,' she said. 'I didn't mean any harm.'

'If you will direct your responses to the court,' the judge said to Claudia, gently.

'Yes, Your Honor,' she replied.

Several other witnesses filed through. The fisherman who had watched her walk into the water. The paramedics who had pulled her out. A neighbor who had seen her drive her car out of the driveway that afternoon. She remarked that, 'Mrs Mercer was very highly strung, running back and forth from the car to the house several times before backing out of the driveway at high speed. I almost went over to check on things. Since the poor boy was lost, that house had a darkness to it, so I didn't.'

The mental health court investigator described Clair's

state on admission, her psychotic delusions, disorganized and tangential speech patterns, and determined that at that time she was experiencing psychosis and was mentally ill.

Staff attested to her cooperative behaviors on the unit. Jet was called.

'Dr Juliette Elena Taylor, forensic psychologist, Harbor Hospital,' she cited.

'Dr Taylor,' Clair's defense attorney asked. 'Do you agree that Clair Mercer does have a mental illness and that at the time of her attempt to murder her husband, Adam Gage, she was mentally ill?'

'Yes, I do,' Jet replied.

'And do you think that she continues to present a danger to herself or any other person at this time?' he asked.

'I do. Dr Mercer continues to have suicidal ideation and I do think that if not under safe and structured conditions, she will attempt to kill herself again. I do not think she presents a danger to any other person at this time.'

Adam Gage was called. He looked less than his former self, as though life had taken an erasure to his charisma. All the features were there: the craggy face, lines like ski runs marking his way through life, from his soulful blue eyes to his full, wide mouth. His hair, silver blonde, shined like a new coin. He dressed for the part, Clair thought, studying him from her chair. Dark, charcoal pants, silk shirt, light navy cashmere sweater draped loosely over his shoulders. But she could see it was an act. That his assurance was lacking. She almost felt sorry for him. She pondered this thought for a moment, as he was sworn in.

Clair had never been one to speculate on the unknowable. She preferred the smooth electric slide of numbers to the intractable tangle of meaningful questions that held no answer. Devon had opened a new world to her. A world where the unknowable became known through feeling, not thinking. When he had smiled at her, his whole being would light up like a shooting star, and she knew then what was true. Adam couldn't see it like that, never found a way in, to be a part of that wonderful mystery. They had split on this and never found a way back. He had discounted their son and, because of that, carelessly lost him that hellish day on the beach at Seal Cove.

This sudden understanding shocked her. She gasped. She had not been able to place the pieces together in this way, like her equations, that made sense. But now, she could see the algorithm. Her attention turned back to Adam's questioning. He was telling the story, as he saw it.

'And was there a time when you began to fear for your safety?' the DA asked.

'After the accident, Clair didn't sleep. She would roam the house all night, sit in Devon's room, on the floor or lie in his bed. She had become obsessed with watching the Weather Channel, following storms all over the world. She had stopped eating meals. I would find her standing at the kitchen counter, a bowl of cold cereal or microwave noodles in front of her, forgotten. She had tried to return to work. She would leave the house in the morning, dressed for work, but she would return earlier than normal. Then her pacing would begin again. If I tried to help, she would either shun me or scream at me that I had already done enough harm. Not to try to do any more. Once I did wake up and find her standing over me, just staring down at me. I wasn't afraid for my safety so much as for her own. It was unnerving, though. I knew she needed to see a therapist, but she refused.'

'And that day, September the twentieth, was there anything different about her?' the DA continued his questioning.

'She did seem happier. When she came in from work or wherever she went during the day. I had heard from colleagues that she would leave campus right after her class, missing her student advising sessions, department faculty meetings. But I never knew where she went. And yeah, that day, she had been more, well, just there. She had offered to make me a drink, fixed me my favorite snack, cheese toast. I had thought maybe things were turning around for her, for us.'

Adam had been speaking directly to the judge, not looking around the small, crowded room. Clair stared hard at him, willing his eyes to reach hers. This wasn't how she remembered it, not at all. Clair heard her name being called.

'Dr Mercer, do you want to speak to the court?' her attorney was asking.

Clair started to stand, then settled, feeling all energy leaving her body like air from a released balloon. She folded her hands between her legs, as though they were startled birds that might fly away. Her heart was racing. She felt her breath catch in her throat, and was afraid she might be sick.

'No, I have nothing to say. I don't care what you do with me. Send me away, leave me here. It's all the same.' Looking at Adam she said, 'I don't want to kill you anymore, Adam. If that is worrying you. I see now that was wrong. I'm to blame more than you. You never even wanted Devon so why should I have expected you to safeguard him. You're free now.'

The judge reviewed all testimony and announced that given the evidence presented in the court, she ruled that Dr Clair Mercer was not guilty by reason of insanity and would remain in the behavioral health unit as an involuntary committed person for a period of time not more than 180 days. At that time, if the district attorney should decide to file charges for attempted murder, a follow-up hearing would be held. She struck her gavel, dismissing court.

Clair sat still, watching as the community room emptied out and patients, who had been exiled to their rooms, began filing back in. They cast curious glances her way, wondering what had happened, and what her reaction would be. She smiled at Gabe, who looked worried.

'I'm OK. I'll be here with you for a while longer, Gabe. We can play lots of Yahtzee. Maybe I'll even be able to beat you once or twice.'

'Yeah? That's great. Do you want to play now?' he asked in his soft, melodious voice. In another life, Gabe could have been a singer, opera or Broadway. Schizophrenia had put a stop to his and his doting parents' dreams for him.

'No, not now, I'm beat. I'm going to rest a bit, but maybe after dinner? she said.

'OK, sure. I'll be right here.'

'I know, and so will I it seems,' she called over her shoulder, walking out the door.

Chapter 8

Clair

Hours drifted into days, swelled into weeks. Each morning Annie would write the date on the large whiteboard hanging in the community room. Holiday decorations marked the changing seasons. Halloween was approaching, with pumpkin decorating contests using colored pens and paint, and baskets of apples and sugarless candy corn.

Clair navigated through time based on how long Devon had been gone, or attaching a memory to a particular date. It hurt, but she welcomed the pain, as her penance.

As she settled into the routine of the unit, Clair felt an echo of old patterns that brought her a sense of calm. Her life was at a stand-still. Surrender was her only option. Staff had allowed Adam to bring her cello to the unit. Clair was able to play in the community room, under the watchful eye of the psych techs. Patients could sleep in on Sundays, not roused by the cheerful nurse assistant Linda at six for morning hygiene. Clair couldn't rest; she was fretful and anxious. She had the dream again. The one in which she was hurtling through the cold darkness of water towards the light, Devon's energy pulsating and carrying her to him, space and time morphing into the vast space. As much as she wanted to stay there, her mind forced her back to here and now.

'Linda, is it too early for me to play?' she asked. 'I'll stay here in my room. I promise I won't bow myself blind or strangle myself with a string.' She smiled as she said this but Linda didn't smile back.

'I'd have to close the door, Clair, and you know that isn't OK. How about if I let you play in the conference room? That way we can see you on the monitor.'

'OK, that's fine. Thanks, Linda.'

Clair began playing softly, remembering how Pachelbel would soothe Devon when he became agitated. As she played, images flooded across her mindscape, like a video reel playing backwards.

'He is such a good baby,' she had told their pediatrician, Dr Chong, at his three-month visit, as she listened to his heart and lungs, tested his reflexes, and talked to him in her musical voice.

'Does he make eye contact with you or your husband?' Dr Chong had asked, holding Devon several inches away and looking into his eyes.

'I guess so. I've never really paid that much attention to that specifically. He eats, sleeps, lets me hold him. I think we make eye contact enough. Why, Dr Chong, is there something wrong?' Clair had asked, her stomach beginning to flutter.

'I don't know, Clair. Infants at this age should be making frequent eye contact, I am not seeing Devon do this. Let's see what he does when you hold him.'

The doctor had handed Devon back to Clair. Her boy felt so sturdy to her. They had worried about Down's Syndrome, because of her advanced maternal age, but the chromosomal testing had been negative. She had told Adam that it wouldn't have made any difference to her. She would have had Devon, loved him with or without any sort of developmental disorder. But he had been perfect. Clair had thrilled at her first sight of him. He can't be sick, she had thought, considering Dr Chong's words. She had held Devon close to her, then away from her. She had talked to him in her mommy voice. His eyes would drift off to the side, and she would smile, believing he was soothed.

Then, at his eighteen-month visit. The words that changed everything for ever.

'Clair, toddlers at this age should be following commands, and starting to say words. It's still early to make any sort of definitive diagnosis, but I would like to have Devon tested. These may be early signs of autism,' Dr Chong had said.

Clair's world had fallen out from under her, like an elevator hurtling towards the end.

'What should I do?' she had asked, the scientist in her wanting action, a plan, holding off the unknown.

'Let's set him up for some testing. We have therapy, applied behavioral analysis, that can help with symptoms. Clair, this isn't a diagnosis. It is just a precaution at this time. We can't really diagnose autism until around age two, but we don't want to wait to begin treatment.'

And so, it had begun, the daily visits to specialists, hopes soaring and then dispelling under fresh hits. Normal infant, toddler, then child developmental milestones left behind. In their place, her sweet boy who had lived his life alone.

'Clair, are you OK?' Jet asked from the open doorway.

'Oh, hi Jet. What are you doing here on Sunday?' she replied, startled back to the present. A memory so tender, feeling her cheeks wet. Had she been crying?

'I had to come in, finish up some paperwork. You were

crying, Clair. Is there something new? Has something happened?'

'No, I'm OK. I was just thinking back to Devon's baby time. How dear he was.'

Jet sat down on one of the chairs opposite Clair. Maggie lay down at her feet. 'Tell me.'

Clair stared into the inner distance, reconnecting with a thread of history. 'You know, we really can't ever go back,' she said. 'We have to bring our past with us forward, but we can't circle around and reclaim it or repair it. That makes living so hard.' Clair began drawing the bow across the strings, not playing a tune so much as creating a drone as backdrop for her story.

'I could feel my life tunneling in on itself, our future, lost.' Clair talked over the sounds of deep droning. In fits and starts at first, then gaining momentum. 'A woman's life is a series of sacrifices, right. There is a proverb about a parent only being as happy as their saddest child. Devon wasn't sad. He just wasn't fully present. Adam at first tried to be a part of the therapy, of the hope that therapy implies. But over time, he withdrew, mentally. Physically too. With all the doctor and therapy visits, our schedules had pretty much been set. Adam went to work. I stayed with Devon.'

She was quiet for a while, continuing to stroke the strings, a deepening line of melody beginning to sort out. 'That day at the beach,' Clair said, shifting in her chair, laying the cello aside. 'It was going to be a change for us. I had found a program for Devon, two days a week for four hours. It was an applied behavioral analysis program and was supposed to be the best type of treatment. And, it was going to allow me to return to teaching on campus, at least on a part-time basis. I was getting pressure from the dean and my colleagues, and I missed it, the interaction, distraction. This day out, I was anticipating good things. Maybe with time away, Adam and I could also fix our relationship. Buddhists are right. Expectations are the cause of all suffering.'

'What do you mean, Clair? What happened that day? We've never really talked about it, you know.'

Clair looked at Jet with torment in her eyes. She looked up at the marine painting, then back at Jet.

Clair stood up and walked over to Maggie. They had become good friends now, and her large, warm body gave such comfort. Clair sat down on the floor, cross-legged beside the dog. Her gaze turned away from the painting. And from Jet.

'I can't. The words, they won't come out,' she whispered; eyes closed tightly as though warding off unsought images.

Jet stood, gently taking her hand. 'Go put some clothes on. We're going on an outing.'

Chapter 9

Clair

At first, her steps were hesitant, a novice pianist's notes, unsteady, shaky. Then slowly, as she adjusted to being outside, walking on ground covered by roots and debris, looking up into a gunmetal sky sprinkled with clouds like spilt milk, her legs felt stronger, steps quickened. She knew this place in her heart. Each rustle of leaves and swish of branches, ripple of stream, roar of ocean just beyond the next turn in the path. These sounds had lived in her head for the past months, eclipsing all other sounds. She looked at Jet, questioning.

'Are you sure?' she asked. 'What if I can't? I feel like an unexploded bomb. I'm too frightened, all bound up.'

'Then we'll go back,' Jet replied, gently holding onto her arm. 'I think you'll be OK, though, Clair. And I think this is the only way for you to be able to get past the block that is in your throat, so you can speak of him and your life together in a way that allows you to live. Maybe here you will feel safe enough to talk about what makes you feel unsafe.'

The way was rough and Clair's leg muscles were weakened by days of immobility. She was breathing in the cool, moist salt air, stumbling and righting herself. As they turned a bend, she caught a first sight of the cove. The last place she had seen Devon alive.

'Oh,' she exhaled, collapsing into a squat, hugging her knees to her chest.

Jet waited. After a few moments, Clair stood again, nodding her head. 'I'm OK, I can do this. I must do this, for Devon.'

Maggie came beside her, nudging her big head under Clair's hand, leaning her weight against her leg.

'Thanks, girl,' Clair said, stroking her silky fur. 'Let's go.'

They came to the end of the path through the woods, walking across a makeshift bridge, two driftwood logs laid side by side, wobbly and slick from condensation. Clair looked up and saw a man standing on the cliff edge, looking down.

'You can send Keith back to the hospital,' she said to Jet. 'I'm not going to throw myself off the rocks or run into the ocean. Cross my heart.'

'Damn!' Jet said. 'You caught us. But he has to stay. You're still under commitment and I'm responsible for getting you back to the hospital in one piece.' She waved at him and motioned for him to move away, giving them privacy. They walked down to the beach, where a creek flowed into the ocean. Massive boulders stood like sentries. An elephant seal lay beached, its ponderous body inching towards the creek. They both stood and watched for a few moments, marveling at this wonder of nature. As the huge marine mammal heaved itself forward, her two white seal pups remained still, waiting for a high tide to carry them back out to sea. The dog eyed them curiously then trotted down the beach, chasing a flock of white sea-birds harvesting the flotsam left by retreating waves.

'Which way?' Jet asked, looking down the curved beach, surrounded by rocky cliffs on each side, a tall wall behind. Clair stood transfixed. Flashbacks of her time underwater, after her suicide attempt, came flooding back. She knew these creatures. They had welcomed her, taken her into their world, breathed life into her as she was crushed against the rocks, pulling her away, to safety. She shook herself like a wet dog. Hallucinating again? Dreams or memories?

'Here,' Clair said. 'Let's sit here. This is – *was* – our spot.' Clair pointed to a smooth table rock.

Someone had built a cairn beside it, several stones placed precariously one on top of the other. A traveler's prayer. They were careful not to disrupt its balance as they settled themselves on the flat stone. Cold and hard, it comforted Clair, something solid to rely on.

They sat in silence, watching the cresting, cascading, and crashing of the waves into each other, up onto the beach, against the rocks. The rhythmic sounds enveloped her consciousness, like an anesthetic. Clair noticed her breathing synchronizing with the patterns, felt the cold water envelop her again, and again. She wasn't frightened. She felt at home. She had read that people with near drowning do this, re-encounter their experience, their death. And long for it. Just knowing it was there comforted her in ways she was not prepared for through her studies of math and science. She believed Devon was sending her information. Like he had sent the seal family. Glancing sideways at Jet, suddenly fearful she might be able to read her thoughts, which she knew would be considered psychotic, Clair quickly shut them off.

'It had started out OK,' Clair began, her voice soft, eyes fixed on the horizon. 'I mean, our usual tussle. Him on the phone, me doing all the work. I didn't care that morning. I was so expectant that this day would change all those old patterns. Like an unequal equation. Once I had found the solution, the elements would all fall into place. We just needed a day at the coast, together, as a family, to initiate our new life. You know, spring break, Easter, resurrection. God, how pathetic it all seems now. But, then, well…'

As Clair talked, the day came into sharp focus. She remembered how warm it had been, soft, and breezy. The ocean had earned its name, Pacific. It was glassy and flat. Not the gigantic waves seen in winter. The morning argument, over packing the lunches, beach paraphernalia, loading the car, all so insignificant now, had continued on the drive from their home downriver to the coast. Anger and disappointment had coursed through her, recovering old neural pathways of thought, speech, and action.

'It's your turn to watch Devon, I'm going to read,' she had told him, flipping onto her belly, the striped beach blanket already coated with a fine dusting of sand. Devon's sand toys littered the area around her. Shovel, bucket, molds for sandcastles.

She had known in her heart that Adam had been talking to his latest girlfriend. Probably the same one from earlier that morning. She had seen him pull his phone out of his vest, as he walked with Devon down to the tidal pools. Part of her had wanted to leave, go home, pretend this variance in their mutual lie of a life had never happened. But the joy on Devon's face when he saw the ocean, his lightness as he raced across the sand, held her back. Instead, she chose the coward's way out, hiding her pain behind a cloak of indifference.

'Oh, how he had loved the creatures in the tidal pools,' Clair said to Jet, looking towards the low rocky area that bordered the cliffs. 'He would watch them for so long, his face serious and intent.' A smile broke across her face like sun behind a thunderhead, and then the thunderhead struck.

'I had pretended to read. But I was watching Adam walk away.' Clair raised her head, breathed in deeply, feeling her chest tighten, nausea rising from her gut. 'I had watched Adam moving away and talking on the phone. I didn't watch my son. When I looked back, he was gone.' A cry caught Clair in her throat. Seeing this, telling this was living it again.

'I ran to the place he had been. I screamed his name over and over. I ran all around looking behind every rock, sand dune, clump of grass. He was gone. I yelled at Adam to call 911. Soon the place was flooded with police, fire, the coast-guard helicopter flying in circles. News people. Gawkers. And then, it was over and we had to go home, without Devon, and the terrible knowledge that I would never hear my name, Mommy, called again.'

She looked up at Jet as though this fact alone was enough to lock her up for life. That she had allowed this to happen. That she had survived this happening was in itself a travesty. Grabbing handfuls of sand, squeezing it between fingers that were trembling with dread, Clair looked down, eyes closed as though seeing was too much to bear.

'The first time I walked into my house, into his room, that is when I lost my mind. The drive home was a blur. The paramedics had given me a shot of something and wanted to admit me to the hospital, but I refused. I was numb, sedated but awake enough to know how empty the car was. How empty the house was, his room, this space where he always was. My Devon.' Clair broke down here, shuddering sobs rocking her body back and forth. Jet sat quietly, letting her cry.

After a time, Clair raised her head. Above, a coast-guard helicopter flew in wide circles on the horizon. A regular sight as helicopter trainees practiced their skills in calm weather. The sound cast Clair back to that morning. The response, active and optimistic soon shifted to recovery and then, after days without finding a body, the relinquishing of all hope.

Running her hands through her hair, she cried, 'Oh God, it just never ends, it never ever stops. How can this be real? I've always looked outward, towards infinity. Now, having to look inward, to find a way to coexist in this life with pain, finding a way to hope, to believe. I don't think I can do it. I don't want to do it, Jet. It just hurts too bad.'

Jet reached over and took Clair's hands, holding them in her own.

'It is, Clair. I'm so sorry but it is real. You're real. And this is what happened. Now we have to find a way for you to live through it and into a future. Healing happens now, in the present moment. This one moment, then the next. That is all any of us have. And for you, it is a journey towards peace. A way to find something more enduring than self.'

'But why?' Clair asked. 'Seriously, I am asking this as a scientist, not as a mournful mother. Why must I live?'

'Oh shit,' Jet said, standing up, brushing the sand from her bottom. 'I was wondering when you would ask this question.'

Clair looked out to sea; her eyes focused on a ship passing through the barrier rock cliffs creating the small cove. Out there, in the vast dark deepness, was her son. His blood, bones, flesh, hair, everything mixed with the salt and water, and all living things. She knew that energy never dies, it just changes form. She turned to Jet. Noticed how her hair, so fair, like light itself, formed a halo around her head. She remembered that hair, that face.

'You were there, weren't you? When they brought me in after my suicide attempt?' Clair asked her, standing up beside her.

Jet turned, eyed Clair. 'Yes, I was. And I was there before; the first time. After Devon. I saw your pain, Clair, your devastation. I knew you'd be back.'

Neither spoke for a few minutes. The wind had picked up, as it did in the afternoons, when the valley warmed, drawing the cooler air from the ocean, creating wind and fog.

'What happened to you, Jet?' Clair asked. 'Why are you always there, at the hospital? Don't you have a home to go to? People who care?'

Jet shook her head, smiling. 'Oh, the patient becomes the therapist, the therapist patient,' she said, looking at Clair with amusement.

'Let's walk. Yes, I do have a home, with Maggie, and a cat named Midnight. I swim laps every morning and teach yoga at a local gym three evenings a week. I also play piano, garden, knit, and read voraciously. I have several women friends with whom I enjoy lunch and an occasional movie. Satisfied?'

'Hmm, that sounds much like the life I had before Adam and Devon, which means, not much of a life at all. Why not?'

'You mean, why don't I have a husband and children? The female dream?'

'Yes. You're young, beautiful, smart. Why the fuck not?'

'I had a twin. Gwendolyn, Gwen. She died of leukemia when we were seventeen, just after graduation from high school. Our parents had been killed in a small plane crash when we were eleven. We lived with our grandmother but it was really just the two of us, together. When Gwen got sick, I contributed bone marrow and it looked like she would beat it, survive. But she got a bug bite, that turned into staph, that turned into sepsis, that killed her. I keep waiting for my turn.

You know, my turn to get sick. So, I'm not going to subject any man, or child to that. End of story.'

'I get it. Some of us are accursed.'

'No, Clair, that's not it. Each of us is an infinite number of possibilities. I love my life. I don't need a husband and children to have meaning and purpose. I am aware, informed, and intentional in my choices, yes. But, cursed, no. My sister was, is, a blessing in my life. I feel her near me always.'

'Then you understand,' Clair cried, stopping beside the small stream that ran down through the forest onto the beach. 'Oh, when I was dead, you know this time, Jet, I saw what it was like. And it was beautiful. Calling me in, not terrifying. I felt such love. He was there, not in his precious little boy form, but vast, ancient, unnamable. I wanted to stay. How I wanted to stay. But I felt a jolt in my chest, in my heart. Pounding, gagging. Hands, pulling me away from him, from that miracle of a billion lights. The warmth, then cold, so cold. So, you see, my yearning for death isn't a running away from, it's a running to.'

The cold fog had rolled in to the cove, shrouding the cliffs overhead. A bell buoy sounded its warning to all ships entering the dangerous waters of the Coos river cut.

'Let's go, Clair, it's getting late.'

Clair tripped over a root stepping onto the forest path. She unconsciously cushioned her left breast with her palm as she righted herself.

'What's going on with your left side? It looks like it hurts,' Jet asked Clair.

'Oh, just a tender area. It feels like when I had mastitis, while I was breastfeeding. It just sort of started, on the walk down here.'

'OK, we'll have Dr Bernstein take a look when we get you back on the unit. You're going to be OK, Clair. You must be, for him. Won't you?' Jet asked.

'Thank you for this, Jet. For bringing me here. I do feel better.'

'That's not the same as telling me you're going to live. To accept life as it is.'

'What else can I do, right? Radical acceptance? Come on, let's get back, I'm freezing and starving,' Clair said, walking away into the darkening woods.

Chapter 10

Adam

The bright yellow dump truck sat in the grass, parked, as though waiting for the boy to race out into the yard, lay his hands on either side of its sturdy metal bed, and push it over to his beloved sand-box. It had been there since the day he and Clair had returned home, from their wretched day at the beach. Without Devon. Like a talisman, Clair had demanded it remain, a sentry for its lost child. Adam pulled into the driveway, walked over and scooped up the truck. He held it in his hands, uncertain what to do with it. Then he walked around the side of the house, laid it in Devon's sand-box, along with his dinosaurs, Matchbox cars, and other play things. He stood for a moment, feeling more alone than he had ever felt. Who was he without Clair, without Devon? A failed actor? A poor friend who substituted flirtation for connection? He felt alienated from the human community, as though he had lost so much more than his son and wife. He had lost the very connection to humanity. A father is meant to protect his family. He didn't. Desperate, he didn't know what to do or where to go.

Adam walked straight to the drinks table and poured a large whisky. He had been advised not to drink alcohol, the adverse effect of the sedative overdose still in his system, but now he needed it, the burn, the rush, the silencing of his thoughts. He walked into the kitchen, looked out the window onto the leaf strewn yard. August in the north-west was the beginning of fall. Especially after such a long, dry summer. Everywhere, he could see the remnants of months without rain or even much moisture from condensation.

The sand-box drew his eyes, unwillingly. The yellow truck sat in the middle, its small shovel raised like a fist, pummeling the world around it. He felt suddenly exhausted. Without bones, or blood to sustain his upright posture. He fell, more than sat, into a chair, hardbacked, and stiff. The kitchen table before him littered with the crumbs from his poisoned toast. Odd, he thought, that the forensics people didn't clean that up. He half-heartedly touched one with his index finger, putting it to his nose and sniffing. Enough, he thought. Get on with it. He drank down the last of his whisky and walked slowly through the house, to their bedroom, and into the bathroom. He stripped, turned the shower on. He stepped into the downpour, as hard and hot as he could stand it, letting the water beat on his back, run down his face. Tears, sudden and unwanted, stung his eyes. After a long time, when the water turned cold, he got out of the shower, sat on the edge of the bed, his forearms resting on his knees. The raucous sound of Queen's 'We Will Rock You' blared through the quiet. His ringtone. Devon had picked it out, loving the pounding and power of the voices and drums.

A flashback, cutting straight to his heart. Devon, slick and wet from their shower, his hair, hanging in ringlets around his face, dancing as only a three-year-old can to the thumping beat. The image conjured up another scene, a day at the beach, almost one year before the tragedy.

'Daddy, look, faces!' Devon had pointed excitedly at the bobbing heads of two sea-lions, curious and staring. Their big eyes following his and Devon's movements as they walked across the sand, towards the tidal pools.

'Those are sea-lions, Dev. They sound like big dogs when they bark.'

'I hear them,' he had called out, running ahead. 'Orff, arff,' he had mimicked.

'Be careful, Dev, the rocks can be slippery,' Adam remembered warning, smiling at the small footprints left in the damp sand, before the next wave washed them away.

He hadn't seen his son that happy in weeks. They had started him in pre-school for children with autism and other neurological disorders. He resisted the confinement. When allowed to be free of clothes, furniture, expectations, he danced. Adam thought he looked like a tribal warrior just released from captivity, his limbs and torso gyrating and spinning in circles. Adam had laughed so hard, tears formed. And they did again. Now, pooling in the corners of his eyes. *No more*, he said to himself, *I'll cry no more. I have to do something about this. Something; I don't know what.*

The call had gone to voicemail. He pressed play, and heard his sister-in-law's voice.

'Adam, what the hell's going on. We just got back in the country, talked to Ben's parents. She's what? Incarcerated? Are you OK? Call us.'

Adam stood, looked at himself in the full-length mirror on the back of the closet door. Clair had hated it, he remembered, calling him vain for wanting to see so much of himself. Now, as he looked, he had to agree. It was a bad idea. He had lost weight, his skin sagging around his bone structure. He opened the door, pulling out clothes at random. Pants, a long-sleeve tee, wool sweater. He couldn't get past the chill the hospital had infused into him. Cold crisp white sheets. At home, they slept under flannel year-round. Socks, slip-on loafers, and then maybe he could call them back. But first, another drink.

'Hello,' he said, fatigue and uncertainty measuring his usual self-assured tone.

Later, after assuring them that Clair was not in jail, that it was a hospital and she was being cared for by professional medical and nursing staff, arrangements were made for Adam to pick them up at the airport in Eugene. The local airport only served small, commuter traffic. Adam liked his in-laws. He only saw them once or twice a year. It hadn't been that long ago this time, though. The memorial for Devon. Adam winced inwardly remembering that.

The coast-guard had called off the rescue mission after a few days. Then, it had switched to a recovery mission, if even that were possible, given the elements and natural predators. Adam had wanted a way to acknowledge the loss, and to close this event. Clair had called it staging a scene. 'You just want to be the star, the grieving father, the wounded hero,' she had scorned. 'I won't have it, and I won't be there. Have your pity party on your own.'

But it hadn't been like that. Her parents, stiff and reluctant; Ben and Jodie plus many of their colleagues from the college. He hadn't invited any of his family. They had never met Devon or Clair. He had arranged for the chorale singers along with their small but talented chamber orchestra to perform. The day had been just like the day Devon disappeared and it almost seemed like a holographic image, except for the fact that Devon wasn't there. Robin egg blue sky, not even a breath of wind.

Adam had invited Devon's classmates but only a few attended, more out of their parent's curiosity than caring, he surmised. After a short ceremony, balloons were let loose over Mingus Park, Devon's favorite playground, and floated over tree-tops, rooftops, and away. Clair refused to come to the park. She had joined in later for drinks at their house, ignoring Adam and spiriting Ben and Jodie away into the study. Their parents had sat like rejected manikins on the couch, itching to leave.

He couldn't stand being in the house alone. Empty, it felt hollowed out, desolate. Before, coming home was like walking into a minefield, uncertainty guiding each step, each word and action. That last day had felt different, almost like their early days. But that had been just too near perfect, he mused. Like a vine pushing against a wall, there must be tension in a life, in a love, to make it grow. Too little, stagnation, too much, turbulence. Fire or ice. They had not been able to hold a middle ground.

Their house was so far from anywhere. Another thing they had argued about.

'This is a good twenty miles from town,' he had complained, when she had driven him out to see it, when Devon's diagnosis of autism was first confirmed.

'Yes, but look at the space. He can have animals, a playhouse, fish in the creek. All the things a boy's world should include. We can let him run free, without worrying about cars, weirdos or other town issues. It will be safe here, and quiet. You know how noise makes him anxious. And look, you can convert that old barn into your acting studio. You've always wanted to do that, right?'

And as usual, Clair had gotten her way.

He felt untethered. So many times, he had felt the pull of

this, this freedom. He needed to be with people, near noise, laughter, life. There was a bar, the Halfway Bar and Grill, a few miles further upriver. Mostly fishermen, hunters, in season or out. It was a crossroads. Turn left, you went further into the back country. A long, winding mountain path to the end of the road. Turn right, you circled back into town, taking the high road around the mountain. It was halfway to getting lost or halfway to being found. Tonight, he wanted to be found.

Chapter 11

Clair

Clair walked into the cold hall, wrapped in a warm kimono, the heat lying close to her skin, bringing goose pimples to the surface of her arms. She shivered. The attendant, or technician, she wasn't sure what to call this kind woman, ushered her into the screening room. Large metal objects hung from the ceiling. Women's magazines about "House Beautiful" and "Coastal Living" placed strategically on love seats aligned along the wall. Imagining herself sitting there, calmly reading about the perfect dinner party made her cringe.

'Hi, I'm Megan,' the tall woman, wearing a white lab coat, standing next to one of the behemoth machines said, a broad smile lighting up her face, as though they were gathering for that perfect dinner party. 'Come on in. Stand right here. This is our new imaging radiography and it is so much nicer than the other one we had. Are you doing OK? Can I get you anything? This won't take long.'

She stood in the center of this white, startling room, trying hard to get her bearings. Her keeper, or guard from the psych unit, Linda, stood next to her, trying to be innocuous but not succeeding. How many patients come for a mammogram, from the locked psychiatric unit, with a guard? Clair thought not too many. So, here she was. If she had just kept quiet about that pain in her breast this wouldn't even be happening. She'd just go on like nothing was wrong. But she had flinched on the beach with Jet. And damn that Jet, she had noticed and insisted on the doctor checking and now she was here. It had all happened so quickly; she was still stunned. She turned as the woman named Megan began to remove the kimono from her right side.

'If you could just step close to this plate,' she said, gently guiding her towards the mammography unit. Clair stepped up, allowed Megan to situate her breast on the flat surface, reach her arm up overhead, and flatten the breast between the two plates. She followed her instructions to the letter. It was comforting to be so controlled. So maintained.

'I'm sorry, this might pinch,' Megan warned. 'OK, we're almost there, let me take a look. OK, that's good, hold your breath, hold, and OK, now breathe.'

Clair stepped back from the vice grips, covered herself with the sleeve of the kimono. She stood still in the room, not moving as Linda read the magazine and Megan changed films.

'OK, let's do the other side. I didn't ask but is this a routine mammogram or is there a problem? You were placed on the add-on schedule without much background.'

'Ah, I am having some pain over here,' pointing to her left side.

'OK, let's see what it looks like,' Megan said as she gently guided Clair back to the imaging machine.

'Like before,' she said as she pulled the kimono off the left side, bearing the left breast that made her gasp before she knew how to stop. The redness was evident even from her angle.

'Oh, well, yes, that is red. Let's see if we can get a picture of this.'

The small movement of taking hold of the left breast caused Clair to cry out. The pain was intense. Megan gently released her hold, easing Clair away from the machine.

'Let's stop,' Megan said. 'This won't work. We need another tool here. Something that won't hurt so bad. Are you OK?' she asked, laying her warm hand on Clair's arm.

Tears came to her eyes, unbidden, unwanted.

'Yeah, I guess I'm OK. What now? She said, stepping back, covering herself up again.

'Clair, we need Dr Michaels here. I think we will switch to an ultrasound examination. It will be less painful and also provide us with a better picture. Can you and Linda wait here for a bit? I'll give Dr Michaels a call. It shouldn't take long. Can I bring you anything? Coffee? Tea?'

What could she say? She was their prisoner. Their mental patient. Did she even want to know?

After what seemed like an hour but was only ten minutes, another woman entered their exam room. She was also tall, like Megan, but so slender, it seemed she might break in two, like a twig. When she extended her hand for Clair to take, it felt strong, capable. Clair liked her immediately. Her hair was short, curly, brown with specks of gray. She wore no make-up, and her eyes shone with intelligence and kindness through wire-framed rectangular glasses.

'Dr Mercer, hello. I'm Sarah Michaels, radiologist. I am sorry that you're having this problem today and I'm going to do all I can to help you through the examination so we can know what is happening in your breast. How does that sound?'

Linda had reached over and placed an arm on Clair's shoulder, as though to steady her.

'Do I have a choice?'

Dr Michaels sat down on the seat beside Clair. 'Yes, you do have a choice. In fact, I have a consent form here for you to sign. This exam is invasive. First, we will locate the mass using ultrasound. Then a technician will insert a large needle and aspirate fluid for biopsy. It may be uncomfortable and we can give you a light sedative, if you would like. It's the best way for us to determine if that lump in your breast is cancer or not.'

'And if I refuse, what then?' Clair asked, gazing into the other woman's steady brown eyes.

'Well, if this is cancer, it will get worse. It will most likely spread throughout your body. The fact that it came up suddenly, is painful, and the area around it is red, makes me think that it might be a form called inflammatory breast cancer. If so, you will need to get started right away on treatment.'

'And if I don't want treatment?' Clair asked, feeling a bit like a stubborn two-year-old talking about eating her vegetables.

'Well, I don't know, Clair. Every individual is unique, every cancer is unique. Maybe we should just take this one step at a time. Beginning with an ultrasound exam to clearly visualize the area in your breast that is causing the pain and redness. May I touch you?'

Dr Michaels pulled back the kimono, exposing the left breast. She gently palpated the reddened area. Clair winced but didn't pull back.

'I can feel a hardened area. Clair, we will need to biopsy this area to know if it is cancer or something else, like an infectious process. We need to know before you can make any sort of informed decision about what comes next. Can we do that today?' Dr Michaels asked.

Clair looked at Linda. 'Do you need to get back to the unit? Can you stay with me?' she asked.

'I'll call over. Let them know what's happening. I'll stay, Clair.'

'OK, then, let's get this done.'

Chapter 12

Adam

The drive over the Coastal Range mountains to Eugene took Adam close to an hour. This time of year, the river was low from lack of rain, gurgling over the rocks and fallen debris. The hillsides were dotted with sheep and grown offspring, many still trying to nurse, even though often bigger than their ewes. Cows, horses, llamas, and goats lay about under large oak trees, soaking up the last of the late summer sun. Weathered barns and outbuildings caught the shadows, inviting reverie for times past.

He felt twisted inside out, hungover, depleted. Still wearing the same shirt and jacket, pants, even socks he had on at the bar last night, he knew he smelt of beer, smoke, and old sweat. He had closed the place down, playing pool with the bikers, dancing with the woman who, like Cohen sang, must have been a hundred but was wearing something tight. He didn't remember how he had gotten home. He had woken up, head throbbing, mouth dry, his phone alarm jangling. When he had looked at the calendar reminder, it said to pick up Ben and Jodie at the airport at 6 p.m. It was 4.30 and he knew the drive would take at least an hour or more, depending on traffic and road work. Somehow, he made it in under an hour.

Ben was the first to emerge from the security area. Jodie close behind, both wearing backpacks and carrying large canvas totes. Not for the first time he marveled at how different they were and yet, banded together for many years now. But maybe that had been as much circumstance as character. Ben took after their mother, small, pale complexion, hips wide, almost feminine. Clair had inherited her father's height, aristocratic personage, but not his arrogance. Jodie's skin and bone structure showed off her South African heritage. Her father, an Anglican bishop during apartheid, had moved the family first to South Carolina, where they were granted protected status, and later to Washington. Jodie's accent mixed her original Afrikaans, with deep south and her own unique musical and articulate voice. Beautiful and kind, she was a strong balance for Ben's quick-fire nature.

They wanted to go straight to the hospital, not stopping at the house to change or rest. And that was fine with him. He hoped they would decide to stay in town, rather than at his house, seeing as it was so far out. He might find a way to suggest this. For now, he just wanted get this visit over with, then go home and sleep.

The drive back to the coast gave him time to catch them up.

'All I know is that she is under commitment,' he said when Ben asked why she was being kept on the psych ward.

'Why can't she go home?' he had asked.

Adam tried to explain the convoluted mental health laws in Oregon to these people who had spent the better part of the past twenty years living and working in countries under attack, or in refugee camps. The idea that a mathematics professor could be kept locked up for six months because she was grieving for her lost child was incomprehensible to them.

'Crap!' Ben exclaimed. 'Did she have a lawyer? Anyone to argue for her?'

'She refused to let me pay for one. She insisted on having the legal aid attorney who, like most of them, was fresh out of school and hated the 'mentals' as they are called. He was less than helpful. But Ben, it might be the best place for her now. She still perseverates on dying and being with Devon. She had a near-death experience and it has left her psychotic. She believes she saw Devon while she was in the ocean, and that he is out there waiting for her. You can't reason with her. It just is this way.'

'In my culture, we believe in the division of the body, and that the spiritual parts of the body and sometimes the physical body itself will survive death,' Jodie said from her seat in the back. She leaned forward, placing a hand on Adam's shoulder.

'From an anthropological and theological perspective, it is understood that during the near-death experience, the mind or spirit leaves the body, and this idea is not a strange or new phenomenon to many people. I think Western thought and maybe the criminal justice system has some learning to do.'

'That may be so Jodie, and I respect and honor your knowledge on this, but it isn't helping her now. And she has this therapist, Jet, who I am afraid is feeding into her psychosis. I just want her out of there so I can find her some real help. She needs to be on medication but she refuses.'

'I thought that was the purpose of commitment,' Ben said. 'To force people to take meds?'

'Only if they are violent. She's committed but still has her rights to refuse treatment. It's a fucking wreck.'

'What can we do Adam? How are you? We feel so out of touch,' Jodie said.

'I don't know. Your being here might be good for her. To see, and know about the world outside. I just really don't have a clue.'

They were quiet the rest of the ride. Both Ben and Jodie slept, exhausted after their eighteen-hour flight from Amsterdam. Following the river back, retracing earlier miles, evening settling in, his mind wandered back to the first time he had seen Clair. He had been at the annual Arts Showcase, a sort of final exam for students, and a chance for faculty to show off their own skills. Clair had been on stage, playing cello, while dancers performed a passage from *The Rite of Spring*.

'Who is that?' he had asked Claudia, his theater department chair and sometimes lover. They had both viewed their sex as recreational and avoided the romantic pitfalls so many faculty colleagues fell into, always with awkward and sometimes fatal consequences. Loss of tenure prospects, loss of job. Loss of family, reputation. With Claudia, it was mutually beneficial and superficial. At least he had believed.

'Oh, that's Clair Mercer, theoretical mathematics,' she had replied, sipping her champagne.

'So, that's the beautiful and enigmatic Dr Clair Mercer,' he had thought out loud. Stories had circulated among faculty, about this brilliant woman who kept to herself, didn't engage in the usual social activities that seemed to infect college campuses, giving rise to a culture of sophomoric competition.

Claudia had given him a funny look, then turned and walked away. He had watched mesmerized as Clair played. She had been dressed in a full black skirt, tucked modestly in so that she could hold the cello between her knees. Her every

91

stroke and caress of the strings had caused her to bend and sheer to the side, her hair, tied back in a bun at the nape of her neck, came loose, and feathered her face. He had wanted to reach out and tuck it back, reveal her. As she dipped and swayed, taken over by the music, occasionally throwing her head back in pure ecstasy, he had been captured, unable to take his eyes off her. After, he would watch her cross campus, long, confident strides making her seem to glide. Occasionally she would stop, chat with the groups of students, easy and natural with them. During a faculty meeting, he had overheard her talking to a math colleague about fractals. Patterns that expanded, but held onto their original seed pattern, a spiral dynamic that always contained its beginning. If only he could help her find that seed inside herself – that person before all of this, before him, before Devon. If he could help her remember, and let go of everything else, maybe she could find a way to live. Even if it meant living without him.

When they pulled up to the front of the emergency department lobby, Adam directed them to the Psychiatric Unit, on the third floor.

'I'll just park, and be there in a minute,' he said, looking forward to a short power nap in the car. His eyes burned and he thought he might pass out.

He parked the car, let his seat down, pulled his jacket over him, locked all doors, closed his eyes and was gone in a moment's time. He woke with a start when he heard his phone's ringtone. Dark now, the lights in the parking lot casting a yellow glow, he was momentarily disoriented.

'Where the hell is she?' Ben's voice cried into the phone. 'They're saying she's not there, on the unit. That they've never heard of a Clair Mercer.'

'Oh fuck. They are so obstructive. I'll be right there. Wait for me in the lobby.'

He used the door handle to pull himself out of the car. Stiff, sore, he stretched tall, lifted his face to catch the cool mist drifting down, allowing a moment to breathe in its velvety softness. Pulling his jacket hood over his head, shoulders slumped, he lumbered off across the tarmac.

* * *

The intercom buzzed.

'It's Adam Gage, here to see Clair Mercer. Belinda, you know it's me. This is Clair's family. Please, let us in or at least let Clair know we're here.'

The voice coming through the speaker was tinny. 'Dr Gage, it's Charles. Hold on, I'll come out and talk with you. Better yet, come in. I'll let you into the conference room.'

'What the hell is going on?' Adam said to Ben. 'I don't get it.'

The buzzer, indicating the door to the sallyport unlocking, sounded. Adam pushed through, holding it for Ben and Jodie. They waited in the center of the small cubicle, for the second click, indicating they were released to enter into the locked unit. Charles, a middle-aged nurse with shaggy, gray hair and a gold stud in his earlobe, stood sentinel, shepherding them into the conference room to the right. But before they were able to enter, two surgical technicians, wearing the green scrubs of the operating room, wheeled a gurney towards them. As they moved aside to make room for the team to pass, Adam saw Clair, her head covered by a surgical cap, IV line dripping from her arm. She caught his eye as she passed, and mouthed the words, 'I'm sorry,' as they pushed by.

Chapter 13

Clair

Clair laid still on the white sheeted bed, an IV-line snaking into her right forearm, a sting, each time the machine beeped, pumping a hit of morphine into her fragile vein, followed by immediate and intense nausea then blessed nothingness. She would drift off for several minutes, then awake again with a start, panic and dread chilling her blood, her entire body shivering in spite of the room's sticky warmth and the heated blanket thrown over her near naked body. A thin cotton gown, untied to allow for easy access by the nurses barely covered her. She felt carved out, unmasked, and vulnerable. The only thing keeping her connected with reality was the punishing pain in her chest, where her breasts used to be.

A soft knock sounded at the door, followed by a voice.

'Hello, Clair. How are you feeling? OK if I come in?'

Clair turned her head, eyes trying to focus through the morphine cloud.

'Hmm, Jet, come in.'

Jet stopped at the sink to wash her hands, then walked over to the side of Clair's bed. A stool on wheels sat in the corner. She pulled it over so she would be at eye level with Clair. Clair had turned her head away again, looking out the window at passing clouds cutting through the tops of tall evergreens. The light was fading early, fall bringing shorter, cooler days, longer nights. Jet noticed her hands gripping the blanket on the bed.

'Are you hurting now?' she asked. 'Do you need your nurse?'

'I'm OK,' Clair said, keeping her head turned so Jet wouldn't see the tears glistening in her eyes. 'I don't like the morphine. It makes me sick. I prefer the pain.'

Jet didn't say anything. They sat there, in quiet, for several minutes until another knock sounded at the door. They looked up together, seeing a tall, slumped-shouldered man, with short, dark-brown hair standing there. He wore a bright purple shirt, lime green tie, and jeans. He wasn't old, but not young either. He looked like he might have looked since he was a high school student, except for a receding hairline.

He walked briskly over to the side of the bed. Jet had to scoot over on her rolling stool to make room for him. He held out his hand, eager as a puppy. Clair began to reach up to take it then winced, tucking her arm back down by her side. He smiled and tucked both hands in his pockets, nodding at Jet. They knew each other from having worked together over the years, Jet consulting on his patients with depression and anxiety. Jet stood up, offering him her stool, the only available seat in the room.

'Hello, I'm Robert Ellerby, oncologist. I've been asked to review your case, and I did. What I found is not good, in fact it's about as bad as it gets, but the good news is we have treatment that can slow it down and, sometimes, send the patient into remission. We should get started right away, with several treatments of chemo, followed by radiation. If we do, I think you can plan to live out most of your life expectancy, maybe with some recurrence but we can treat that too. First, we need to do a PET scan, but that has to be done as an outpatient. So, that first, then we start the chemo. Questions?'

Clair was stunned. She looked at him, shaking her head slightly from side to side, eyes trying to focus on his face, his skin, his hair, anything but his eyes, which were so kind. His words had spilled out like foam, bubbling away so that all that was left was the bitter taste of bile rising in her gut.

'Are you saying I have cancer?' she asked, eyes now seeking his.

'Yes, sorry, I thought I had explained that. You do have what looks like stage IV, inflammatory breast cancer. We'll have to wait for the full biopsy results but just based on the number of lymph nodes involved, and the presentation, I am pretty certain this is what we are dealing with. And you did just have a double mastectomy. Sometimes patients are a bit confused after anesthesia. What do you remember?'

'I remember everything. The mammogram. The ultrasound. Everyone rushing around like I was an infectious disease, just about to spread. Consents signed. God. I don't know. I do remember seeing my brother and sister-in-law, and my husband or who used to be my husband, crying. I'm just so tired now. Everything has happened so fast. In the past month, I've almost killed my husband, almost drowned, been committed, and now this. I just want to sleep, be left alone. So, what is it that you want?'

He sat, head bowed, hands on both knees. His hair, like a boy's, falling forward into his face. She watched as he stood and walked over to a computer terminal set on a mobile stand, typing in instructions. Soon images appeared on the screen. He turned the screen towards her, pointing out areas with his index finger.

'See here and here? These are patches on the CT scan that might be metastasis so we need a test called a positron emission tomography, or PET scan to make sure. Like I said, this is one mean cancer and we have to be aggressive. We also need to get a bone scan, more blood work, and then we'll start you on treatment as soon as possible. There are protocols to follow, clinical trials. You're relatively young, healthy, so you should do fine. We can't cure it but we can slow it down. You will be able to live a good life, possibly with remissions. And we can treat recurrence as they appear. Every day we are learning more and finding new ways to treat metastatic breast cancer. It isn't as hopeless as it once was.'

Jet had reached over and laid her hand on Clair's arm. Clair didn't seem to notice. She stared at the ceiling, as though looking for a sign.

'Will I die if I don't take treatment?' she asked, eyes still on the ceiling.

He had walked back over to her, sitting on the side of the bed, his hands folded in his lap.

'Well, I can't say for certain, but statistically, the odds are not in favor of your surviving for longer than a year to eighteen months.'

'Good. I don't want chemo or radiation,' she said, shifting her gaze to Dr Ellerby. 'I won't do it. I want death with dignity. Just give me the goddamn pill.'

* * *

The family meeting took place in Clair's room. She sat cross-legged in the middle of the bed, her hair brushed back, revealing a face drawn and tired. Two drains snaked down on either side of her body, serosanguinous fluid coursing down, gathering in small plastic bags that sat on the bed. She tucked them both under the bright colored fleece blanket covering her lap.

Adam stood quietly in the corner, arms crossed, leaning against the sink. He looked so out of place, Clair eyed him curiously, as though seeing him for the first time. Ben and Jodie sat side by side on the window seat. Dr Ellerby sat next to her bed, along with a palliative care nurse named Lorraine. Her psychiatrist, Dr Rebecca Bernstein was there, presumably to attest to her ability or inability to make a rational choice, given her status as a committed person. Clair had spent more time with Jet than the psychiatrist but felt safe with her, nonetheless. Jet sat on the other side, in eye shot, but not part of the circle of family.

'It's your party,' Clair said to Dr. Ellerby, holding out her hands as though offering herself and these people to him.

He in turn looked at Lorraine. She nodded. A woman in her late fifties, she had the look of a nurse who had seen every possible good and bad thing that could happen to a person, and still maintained her equanimity and hope.

'Clair, family, our focus for this meeting is to help clarify what is happening, what you hope will happen, and how we can support your own goals for your care and life, going forward. Now, Clair, first, what is it you understand about your situation?'

'My situation is that I don't have time for any of this, Lorraine, and I do appreciate your support here, but given my situation, I just really don't need, want, nor will I participate in this. I have made up my mind and that's that. I do need information. On how to obtain the death with dignity pill. If you can provide me with that, great. If not, I can find out on my own, through the web, of course.'

Lorraine didn't ruffle. Outside the window, a mourning dove cooed. Clair wondered, what is she mourning? Not my life surely. This unit is full of people worthy of mourning. But not me, not a woman who loses her child, her special needs child, to a wild and cold ocean. That woman doesn't deserve any of this. Not these kind people, not this family, not even this husband who seems determined to forgive her for trying to kill him. She welcomed the pain in her chest, masking the pain in her heart. Lorraine's voice brought her back.

'OK, I can provide you with some basic information. First, you will need to acquire a primary care physician who will write the initial request for you to be considered for death with dignity. Then, once that is done, a second physician will also need to review your case, talk with you, and ascertain that you are rational, not depressed or suicidal, and that you do have an illness that is terminal and will ultimately cause you a degree of suffering that cannot be managed with traditional treatments. Now, all this will take time. You don't currently have a primary physician, do you?'

'No, I don't. Other than maternity, I've never needed a doctor. So, I'll just sign up.'

'Again, it isn't that easy. We currently have a significant physician shortage in our community, and it has to be a doctor – not a nurse practitioner or physician assistant. It could take a while, and then that person will have to treat you long enough to know you. They face big liability if they write for death with dignity without meeting all the criteria. Clair, this isn't a quick fix. This won't be your suicide pill.'

Clair exhaled. Her shoulders slumped.

'I am not suicidal anymore. That isn't what this is about. The issue here is one of failure of you all being able to understand my experience. This is about me, and only me. If I am going to die anyway, and that is what I just heard Dr Ellerby say, then I want it to be on my terms. It won't be suicide because the cancer is the cause, not my own hand. It's just my time. And I want it to be done my way, not wasting away, being a burden to others. What others? There's that as well.'

'Clair, we'll stay here and help,' Jodie cried out. 'You know we will.'

'I don't want you to, Jodie. I want you and Ben to go back to your work, where you are needed. I have money. I can hire a caregiver. I don't want anyone to bother with me.'

'I'll help,' Adam said, his voice uncertain. 'If you'll have me.'

Shaking her head, she brought both hands up to her face. 'I don't want anyone's help. I don't deserve it,' she said. 'Don't you understand?'

Dr Ellerby shifted in his chair, 'Clair, how about letting me at least get the PET scan, while you're going about the steps to apply for the death with dignity? And then maybe, we can just start some treatment. This cancer is fast. And we need to know if it has already spread to other parts of your body. It won't delay death with dignity. In fact, it might look better for you if you are in treatment when the board receives your application. Right now, you do have a choice. If we wait, even a few weeks, that choice will be very different. And Clair, it won't be pretty. It will be painful and messy. The cancer will eat away at your flesh, causing open wounds that will cause terrible suffering. We might not be able to rescue you once it gets that far. I don't want you to suffer. Please, let me help.'

His frank and honest talk moved her. And it made sense to her. She liked the idea of doing something while waiting for death. It was a form of shedding, losing the bits and pieces of herself, readying for her final liberation. Like Devon, she thought, he began as a tiny spark, grew into an infant, a boy, then like a sun, exploded into an infinite possibility pattern, freed from the constraints of time. She will do the same only in reverse order. And they will meet, she knew, where the edges of time meet space.

'OK, I'll do it. I'll take treatment. But only if I can get out of this place.' She looked at Dr Bernstein. 'If this isn't proof I'm no longer suicidal, then I don't know what is.'

Dr Bernstein laughed. 'I think you're right there. Clair, I'll make up a conditional release from commitment for you and you can go home, as soon as Dr Ellerby releases you.'

'Just like that?' Clair asked.

'Yes, just like that. I'm sure the judge will sign off, once she receives my discharge order. There will be certain conditions that must be met. And you will need to have a responsible adult to ensure you meet them. I will need a home address for you, though, and a plan for regular sessions with a therapist. As well as regular visits with me or another psychiatrist. And I can have our case manager refer you to a primary care physician. I also expect the district attorney will drop the criminal case, especially now. You are no longer a danger to Adam, or anyone else.'

Clair turned her head, looking out the window, at the rain cascading down the side of the glass. Home. The very word sent her into paroxysms of guilt, remorse, sadness at all she had been and not been. There had never been a home for her, she thought, *maybe that's why I failed to create a safe haven for Devon.*

The house she had grown up in was never home. Clean as a realtor's showcase, even her own room was a designer model.

The housekeeper was on orders to pick up every object that didn't fit Mother's ideas of décor. Lavender, yellow, and pale pink. She almost gagged remembering how awkward she felt in that space, unable to close the door, not allowed to bring a friend over. Always on display. The only thing out of order, in her mother's eyes, was Clair's cello. That was tolerated because she received merit for her playing. Accolades and awards to brag about to her friends at the club and on her many boards and committees.

She had wanted the opposite for Devon. She had tried to create a space that was warm, inviting, loving. Giving him freedom to roam, and explore. Even with his disability. Maybe, surely, she had gone too far. Too much freedom, and she had let go. She had lost him.

'I don't know,' she said shrugging her shoulders, gazing around the small group, feeling detached, remote from all that was happening to her.

Adam pushed himself off the wall. He stood, hands in his pockets, rocking side to side, looking like a nervous school boy.

'I'll take you home, Clair. If you'll come.'

She looked up at him, seeing hope in his eyes. Could she do this? The commitment was meant to force her to live, when she only wanted, yearned, to die. Without that, and the safety of the psychiatric unit, if free, what would she do? Now, she was at risk of dying, not from her own hand but from this cancer, and she was terrified. Looking at Adam, standing there, waiting for her answer, she knew in her heart she wasn't ready to die. Not yet. Not now. She had a new purpose, to live, for what she wasn't sure. But she had to at least try and find a different way of being in the world. One without blame, shame, and hopelessness.

Feeling like she was riding a monster wave, moving too fast to maneuver or leap off, time and events outside of her control. She dropped her gaze, exhaustion taking hold, and slumped back against the pillows.

'Yes, I'll come home with you.'

PART TWO

Chapter 14

Clair

As they turned onto the long, narrow road winding through the native Douglas fir forest, half a mile up to their house, she couldn't drive the menacing thoughts from her mind. She was afraid Adam would send her back to the hospital. She had to keep it together. Somehow, separate her fear and dread from some emotion that wasn't despair. Her guts cramped as she began perseverating, a maelstrom of words circling in her mind; I lost him, my boy. My beautiful, sweet child. She felt her breath catch, her heart race. Her hands gripped the sides of the leather seat, as her mind willed her breath to flow into her nostrils. Remembering the practice, engage the parasympathetic nervous system to override the sympathetic. The body will breathe on its own. Just allow it.

She risked a glance at Adam. The north wind was blowing. He had his window down, letting the late fall sunlight in. Low and golden, it cascaded, lighting him up, his hair, too long now, whipping around his face. He was disheveled, she noticed. Not like Adam at all. What had she brought them all to? The car slowed, her stomach churning. She did not want this next moment to come into shape. If only, for the thousandth time she chanted inwardly, if only. But she knew, as a scientist knows, there was never an if only.

Coming to a full stop, they both sat, still and quiet, listening to the wind in the trees, the river, strong from recent rains, gurgling as it rounded the rocky bend. Slowly, cautiously, as though not wanting to disrupt this fine peace, Adam opened his door, stepped out. He reached over the seat, grabbing hold of her small plastic hospital bag, containing medical supplies. She had no clothes or toiletries, only what she was wearing, borrowed from the psychiatric unit's clothes closet.

Adam and Clair had barely spoken on the ride from the hospital. It had been a tearful parting from Ben and Jodie. Clair insisted they return to their work, that she would be fine. She didn't know if she would ever see her brother or sister-in-law again. Ben had called their parents during the visit. The conversation had been cool and disengaged. He gave the phone to Clair. After a few meaningless words passed between she and her mother, then her father, she handed the phone back to Ben. Then, there were papers to sign, appointments to make, prescriptions to fill, and instructions on how to care for her drains and wounds. It was overwhelming. Now, they were here, and it was time to get out of the car, begin again.

'Clair, are you OK to open your door? Or, I can come around?' Adam asked, stepping out of his side of the car, bending down to look at her.

She heard his voice crack. Never had she seen Adam on the defensive like this. Unsure of himself. Part of her wanted to hold him, tell him it was OK, she was OK. But she didn't. There was a river running between them, cold and turbulent. It was dangerous to cross. She didn't know if she was more afraid of being swept away downriver or making it safely to the other side.

The wind whipped through the car, chilling her. She felt so weary. Contaminated by the hospital and all that sterility.

Her body and mind craved mess, disorder, chaos. Anything to unsettle and disrupt this quietude. Her chest ached. Two long tubes hung down either side, attached to collection bags, with reddish, yellow fluid. Her fluid. Her blood, her being. Like when they brought Devon home, newborn and fresh. Her breasts full of milk, leaking through her shirt. Now this.

'Oh sure, I can do this. I'm fine, Adam, really. Go on in. I'm not feeble,' she answered.

'OK, then, I'll just take your bag in… I'll put this in the bathroom.'

She noticed his pause, hesitation. Was he wondering where she would sleep, now that she was home? It had been his bedroom for the past few months while she had been in the hospital. Would she share it with him now? Who else had been sleeping in her bed, she wondered?

'OK, I want a shower first thing so that is good. I'll change my dressings while I'm in there.'

They were standing alongside the car, him on one side, she on the other, talking across the roof. A strong gust of wind lashed hair around her face, causing her eyes to water. She felt an ache go deep into her gut. How Devon loved the wind, running around the grounds, wearing a makeshift cape of old curtain material, pretending to be able to fly. As Adam turned his face away, she saw Devon in him. His silver blonde hair blew back, showing his fine and aging features. A thrill of longing swept through her. Not now, she cautioned herself. Not ever. You tried to kill this man. What are you thinking?

They walked together into the house. It was cold. The kind of cold that comes from not having any life in the space for a long time. No amount of heat or fire erases this cold. She shivered. Adam noticed and rushed to the gas fireplace. He flicked a switch and fire erupted, fake rocks emanating red heat.

'Sit down, Clair. Here, on the sofa.'

Sitting down carefully, tucking her feet under her, she kept her arms close to her body, afraid the two tubes would go crazy and begin flying around her. She had never had so much as a minor wound before. This double mastectomy was like traveling to the moon after never going further than the end of the road. She smelt of antiseptics, and disease. She wanted to get clean.

'I can't sit still now. I need to shower. Change clothes. Is that OK?'

'Of course. Do you need my help?'

'No, I'm fine.'

'You know, you have all your clothes in the closet still.'

'That's good. Polyester has never been my thing. I'll be out soon. And I'll help with dinner, right?'

'OK, sure.'

She heard something in his voice. Uncertainty?

'I won't poison you again, Adam. I promise,' she said, an almost-smile on her face.

He couldn't find a response. He nodded, a crooked grin on his face.

'That's good,' he said. 'Call if you need anything.'

Clair eased herself off the couch, sharp stabs of pain shooting through her chest. She stood, holding her arms around her middle, moving slowly, as though underwater. Each step hesitant. The wide, open living room held ghosts. Devon on the floor, watching *Paw Patrol* on television. Curled in the armchair, staring out the window, daydreaming. Lying on the couch, his head in her lap, reading *Peter Rabbit* and *Winnie-the-*

Pooh together. He had been a precocious reader, recognizing words and finding rhythm to sentences as early as two years old. They had at first thought he was gifted, and he was. Just not in a way society accepts as normal. Neurodivergent is what they call it now. Before his autism had been diagnosed, he had been set aside in his public pre-kindergarten class, left to play on his own, a distraction from the daily routines. The memory saddened her.

'How long has this been going on?' she had asked his teacher that day she had arrived early to pick him up, finding him in a corner, by himself, a line of toy metal cars surrounding him.

The early testing had been inconclusive, and she had willingly deluded herself that he was OK, or would be with the right school, the best environment. Now, they had to do more, extensive and definitive.

'I don't believe it,' Adam had said. 'I'm taking him to a different specialist. They're wrong, he can't have autism. He's my son.'

She would find him watching Devon with tears in his eyes, but if she said anything, he would look away, walk away. And their distance had begun to grow. The closer she clung, the further he drifted until they had become shadows passing in these rooms, afraid to touch lest their carefully constructed realities shatter.

* * *

As she turned to walk down the hall, towards the bathroom at the end, her skin prickled. His room, Devon's, was there on the left. She stood for a moment, holding her hand on the door, feeling the grainy wood, the raised lettering spelling out his name. She thought about opening the door, looking in, but didn't, couldn't. Unsure of what she would find. Adam had not said. She was afraid to ask. They'd had a big fight about Devon's room, his things. Little boy treasures. Two weeks after they had returned home from the beach, without Devon, he had opened the door to his room. Calling her to come. Waving his arm inside, at the evidence of a boy gone. Dust had settled on the shelves, a cold stillness hung over every object.

'It's time, Clair. He's gone, never coming back. You have to accept this so we can move on with our lives.' he had said.

'Not today,' she had said, and walked away.

Clair had moved about the house like a robot, making coffee in the morning, putting away dishes from the dishwasher. There weren't many. Mostly they ate takeout from the local food collaborative. Eating right from the boxes. Clair would sit in her window seat, looking out towards the river, watching the sun move across the grounds, first lighting the tops of the trees, then shining on the last of the rhododendrons and azaleas banked up along the garden borders. It sparkled when it caught the ripples in the white water, shooting up like crystals, catching on the flat rocks scattered across the areas where the river narrowed, creating small, wading pools. She would imagine Devon there, hopping across the rocks, using his water telescope to look deep into the pools.

That was what he had been doing the last time she had seen him, at the beach. Gazing into the tidal pools. Sometimes she was sure she saw him here, on the river. His red Superman T-shirt catching the glow, like a sun. When she looked in his room, when she would go in and dust, vacuum, straighten the already orderly toys, she felt like she could sense the elephant on the shelf, the bear, larger than Devon, huddled in the corner, look up expectantly as though their boy was coming home. Looking back, she thought maybe that was the beginning of her descent into madness. But then, she felt only rage.

Adam had kept at her, wanting to pack everything up, donate to charity, or throw away. It was that insistence that had led her to madness, to her attempt to kill him and herself. Now, standing here, she was afraid to open the door, of what she might find, or not find. Maybe he had done that while she was away, rid this house of their son, of every last vestige of his precious life, lived here, in this room? Later, she told herself. I'll look later. One last caress to the door, then on down the hall. She looked into their bedroom, bed unmade, curtains closed, a musty, old shoe odor coming from its darkened space. Walking through to the bathroom, she noticed only one side of the bed had been slept in. It surprised her that she noticed and even more so that she cared.

The bathroom looked out onto the wide, sloping yard that ran down to the river. Apple trees, plum, and cherry dotted the landscape, leafless and barren. A large fir, with many branches, old and nicked by time and storm, stood, shaking and swaying in the wind. A rope swing danced from one of its lower limbs. They would swing out over the river, dropping into its waters, clear and freezing cold, even in summer. Devon's laughter and screams of make-believe fear rang out. She took a deep breath, exhaled longer, as the yoga therapist had taught her. Again, and again until she felt calmed. The medical bag was clutched in her hand. Setting it down on the counter, next to the double sinks, she began setting the dressings and other apparatus on a clean towel. The nurse had instructed her to stand in the shower and let the warm water loosen the bandages around her chest, then gently ease them off. Clair had asked what would she do if the drains pulled out. The nurse had said that wouldn't happen. They were sewn in and were secure. Taped up, with plugs for draining, the nurse had assured her nothing bad could happen. *OK then*, she thought. *Here I go.*

The water flowed down her face, her back. She was unsure if she should turn and let the water run down her front, right over the dressings, but soon realized she would have to do that. Slowly, she turned cautiously to the right, each new area of skin being cleansed and massaged by the water jets, bringing her back to herself, to the woman she was before any of this happened. Like a baptism, she thought. I was lost, then found, lost again, and now, maybe found again. Everything that I was is gone. These very breasts I nursed my son from, gone. Soon, my hair will be gone. Broken down, shattered, turned to rust. And then, cells replaced; all new and resurrected. If I live. While I live, she reframed.

Standing with her face up to the water flow, feeling its warmth begin to loosen the tape, the weight of the bandages pulling on her skin, she raised both arms up, pushing wet hair out of her eyes. Tightness burned, under her arms and down towards both wrists. She had been told it was important to reach her arms up, several times a day, to prevent lymphatic fluid buildup. Keep your fluids flowing, the nurse had said, moving her arms in circles around her head. Clair had said she looked like a crazy banshee, and they had both laughed. Still, she understood the concept. Like a garden hose, any blockage in the system would clog up the flow, and we don't want that, do we, Clair? She smiled at the memory.

The dressings were getting looser now. She gently tugged at the corner of one. To her surprise, it came off in one piece, dangling by a few strands of sticky tape to the bottom of her ribcage. Her breath caught. She held it while she pulled the last of the tape, releasing the dressing altogether. The site of her slashed chest made her slip down the shower stall to her haunches, the water pounding on her head. As though by design, the dressing on the other side slipped away, hanging by a few threads of tape, lying on her belly where she slumped, faint and tremulous.

'Adam,' she called, her voice weak. 'Adam,' stronger.

He rushed in, seeing through the glass shower door. 'Oh Clair, darling, what have you done?'

He stepped through, gathering her in his arms.

'These drains,' she cried. 'I have to drain all this fluid.'

'It's OK, Clair, I'll help. Here, let me see.'

He began to open the plug on one of the drains, and Clair cried out, 'Oh God, not here. We'll have this bloody mess all over us.'

'Well shit,' he said. 'I have it open, now what?'

They began laughing, he holding onto the plug, stopping the drain with his thumb. Clair looking at him, soaking wet in his clothes, hair streaming into his face and eyes, looking so much out of his depth she laughed harder. He figured out how to close the plug and yet, they remained. He holding her, stroking her back, as their laughter turned to tears.

'I am so sorry, Clair,' he said. 'So very sorry.'

'I am too, Adam. That day, I was angry. Seeing you, hearing you. Why, why so many women?'

'Clair, I was never with another woman, not like that, not since we married. I flirted sure, hoping to get a reaction from you. But sex, love? Never. From the first moment I saw you, I loved you. All I ever wanted was for you to love me too. Then

Devon came, and all you seemed to care about or notice was him. I knew it was because he had special needs, I loved him, Clair, so much. But you never would let me in. You wouldn't let me share the love or the pain.'

They huddled there, not talking, until the water cooled. Clair shivered.

'Here, let me help,' he said, lifting her up. They stepped out into the bathroom, warm from a small space heater. Adam gently wrapped her in a towel. He led her to the side of the bed, setting pillows against the headboard so she could lie back. He covered her with a soft fleece blanket.

'I did see him, Adam. That day I drowned. He was there, with the selkies.'

'I believe you, Clair. Now rest, let me cook for you.'

'You cook?' she chided.

'Just you wait and see,' he said, pulling off his wet clothes.

She watched as his pale; angular body came into view. He had lost weight, she noticed. His broad chest looked sunken. His waist, slender, sloped down to narrow hips, tight buttocks. His back was turned to her. As his arms reached up to pull off his fleece sweater, muscles rippled along his spine. It was as though she was seeing him for the first time. He looked at her through the mirror in the dresser. Noticed her looking at him. Their eyes met. Held. He felt himself warm, grow, shuddered. Turning slowly, so she could see, he moved towards her, easing himself down onto the side of the bed. She pulled him to her. Laid his head on her belly, tucking the drains up under her arms. He raised his head, kissed her. She kissed him back, rocking him gently side to side.

'Are you sure?' he asked.

'Don't ask,' she said. 'Just do.'

Chapter 15

Clair

The support group was mandated by her nurse navigator, Naomi. At least, it felt like an edict to Clair, along with daily arm exercises, breathing exercises, eating green and yellow fruits and vegetables. Positive thinking. Visioning. Even a glass or two of wine seemed to be on order during treatment. The room was large, surrounded by floor to ceiling windows, looking out over the forested hills, today shrouded in fog and mist. How could this be comforting? It felt if anything too big, too open, too wet and cold. She wanted to turn and run. But Naomi spotted her, calling her over to a cluster of women and, surprisingly, one man, sitting in a close circle. Clair squared her shoulders, still feeling the pull of the scar tissue along her chest. She had been told she might feel pings of nerves reconnecting for several years. *Lovely*, Clair had thought, *I'll never be able to forget. Even if I live to remember.*

There was an empty chair to Naomi's left. Clair sat, folding her hands in her lap, like a supplicant. What was she hoping to receive, she wondered? Penance?

'Clair, so glad you made it. We're just getting started. Let's go around and introduce ourselves, say a bit about what brought you here, your basic facts, you know – diagnosis, treatment stage, prognosis, and also, what is the most important thing in your life, the one thing that gives you the courage and strength to get through all of this?'

Naomi turned to the woman sitting to her right to begin the talking circle. As people shared their stories, Clair's mind wandered back to a week ago, her homecoming. She and Adam's finding each other, maybe for the first time. It was sweet, she remembered. His tenderness, kindness. During dinner, he had talked easily about his classes, students. He had to return to work the next day, Monday, and wondered if she would be OK at home, on her own. She had assured him she would, even though she wasn't sure herself. On a medical leave of absence from her own teaching, she was finding pleasure in not having to think about anything other than the simple moment to moment happenings in her small, and now even smaller world. The psychiatric unit had been a constant hum of voices and actions. Here, home was quiet. Spacious. And pulsating with energy. Devon's energy, she was certain. The scientist in her knew this was a fixed delusion. The mother in her didn't care.

She heard her name being spoken.

'Clair, are you OK with sharing?' Naomi asked.

'Uh, yes,' Clair said, bringing her attention back to the group. 'Hi everyone, my name's Clair Mercer. I was diagnosed with inflammatory breast cancer, stage IV, last week. I don't know what my treatment plan will be yet, I just got my Hemovac tubes out. I meet with the oncologist tomorrow and go from there. I think my prognosis is pretty grim, even with treatment, so I'm just taking this all one day at a time. Having cancer is like a full-time job I'm learning. So, I'll just do my best and whatever happens, happens.'

'And the most important thing to you, Clair?' Naomi reminded her.

'My son, Devon.'

As they went around the circle again, sharing personal stories, Clair relaxed. If any of them did know about her suicide and homicide attempts and stay on the psych unit, they didn't let on. She felt comfortable around these broken people, one very young, and the man wasn't a husband as she had first thought, but a breast cancer patient himself. He had shared how embarrassing it had been for him. His work crew making fun of him. His insurance company denying coverage for his surgery, saying he was making it all up to get out of work.

'Oh sure, put myself and family through this hell just to miss a few days driving a truck?'

The young girl, Brianna, was sixteen. She had been diagnosed with invasive ductal carcinoma in situ. Because of her young age, a double mastectomy had been done and she was going to have reconstruction. She had laughed, talking about how all of the dancers on the dance team, where she was captain, shaved their heads to support her for their prom. She wore a strapless gown, stuffed with foam rubber. The girls had all sprinkled glitter on their bald heads.

'My date was horrified at first, then it was OK. We've been best friends since grade school, so he said he wasn't that surprised by my costume. It was my mom who had the hardest time. She wanted me to cover myself head to toe. No way, I said. I'm not hiding from this. I'm meeting this thing head on and I'm going to beat it.'

The group cheered and clapped for her. Clair was amazed at how connected she felt. Her eyes teared up. A lifetime loner, she realized these people didn't care who she was, what she had done in her life, or what she would do or be after this. They only cared that she was here, now, with them, to share and be a part of their story.

When the talk came back around to her, she told the story of having her drains removed. She described how Adam, her husband, had fainted dead away when the doctor began pulling one of the long tubes out. They all heard a crash and thud, as Adam fell to the floor, taking the sterile instrument tray down with him. That led to other stories of partners, spouses, and friends. One woman told how after her double mastectomy, Tommy, her former professional baseball-playing husband and devoted lover of her double D breast cups, had taken her to Walmart, personally selecting an assortment of Nerf balls for her to wear inside her bra.

'Everything from a double D to a G,' she said, bringing laughter again to the group. Clair realized she had laughed today more than she had in months, maybe years. Her stomach ached from laughing. Maybe she could do this, she thought. *If these people can, then so can I.*

Clair still wasn't allowed to drive, so she waited outside for Adam to pick her up. They had set the time for 4.15 p.m. It was now only 3.30. On Friday afternoon. Was it possible it had been less than one week since she had been released from the hospital? Looking across the parking lot, through the large bay window, at the four-story tower, which housed the psychiatric department, she wondered for a moment what Jet was doing. Taking her phone out of her tote, she scrolled through her contacts until she came across Jet. She considered how their relationship had begun morphing from client/ therapist to friends. Jet had cautioned her about this, saying it was unwise for these relationships to go beyond professional. Clair had reasoned with her, saying she understood but that theirs was different. Clair wasn't a normal crazy person and Jet wasn't a normal therapist. So, in her world view, they could and should be friends. At the time Jet hadn't argued back on the issue. Clair tapped the number. A green light glowed on the screen.

'Dr Taylor,' said a soft, husky voice.

'Jet, it's Clair.'

'Oh, hey, how are you doing? Your name didn't come up on my screen. I thought you were a normal client,' she said, mimicking Clair's own words back to her.

'I'm good, really. I'm just across the lot, at the cancer center. Do you have time for a coffee or tea?'

'Yeah, I think so. Hang on, let me double check. OK, yes, I can. Meet you downstairs in the café in ten?'

'Great, see you then.'

Clair felt buffeted, lifted and lighter. It would be good to talk with Jet, get her perspective on things. Pulling her coat close to her, she walked, head high, and feet planted across the tarmac, large raindrops beginning to fall. She lifted her face up to the sky, catching one on her tongue.

'So, what's new?' Jet asked Clair as she slipped into the chair at a table by the large, plate glass window overlooking a rose garden. Only a few fragments of blossoms remained, and those were surrendering to the late fall rains, their tender petals drifting like confetti to the browning grass below. Normally, such a sight would have filled Clair with melancholy, dread for the coming winter. But today, she found a comfort in the cycle of fall, winter, spring, and the knowledge that if she could just keep showing up for her treatments, she might live through this. And then what? *Don't wonder,* she told herself. *Just stay here, with this now.*

'First support group, with Naomi. Do you know her?' Clair asked.

'Naomi, yes, she's great. A bit cheerful but maybe that's what her job calls for. What did you think?'

'It was OK. I sort of enjoyed it. There was a young girl and a man. I was surprised.'

'Yeah, cancer doesn't discriminate. Like mental illness, Clair, it can happen to anyone. So, how's it going at home, with Adam? Are you two talking?'

Clair got a look on her face, eyes crinkling at the corners, mouth turned up in an almost smile.

'What is that look?' Jet asked.

'Um, yeah, we are talking and a bit more than that,' Clair said, smiling fully now.

'Oh my God, Clair, is that OK?'

'It is, I think, I mean, it just happened, but we were, we both, well, it happened. You can't fake that, right?'

Jet laughed. 'No, at least the man can't. Clair, I'm touched. I was worried and now, I feel so much better about you two being there, so far away from town, from me, alone.'

'You mean from the psych unit, don't you?' Clair asked, but with a smile. 'Jet, I'm not insane anymore, remember. I've been released from commitment. I'm normal.'

'Ha, we could argue that for days, months, and many have – the differences between legal insanity and just pure crazy. But, no, that's not what I meant, Clair. I mean, being there, without Devon. Going back through all of that. How's that going?'

Clair picked up her cup of tea, holding it with both hands. Took a small sip. Looked back out the window, at the wind, now stronger, blowing cat paws across the puddles in the parking lot to the side of the rose garden.

'I'm not, dealing with it, not yet. I know I need to go in his room, clean it out. Open that space. But I can't.'

She took a long breath, set her cup down, looked at Jet.

'After I first went home, you know, that very first time. After Devon disappeared, I would go into his room, lay on his bed. Smell him. Just wrap myself in his blanket, hold his pillow to my face. Breathe him in. The sunlight was fierce that summer. Each day, shining right into his room, onto his rows of toy cars, arranged in a perfect circle, each one exactly equidistant from the next. Before, when I would go in to clean and accidently dislodge one of the cars, he would quietly, without anger or emotion, place it carefully back in place. So, even after, I would walk so carefully around those cars. That was what did it for me, that last day when I lost it. Adam had moved all the cars, packed them up in a box, set them in a corner of his room. I knew the bed, the pillow, blanket would be next. I couldn't let that happen. I emptied the box, rearranging the cars in Devon's order, the way he always did it. I found his little red truck. It was his favorite. I picked it up, tucked it safely in my pocket. I carry it with me always now.'

Clair patted a large black tote bag hanging off the back of her chair.

Jet reached across the table, patting Clair's hand. Clair's gaze wandered around the coffee shop, noticing people moving about, not wanting to look at Jet, sensing a conversation was coming she didn't want to have. She looked at Jet. They easily slipped back into patient, therapist mode. Clair didn't mind. It comforted her.

'Clair,' Jet said, holding her gaze, 'there is a concept in psychology and grief work called ambiguous grief. It is that grief that has no end, no closure. It abides in us. Clair, this is what you are facing. T.S. Eliot said that what we do not know about a missing loved one becomes all that we know. You are facing this new threat, immediate and real. It might help to bring some ending to the past, not closure. We know that doesn't exist in real life, but it can be a next step. So, you can focus on your treatment now. This is going to take all you've got, energy, willpower, hope.'

Clair took a breath. Smiled at Jet, her eyes looking back over the parking lot.

'Oh, there's Adam,' she said, standing up quickly, jostling the tea and coffee cups on the table. 'I have to go now, Jet. I appreciate the lesson, or session, whatever this was. But, I'm OK, really.'

'Clair,' Jet said, standing up to meet her gaze. 'Call me, anytime. Don't do that on your own, OK? Let me help you pack the rest of his things.'

Clair didn't answer, just waved backwards, as she hurried out the double glass doors. Adam's car was driving into the lot across the street.

Out of breath when she opened the door, wet from the rain, driven hard by the wind, Clair fell into the front seat.

'Where were you?' Adam asked. 'I thought you were in here,' he said, pointing to the lobby of the cancer center.

'I was, but we finished up early. I had a tea with Jet, over in the main building.'

Adam was silent for several moments. The car was running, the heater blasting warm air. Soft jazz playing on the radio, tuned to National Public Radio.

'Is that wise, Clair?' he asked, his voice tense.

'I don't know what you mean,' she answered. 'Wise? Jet's a friend now, Adam, not my therapist. I can see her anytime I want.'

'But she is still a therapist, Clair. She can't not be a therapist. And she has the ability to get into your head, and mine, and well, I just don't think it's a good idea for you to spend time with her, now you're out.'

'What are you afraid of Adam? That I'll share too much? That I might actually become whole again? Would you want that? Or do you want to keep me sick, at your mercy?'

It surprised her, how quickly this virgin peace could be shattered, returning them to their former state of adversaries. Her anger came quick and hard.

'That's not fair, I only want you to get better. I want us to get better. I want you, Clair, however you come, cancer, crazy, healthy, whole. It doesn't matter to me. As long as we can be together. We'll find a way, work this out.'

'Then don't worry, Adam,' Clair reached over, placed her hand on his forearm, resting on the gear shift, feeling herself soften. 'I'm going to be OK. I can feel it in my bones. And we're going to be OK too.'

He put the car in drive, glancing over at Clair.

She smiled, her eyes shining with anticipation. Of what, she wasn't sure. But she felt ready. Maybe it was a fool's paradise, her new-found optimism, she feared, but she'd take it. Anything was better than the darkness looming inside every open space in her mind, every single moment without intentional thought. Points of light broke through, like the sunlight scattering rainbows across the oil slicks in the parking lot, as the black Mercedes eased forward, toward Highway 101 and home.

Chapter 16

Adam

Clair had been sleeping when Adam looked in. She looked pale and thin, insubstantial. Her bare shoulder had shown above the comforter. He gently pulled the duvet up to cover her. He had been sleeping in the guest room, not wanting to disturb her rest. He smiled, remembering their lovemaking that first day home. It had been sweet, gentle. He was afraid he would hurt her, or dislodge the drains again. But she had kept saying to him, 'It's OK, Adam, I'm OK.' It was the first time they had made love in months, maybe even years, since Devon's birth. Really connected, in this way. Not just sexual release. No wonder she thought he was fooling around. And he had allowed her to wonder. That had been wrong, he knew. Time for a fresh start, all around. He was feeling better this morning than he had in a long time. Their almost argument yesterday on the drive back from her support group meeting was an early alert for him, showing just how fragile their new-found peace still was. He would nurture it, fan it, amplify it until this new way of being together became the only way. Now, he was eager to get back to work, to see his students, right his world.

He slipped around the room, quietly opening drawers, his closet door, extracting clothes for the day. He could hear the rain pattering on the roof, not a downpour but steady enough to need a raincoat and boots.

'Are you off then?' Clair's voice called from the bed.

'I'm sorry, I didn't want to wake you,' he said, walking over to the bed, sitting on the side. She was turned on her side facing him, all but her neck and face covered by the down comforter. He reached over and brushed a lock of hair from her eyes. Cupping her face in his hands, he gently kissed her mouth.

'Oh, God no, not now, I have morning breath I know,' she chided, pulling back, but smiling.

'I don't mind,' he replied. 'Do you want some coffee, tea?'

'Hmmm, yes, black coffee please, really strong. I can't seem to get enough of real coffee. They made us drink decaf on the unit.'

'Cruel and unusual, right?' he answered, getting up. 'I'll just get it going. Then Clair, I have to go in to work today. Will you be OK, here at home?'

'Do you mean will I walk into the river, or slash my wrists?' she answered.

He sighed. Will they ever get past this, he wondered?

'No, I just want to be sure you're OK, you know.'

'Oh, right. Yes, I'll be fine. I'll just eat, rest, read, and relax. I have a treatment soon so I want to enjoy my last days of freedom from nausea.'

He turned and walked out, carrying his clothes with him. For some reason, he felt shy dressing in front of her. He decided he would think about that later. Now, he needed to get to work. He took the cup of coffee to her, made certain she had her phone charged, within reach on the bedside table. He felt a deep sense of relief as he settled into his car, looking forward to the day. Enjoying the rain cascading down the windshield, and the hum of the motor as he set off down the drive, he turned onto the river road towards town, and college. He changed the radio to Bluetooth and Spotify, not wanting to hear the latest rounds of political bickering.

The rain was coming down hard now, mixing with the drone of Yo-Yo Ma's cello. He felt vitalized, as though his purpose as a man and husband, even father was finally going to be realized. He could mourn his son properly now. Tapping his fingers to the rhythm of the piece, he let his mind imagine what their future might be like. The doctor had said she was really sick, and that this cancer could very well kill her, but looking at her this morning, he refused to believe it. Clair was alive, he was alive, and they had their whole future ahead of them. That was that.

Adam parked his car as close to the theater department building as possible. He pulled his anorak hood over his head, tucking his leather messenger bag up under his arm. Walking across campus, he was greeted by students and faculty, welcome backs and well wishes. It felt good. He felt good. Settling into his office, turning on the coffee maker, adjusting the thermostat, which didn't work but everyone did it anyway, he heard a soft knock on the door frame. Turning, he saw Claudia standing there, backlit by the hall lights. His office was still shadowed by the dull rain-drenched morning light. Her hair, a golden sheen, created a halo effect. She was dressed in one of her modern designs, all geometric angles and sharp edges. Thin as a wafer, she reminded him of a spirograph, reds and yellows vying for dominance on a black background.

'Welcome back,' she said. 'May I come in?'

'Claudia, yes, of course. You're the boss, right?'

He cursed himself for his edginess. Feeling his former sense of energy draining away, he mentally reframed his attitude to one of 'get through this and then get her out of his office'. She walked in, shutting the door behind her. She stood there, leaning her back against the closed door. He rearranged items on his desk, moving a paperweight from one corner to the next.

'So, what now?' she asked, continuing to lean against the door.

'I don't know what you mean, Claudia.'

'Come on, Adam. We both know you have just been waiting for Clair to be released from the hospital so you could leave her without looking like a total jerk. Well, now, that's done, right? She's back home and so, we can now be together again, finally.' She had walked over to him, leaning over his desk.

He drew back, sitting down in his desk chair, holding his head in his hands. He ran his hands through his hair, looking up at her.

'What the fuck are you talking about?' he said.

'Christ, Adam. I've been waiting all this time. Putting up with your crazy wife, waiting for you to be free of her and her bullshit. Now you are. And, like we've talked about, we can be together. How can you not remember?'

She reached a hand out to touch his face. He pulled away.

'Claudia, I don't know how you can think that. I've never given that a thought and I don't understand how you can even begin to imagine this. Since I've been with Clair, we've never ever had any sort of sexual relationship. I haven't with any woman.'

'Well, maybe not literally, Adam, but you led me to believe you were just waiting. All those glances during rehearsals. Those brushes when we stood next to each other… even once, I know you meant to, you touched my breast with your forearm when reaching across me. I didn't imagine those, I didn't.'

Claudia was pacing around the small room, her colors flying in the dim light. Bookshelves, stacked tight, vibrated with her movement.

'I'm sorry, Claudia, I never meant to let you believe that. I was angry, in turmoil, you were so available. I thought you understood; it was a game. A flirtation. We all did it, didn't we?'

'But I thought you were different, Adam. We were different. I have waited for you now, for five years. Since before your son was born. Waited through the pregnancy, his sickness, her obsessions, your sadness and regrets. I held you up, so you could do your work, win your prizes for best directing, best stage play, best professor. I saved your life. I was your wife in everything but the bedroom, and now, it's my turn.'

She had stopped pacing and sat in the chair opposite his desk. She crumpled over, holding her head in her hands, resting on her upper thighs. He could see her back shaking but was curiously unmoved by the sight. She's acting. She's dangerous, he thought.

'Claudia, I have to get to work now. I have a lot to do to get caught up. Can we talk about this later? Maybe over a drink?'

He knew she would put the department first; of that he was sure. So, he could appeal to her sense of professionalism, for now at least. And a drink, that was not a good idea, but he could find a way to put her off. Until he came up with a better idea. He didn't want her going to Clair. And if needed, he could always pull the sexual harassment card, she was in fact his superior. She'd had trouble in the past with that, with a male student. For now, he just wanted her out of his office.

She looked up, eyes reddened by rubbing, but not wet.

'OK, but we're not finished here. A drink, after work today?'

'Not today. I'll need to get home.'

He wasn't ready to talk about Clair's cancer. And certainly not with Claudia.

She looked at him. He held her gaze.

Finally, she stood, and walked to the door. Sensing her need for a final word, commitment to a date, he hurried to open the door for her. Placing his hand on the small of her back, he gently guided her through.

'I'm sorry, Claudia. It's the best I can do.'

'That's always been your final escape, Adam. But you know, it isn't about doing your best, it's about doing what's right.'

'Maybe so, and if that is true, then what's right is that I stay with Clair.'

He felt anger at her insinuation that she was right for him.

He heard her stacked heels clicking down the linoleum hall. Closing the door to his office, he felt his bowels tighten. An all too familiar feeling that he remembered happening for the first time when he was fifteen. The first time he realized he had power over women, and that sometimes, it went too far.

Chapter 17

Adam

Adam stood still, the vibration of the slammed door vibrating through his cells. Old feelings of confusion and remorse surged through him. Had he brought this on? Did he send out signals that made Claudia think he cared in that way? That he wanted her as a lover? Before Clair, yes, probably, he thought, but not since, surely.

He slumped back into his chair, staring at the door, his breath coming in short, staccato sips. For the hundredth time he wished he still smoked. He opened a drawer beside his desk, pulling out a bottle of Scotch he kept there for special needs, good or bad. Never a man of action, he found relief from others' expectations in presenting an aura of mystery, as though he was too deep to be understood. An escape artist, he rode the rip tides of passion and desire until he found an eddy where he could ease out, leaving no wake behind him. Or so he thought.

The whisky burned going down. He took an imaginary drag off a camel, unfiltered, feeling the acute sensation of loss of neurons, bringing an immediate placebo high. Holding his breath, he looked around his office, his sanctuary. Degrees, certificates, honors, awards, photos of productions, graduations, all the hallmarks of a successful career. And inside, he felt like an imposter. Exhaling, he took another sip, savoring the burn, the feeling of calm that came with it. It wasn't his fault, he thought. It never was. Old memories surged up, like spring bulbs, underground through the winter and, with heat and warmth, pushing through to the open.

He had been a magnet for women of all ages. Since his earliest memory, his mother's female friends had fawned over him, saying how handsome he was, even as a young boy. They would go out of their way to smooth his hair, brush his cheek. When he had reached adolescence, they would do more. At thirteen he looked eighteen. At fifteen he looked twenty-one. The first time he had sex was at thirteen. He had gone to visit his girlfriend. They had just begun dating, as much as teens too young to drive or be away from home for any length of time, could date. Within their small circle of friends, it was known that Adam and Carolyn were a pair. When he would visit, her mom, already intoxicated and slightly manic after school, would sit in his lap, pull him out onto the living room rug to dance with her. Wearing clothes that were too tight, too bright, her full body overflowing the seams, smelling of cigarettes and gin, Patty fed him lust in small bites, but enough that he knew he wanted more. The girlfriend, hurt and embarrassed, would go to her room, waiting for Adam to free himself from her mother's hold on him. On a sunny Sunday afternoon, he had gone to visit Carolyn, forgetting she had a swim meet out of town. Patty invited him in. That was his initiation into sex.

His first serious romantic relationship was with his ninth-grade literature teacher, Miss Corrigan. He had just turned fifteen. Tall and rangy, his hair yellow gold, Adam vibrated with poetic potential. His father had left, stranding Adam in a house without joy or hope. His mother, emotionally isolated, depressed and angry, blamed Adam for his father's absence. He wrote beautiful, sorrowful verses, full of longing for love, connection, and Lisa Corrigan, an almost young woman in her early thirties, was drawn to his beauty and pain. It began innocently enough. Talks after class. Walks on weekends, in parks and along beaches where they weren't seen by anyone who might recognize her, or him. But if they did, so what? She was being a teacher, providing counsel to a troubled youth.

Then it did become more, a relationship. It was not wrong, they had believed, because it was love. Simple, pure, and theirs alone. Until it wasn't. Discovered, shamed, and separated, he had felt adrift. He had known the one thing in life that brought him comfort was love, or sex, he wasn't sure of the difference. And to him, it didn't matter. He had found a niche. A place where he could rise, achieve, and not be himself. He had found the stage.

The teacher had also been the drama coach and theater director. She had chosen him to play the part of Macbeth, and he had done well. It felt natural to him, to assume a separate reality, become someone else. It was as though he had been waiting for this moment all his life.

Thinking back to all of this, after Claudia left, he wondered, for the thousandth time, what might his life have been like if he hadn't followed this path, caught up in the dream of himself. What had he missed? Looking around, at his room, his space, this one place in the world that he felt at home, so much more than in any house he had lived in, even the house where he had lived with Clair and Devon, he burrowed deeper into his chair. Easing back, allowing the soft, buttery leather to enfold him, he remembered the first time he had come here. Newly hired, still finishing up his master's degree, he immediately felt a sense of belonging, like no other time or place.

This room with its high windows, all new and modern, in such contrast to the rest of the college. His building was filled with music, dance, song. Walking in, at any time of day or evening, sounds of rehearsals, practice, and students' voices, excited about their lives and changes to come. Opera, theater, jazz, hip hop, ballet, all were alive and vibrant in these halls. Here he belonged. A knock on the door startled him out of his reverie. He was afraid it was Claudia, returning.

'Come in,' he called, steeling himself for another round of argument. Walking to the door, he grabbed the handle just as the door swung open towards him.

'Clair, what are you doing here? How did you get here?' he asked, surprise causing his voice to rise, a note of panic ringing through. He knew she wasn't supposed to drive, because of the effects of the chemotherapy and drugs. 'And, wow, your hair!'

She stood in the filtered light coming from the high cut glass window, her skin pale and translucent. She had taken scissors to her hair, then a clipper, so that only stubbles ringed her perfectly shaped crown. Wearing a long, bulky knit pullover sweater, she looked like a waif, needing a hand out.

'I couldn't stay in the house,' she replied, looking around his office as though seeing it for the first time. 'I called a cab.'

'Here, sit down,' Adam said, walking to her, gently taking her arm, guiding her to a leather armchair pulled to the side of his desk.

He marveled at the lightness of her. She had no heft, no substance, as though already having passed over the horizon to beyond. He questioned his own reality. Who is she and if not Clair, then who am I? He shook this off, a mid-morning post-drunken delusion. Good God, man, get a grip, he told himself.

'Can I get you some tea? Coffee? Whisky?' he asked, pointing to the bottle on the desk.

'No, I'm fine. I just had to get out of the house. I want to get into my office, you know, sort things out, and talk with Raj about coming back to work. She ran her hand across her scalp, feeling the sharp stubbles.

'Oh, and yeah, the women in the support group advised me to go ahead and take it off, rather than wait for it to fall out in clumps. So, I used your clippers. Punk, huh?'

Shaking his head, 'Punk it is. You have a great looking skull though.'

He felt taken aback. The thought of Clair returning to work so soon, ever, surprised him.

'Are you sure, Clair?' Adam asked, concern coloring his words. 'What about your treatments? And I don't know, just being here, after everything.'

Clair stood, walked over to the floor to ceiling bookshelf.

'I don't know how much everyone knows about what happened,' she said, 'but, I need – want – to try. I'm sure the gossip mill is on fire, but I don't care. You know I've never paid attention to what anyone else thought about me. Or us, for that matter. Except for the few that matter to me, Raj, Emil, my students.'

Suddenly starving, he looked around for anything to eat. A package of saltine crackers sat on the edge of his desk, left over from a salad, who knew how long ago. Tearing the plastic off, he ate, greedily. Too late, he thought to ask Clair if she wanted one.

'No, I'm fine. You must be hungry, though?' she asked, eyes questioning, wondering.

'Yeah, I don't know why. Midday. Hard time of day for me.'

'I'm OK. The treatments hit me hard the first few days then I start feeling better. I need to work. I need to not be in the house,' she said, as she walked back over to the chair by his desk. Sitting, she folded her arms around herself.

'And Ellerby, he thinks I should work too. Engage, you know, in my life. Keep busy, as much as I feel like. He said the chemo, it comes in waves. When you're down, you're really down, but in between, you have to get going again.'

The sound of heels clacking on linoleum broke through the silence between them.

'Oh, sorry Adam, I didn't know you had a student,' Claudia said, standing in the half-opened door.

Clair turned in her chair, looking across her shoulder at Claudia.

'Clair, oh my God, I didn't know you were here. Are you OK?' Claudia asked, staring at Clair's shorn head.

Clair stood and walked over to the door, taking the handle and opening it wide enough to slip through, past Claudia.

'I'm fine, really.' Looking back at Adam, she said, 'I'll be over in my office, if you want to come find me when you're ready to leave. I'll ride home with you.'

Adam nodded, his eyes on Claudia. 'I'll do that,' he said, a quick smile, glancing at her. Then back to Claudia as though waiting for a snake to strike. His heart was hammering in his chest. His feelings of protection for Clair, his dread of old habits finding a way through his new-found honor, and the whisky all swirling around, like a water spout. He feared what might be brought up to the surface.

Chapter 18

Clair

Clair kicked through piles of dry, crackling autumn leaves as she walked across campus to the original buildings, housing the graduate math and science schools. She wasn't sure why, but she felt a flicker of joy in the day, and in her own presence. As she passed huddles of students, the pond, spotted mallards and geese, her mood lifted so that she could almost imagine being happy again. Maybe there was hope, here in this life, for another simpler way of being together. And between the two of them, perhaps they could keep Devon alive, his spirit vital. She could teach again, play her cello in the orchestra and the string quartet. Maybe even teach cello. She was happy before Devon. She could be happy again. Now, she had Adam back. She believed him when he told her he had not been unfaithful. Didn't she?

Classes were in session so the halls were mostly empty. Clair had always reverenced these moments, the quiet intensity of learning. All those young minds, soaking in knowledge, integrating it with their own experiences and aspirations. By the time they got to this building, graduate studies, they were motivated. There was no need to compel, only to provide the support and resources. They did the rest on their own. School had always been a haven of calm in the quiet chaos that had been her life. And today, she found deep solace sitting at her desk, watching the dust mites swirl around in the afternoon light filtering in through the southern window.

Outside, a murder of crows was cawing, announcing the end of day. A rush of sadness and longing so fierce it took her breath away coursed through her. Doubling over, she felt faint. Out of the corner of her eye, she caught a glimpse of movement but when she turned her head, nothing was there. This had happened to her many times since her walk into the ocean. She hadn't told anyone. Spirit beings, she believed. Not quite ghosts. The wave of emotion passed. Dr Ellerby had warned her about hot hormone surges that would feel like being pulled along in a truck's tailwind, being swept up in a volcanic eruption. Wait it out, he had advised. Run cold water over your wrists, Naomi had advised. Take drugs, Rosemary from the support group had advised. She waited it out. Beethoven's ninth opening strings broke the silence in the room as her phone alerted her to a call.

'Clair here,' she said, sitting up straight and leaning back into the soft fabric of her desk chair. Surprised by the caller ID, a smile sounded through her voice. 'Ben, or Jodie, which one of you is it, or both?'

'Hey, it is both of us, using our one tiny, out of date phone. But we have service, for a few minutes anyway. We're traveling across southern Africa now, going to the latest cholera outbreak.'

'Why?' Clair asked. 'How is a trauma surgeon going to help a cholera patient?'

'All hands on deck, and mainly it's for Jodi, she was called to help with moms and babes and where she goes, I go.'

'I think he doesn't trust me not to run off with the fortune we get paid,' Jodie said, laughingly.

'Fortune indeed. We barely make enough to keep us in medical supplies much less enough for an adventure. But, that's enough on us. How are you? We haven't caught up since you left the hospital. Have you started treatment yet? How's Adam? Tell us everything.'

Clair closed her eyes, imagining them at a train stop, colorful people moving about, the smells of life and energy pulsating across the miles. Their love, and authentic happiness proved the belief that this is what makes us human. The need to love and be loved. And their ability to share this with others, strangers as well as family.

'The treatments are going well. I'm sick as shit the first few days then OK for a few days, until the next round. I'm in my office right now, getting ready to come back to work. Can you FaceTime? You should see my head. I look like an artichoke.'

'No, ha, we can't FaceTime but I can picture you without hair. I remember that time you bleached your hair with peroxide, you and that friend, Missy. It turned out orange and Mother Dearest made you have it clipped almost to the stubble. Hopefully you aren't going to dye it purple or something.'

'Now, that gives me ideas,' she said. 'Maybe I'll stripe it.'

'Seriously Clair,' Jodie cut in. 'What's going on? What does Ellerby say.'

'I find out tomorrow. He'll review my latest blood work and scans. I'm going to a support group, and it's great. The women, and one man, believe it, were so funny and supportive. Jodie, I think I can do this.'

'I know you can do this,' she said. A strong crackling sound broke into the conversation.

'Damn, we got to go sis,' Ben said. 'Train's pulling out. We're losing connection. Love you.'

And they were gone. Clair sat for several moments, savoring their voices, their closeness, and adventure. Maybe once this was all over, she and Adam could go on a trip, just take off, travel, on a train, bus, boat, any way. Walk. Just to move and breathe.

She looked around her office, at the books stacked on shelves, on the floor, hovering in piles on side tables. Manuscripts of her doctoral students waited for her review. She had passed them on to fellow faculty so her illness wouldn't interfere with their progress, but she wanted to read them herself, comment and provide feedback. She had taught and shepherded them through their early years, learning how to apply evidence to questions, and more importantly, how to ask the right questions.

A knock sounded, then a soft 'Hello' as her office door opened a crack. A head showed around the edge of the door, red hair, beard first, then massive shoulders followed.

'Emil, come in,' she called, standing and walking around her desk. She was scooped up in a bear hug, causing her to grunt.

'Oh God, I'm sorry. Did I hurt you?' he asked, setting her down gently.

'No,' she laughed, 'I just felt like a balloon being gutted. Kidding, Emil.'

Stepping back, she looked at him. Long her best friend on campus, Dr Emil Marchand had been absent from her life since Devon died. She had banished him, like so many others who had tried to help her. Time to make amends, she thought. She motioned to a corner of the office where a small, round table held a stack of texts and manuscripts, circled by two hard-backed wooden chairs.

'Here, let's sit. I get dizzy if I stand too long.'

Looking at him, she felt a deep pang of remorse.

'God, Emil, I am so sorry. I was out of my mind, you know,' she said, leaning forward, pushing aside a stack of papers.

'I just couldn't face anyone. And then, after my crack up, well, I was embarrassed. I've been gone, but I feel like I can come back, different now, but here, doing my work, again. If Raj and the powers that be agree, that is. Hoping my tenure survives this.'

'Clair, it's OK. I understand. I didn't take it personally, well not too much. As you can see, I did lose about twenty pounds grieving though. So that was helpful.'

Relieved that he was turning to his usual bantering, even though she could see tears glistening in his eyes, it began to feel like old times.

'Seriously, Emil, I just didn't have the heart for anyone or anything but my grief. I'm not going to say I'm a hundred per cent better but I am working my way towards better. And Adam, he has forgiven me. We're trying to be a couple again too.'

Frowning, Emil said, 'Hmm, that was the one thing that disappointed me Clair, that you didn't actually kill the bastard.'

'I know how you feel, how you've always felt about him. But he confessed to me that he never actually had a relationship with any of those women. I believe him, Emil. At least, I do so want to.'

'Clair, I knew Adam and you both before you got together. And I can tell you that he did. Before you, I mean. He was a total misogynistic womanizer. Especially with Claudia. After your marriage, it was more subtle but I am not convinced he didn't mess around. I'm not trying to hurt you. I'm trying to keep you from getting hurt.'

'Emil, I know that was how it was in the past, but we're trying, I'm trying to get past that. We must move forward now. Adam has promised me that he has been faithful since we married, and I choose to believe him. Let's not do this now, please. I just want to get back to some form of normal.'

Emil began to say something, but was interrupted by a knock on the door. Waving his arm at her, nodding an OK, he opened the door and a group of students eased in, surrounding Clair.

'Dr Mercer,' a young woman in her early twenties exclaimed. 'It's so great to see you.'

'Hi, Emma, Josh, Leslie. Come in, it's good to see you all. How is your work going?'

Emil walked through the open door, turning back to say, 'Clair, it's so good to have you back. I'll call and we'll talk, soon. And, I wouldn't worry about Raj. I'll talk to him. He owes me after teaching his summer term last year so he could go sailing around the Galapagos.'

Clair smiled, nodded goodbye, and settled down to listen to her students, reveling in their stories of breakthroughs and frustrations.

Word spread quickly through the building. Soon other students, faculty and even maintenance staff dropped in to say hello and welcome back. Clair was moved and surprised. In her mind, she was a loner. A professional who did her work, engaged in social events as much as required but had not ever seen herself or thought others saw her as anyone special. That so many people seemed to genuinely care astounded her. She felt those waves of emotion course through her over and over throughout the afternoon until before she knew it, dusk was falling. Adam hadn't come to collect her so she gathered her coat, looked around her office, now strewn with paper cups of coffee, soda cans, and chip packets, from their impromptu celebration.

With a satisfied heart, she closed her door, and walked out into the crisp, cold air, the sunlight ebbing into streaks of purple and gray across the western sky. Lighter than she had felt in months, she lifted her chest, still feeling the tugs of severed flesh and muscle, but not pain. No more pain, she chanted to herself, pulling her shoulders back even more. Breathing deeply, catching the scent of curry from the food truck on the corner. She realized she was hungry. Maybe she and Adam could walk over to one of the campus food trucks and get a takeout. Her steps quickened as she thought about home, for the first time with joyful anticipation, not dread.

* * *

It had been such a small thing. Her hope. Fatigue was beginning to envelop her as it did without warning, and she was eager to find Adam and go home. When she opened the door to the theater arts building, as she climbed the fake marble stairs up to the third floor, having to stop on each landing to catch her breath, the feeling fluttered like a dragonfly hovering above a blossom, not wanting to break that perfect stillness, that transitory moment between before and after. Walking down the hall, looking at posters on the walls of past productions, many if not most featuring photos of Adam with a beautiful girl or woman. Really looking now, she saw that Claudia was also in many of the scenes, standing just behind Adam, sometimes off to his side. It didn't mean anything, she reminded herself. Nothing at all. It was his work. Like her work, his students and colleagues were actors, playing parts. She was his real life.

Voices rang out from his room at the end of the hall. She pushed through, eager and hesitant. Then an anger so strong, like a hurricane wind, tore through her. Never had she felt such emotion. She picked up the closest thing at hand, a framed award for Best Director Western Colleges and Universities, and heaved it across the room, where Adam and Claudia were embracing. It hit Adam between his shoulders, causing him to gasp, turn to see her standing there.

'Clair, God Clair, it's not what you think.'

She was running down the hall, down the stairs, to the street. Past the Fusion Food Truck, dark now, lights off, owner hooking up to his van. Tears blinded her, thoughts unraveled. What to do? Devon, she knew, this one thing, this true thing. She had to get back to Devon. A deep intuitive knowing that his spirit waited for her somewhere in the world carried her forward.

Chapter 19

Clair

The cab pulled up to the house. It was fully dark now, a new moon offering no light. Wishing she had left a light on, she dug in her bag for her phone, turning on the flashlight function. It illuminated the front door, which she saw had been left open, only the screen door keeping out the autumn winds and evening insects. Remembering how excited she had been to surprise Adam, to reclaim her office, and role as wife and teacher, rushing out, not bothering to close the door behind her. What a delusion, she chided herself.

'Will you wait here?' she asked the cab driver. 'I'll just be a few minutes, OK?'

Rushing into their bedroom, she pulled open her closet, ripping shirts and pants off hangers. Drawers pulled open, underwear, sweaters, and night clothes were found, tossed into a large fabric tote. From the bathroom, a toothbrush, toothpaste, and body lotion. They'll have everything else I need, she thought. This will do for now. One final look into Devon's room, gratified to see that the cars were still arranged in their circle, she rushed back out into the cold, dark night, the only light coming from the taxi's low beams. She opened the door, falling back against the seat, exhaustion leeching the last drops of energy from her.

'Harbor hospital, cancer center housing,' she said. 'And please, hurry.'

She had called ahead, letting the desk know she was coming. The housing for cancer patients was simple and provided small, studio-type apartments, with a central kitchen and community room. Tonight, only two of the five studios were inhabited, making it easy for her to get one at the last minute. They were set up for patients who had to drive long distances to receive their treatments. She had explained that she needed to stay because she didn't have transportation and had to see Dr Ellerby first thing in the morning. The desk clerk didn't argue.

A woman was standing at the kitchen counter as she walked through the lobby of the housing center. Tall, but stooped, she moved slowly, as though every action required enormous energy. She leaned against the counter, both hands pressing against the edge. Clair didn't want to startle her so she spoke softly.

'Hello, I'm Clair, can I help?'

The woman turned, and Clair saw such pain on her face, she stepped back.

'Oh, no, sorry, I was lost in thought for a moment. Hi, I'm Hope, what a ridiculous name, especially now. Oh, dear, sorry again. I must sound mad.'

'No, really, Hope, it's good to meet you. Can I do something? You look like you were going to be sick.'

'Not me, no, I'm fine. It's my husband, Mike, he's sick. And we just learned he can't have any more treatment. It's futile, they said. So, we have to go home, back down to Redwood City. It's right on the border with California, but inland, about a hundred miles. It is in California actually, what am I saying,

I'm rambling. But we didn't have a cancer center there and we would rather be up here. We love the coast. Always have. So, you're just getting in?'

The tall woman, visibly straining to hold herself together, stood straight, pulling her shoulders back. Clair realized she was standing there holding her large tote.

'Yeah, I live here but I'm not driving right now, and my house is way up the river. It wouldn't have been practical for me to try and make it every day, for treatment, you know.'

'All by yourself then?' Hope asked.

'Pretty much,' Clair said. 'But here, let's sit down. Can I make us some tea? I see a pot and packages on the counter there.'

'Yes, please, that will be good. I can't stay long. My husband is lying down. I came in to make us something for dinner and got distracted. I don't know what we'll do. He's being sent home to die.' Hope disintegrated into sobs, her back heaving.

'Oh dear, here, let me help,' Clair said, although she had no idea what to do to help. 'I'll find us some food, I'm starving too. Come, sit down. Here on the sofa.'

She took the distressed woman by the hand, leading her to a circular sofa, old, battered, covered by several handmade Afghans. Pillows abounded, of every size and shape. Clair imagined how many tears of joy and frustration, anger and rage had soaked into them. Tonight, we will add some more, she thought.

Clair dropped her bag on a chair and began rummaging through cupboards, opened the fridge and was able to put together some eggs, cheese, toast and what looked like homemade marionberry jam. There was also a can of tomato soup she heated up, believing the heat would sooth them both.

148

The kettle whistled, tea was made, and Clair brought it all over to the couch and table.

'Can Mike come join us?' she asked, sipping the warm, rich tomato soup.

'No, I'll take him a tray later. I gave him one of his sedatives, he was so upset.'

'Here, eat, drink. It will ease you. That's first.'

They sat quietly for several minutes, sipping soup, tea, then digging into cheesy eggs and toast. Clair marveled again at the immediate closeness that came with having cancer. Like the people in the support group, it was like all social filters evaporated, leaving only human care and concern for another.

'So, tell me about you and Mike. Have you been married long?' Clair asked.

'Long, long. Going on fifty years. We were high school sweethearts, married after he came back from Vietnam. He learned how to fix helicopter engines, and from there any engine. We had a good life. I worked as a teacher, but mainly, I was a homemaker. Loved making a home for Mike and our three sons. Oh God, how am I going to tell them?'

Hope began crying again, but not so intense this time, more like the final rumblings of thunder as the storm moves out to sea. Clair sat quietly, letting her grieve. She thought about what the woman had said, about being told there was no more treatment. She didn't think this could happen, but that as long as you had insurance to pay, you would get treatment.

'What does this mean for Mike?' Clair asked. 'What will happen now?'

'Hospice. We'll go home, set up a hospital bed, commode, get ready for him to die. I want him to be able to die at home, not in the hospital. But he has such pain. It's lung cancer, you know, very painful. And he can't breathe. Morphine has to be given, every hour. And they gave him a Fentanyl patch today. They don't do that unless it's close to the end, everyone's so goddamn afraid of giving patients pain medicine. It's absurd. So, sure, there are addicts. Help them, treat them, but don't punish us. People with real pain need their medicine. They said it will be quick, you know, his death. Once he gets his pain under control, he'll pass pretty easily. Morpheus, God of dreams, I hope he takes my Mike somewhere beautiful. I'll need to call the boys. They'll want to be here. And the grands. Oh God, the babies. They love Grandpa Mike. This will be their first death.'

Clair let Hope talk, working out her plans for how she would get Mike home. But inside, she felt a cold wave of fear. What in God's name would she do, if this were her, if she were told all care was futile? Just a few months ago, she wanted only to die, to join Devon. She still felt certain that he was there, waiting for her, but she wasn't so ready to die anymore. Life had become worth living again. Even with this new despair about Adam, still, she was more than just his wife, more than a teacher. She was discovering for the first time in her life, that she was a person of substance, with heft. She felt her bones, her skin, felt the blood flowing through her arteries and veins. Lifting her hands to her face, she traced the bones, thinking about Ben, and how they had the same high, strong cheekbones. She might have lost her breasts, but she had found her heart, and it was strong enough for this.

Hope rose, taking her plate and mug to the kitchen.

'Hope, I'll clean up. You go to Mike. I'll see you in the morning, OK?'

Clair stood and walked over to where Hope leaned against

the counter. Opening her arms, she hugged the woman, trying to share some of her own strength.

'Morning, yes, it will come. Whether we're ready for it or not.'

Clair watched her walk across the central floor, around the couch, and into the hallway, leading down the side of the building. Clair looked towards the opposite end, seeing another hallway. She walked down towards a light at the end. A small window opened onto the parking lot, LED lights casting a sulfurous glow against the dark backdrop of dense firs. Looking out, she saw a deer, and then another. She remembered once, long ago, she had an animal spirit card reading. It was a rare party she had attended, a sort of sorority initiation. She had gone along because her mother insisted. As the leader of the reading passed out cards, and then interpreted their meaning, Clair was surprised to learn that a deer was her totem animal. She had hoped it would be something more dramatic like a bear or a wolf. She had forgotten about it until now. A deer was quiet, contained. She kept to herself, was fleet of foot, and would flee at the first threat. She was also a fighter when threatened, especially to defend her offspring.

As she watched the two deer walk slowly cross the tarmac, stepping carefully, alert for sounds of danger, ears moving like satellite dishes, she felt a kinship. Like the deer, each step must be deliberate, without haste. Clair knew she would have to navigate her uncertain future with nothing but her own wits. Watching the two deer disappear into the forested area behind the cancer center, Clair said to herself, *I am OK, I think.*

Chapter 20

Clair

The halls and studios were dark as Clair walked toward the women's locker room in the community fitness center. Waking stiff, sore, and needing heat and movement, Clair had decided to avail herself of the swimming pool, a close walk from her housing. A sudden remembering of why she was in this new place, so similar to her room on the psych unit but yet, so different in ways that mattered, brought her a moment of panic followed by deep regret, and then, calm. *I am awake, alive, and I feel OK,* she affirmed, slipping quietly out the door of the shared living space. The morning air was fresh, cool. Early morning joggers, dog walkers, and transients heading towards the daytime shelter for a hot meal were her only company. The parking lot at the community center was empty except for one older model Honda. The smell of sweat and chlorine hit her as soon as she walked in the door. The club receptionist, a young woman with her head down over her phone, ear buds inserted, checked her in. She knew she would be alone. Or should be alone. Whose voice was coming from the locker room, Clair wondered, hesitating outside the door, listening.

'There is no peaceful war. There is no friendly fire. He killed his three-year-old brother when he was sixteen. He tried to tell them but they didn't believe him. They said it was his Asperger's. Asperger's my ass. I'm talking to my invisible friends because I don't have any real ones. Now he is one of you too, one of us.'

It was a female voice. Clair relaxed. One of the many homeless, she thought, who pitched tents around the outside of the gym, taking advantage of the large old oak trees standing on the edges of the parking lot. For the most part, they were harmless, people struggling with mental illness, poor decisions, and social isolation. But there was always the risk that methamphetamine addiction and withdrawal caused people to act in crazy ways. She listened a while longer then walked inside, putting her towel bag on a bench just inside the door. A row of lockers lined the wall. To the left, around a slight corner was a hot tub. Not wanting to startle the woman, who was sitting in the hot tub, the water still, without the bubbling jets, Clair quietly opened the door to a locker. The woman turned, looked at Clair, standing in a pool of light shining down from the fluorescent tubes crisscrossing the ceiling. The early morning mist had left droplets of water on her blue hooded fleece. She was wearing a pale green woolen scarf wrapped around her shaven head.

'Oh, there you are. I was waiting for you,' the woman said, keeping her gaze on Clair.

'Ah, good morning,' Clair answered, without saying more.

She had been around enough mentally ill patients on the psychiatric unit to know that engaging a person with delusions or psychosis was a one-way conversation that could lead to outbursts of frustration.

'You, you are one of the ones. You crossed over. You made it back. Is he with you?'

'Is who with me?' Clair asked, feeling uncomfortable now, wondering if she should go get the receptionist.

'That boy, standing beside you. Is he with you or is he with me?'

Clair sat down on the bench, in front of the row of lockers. She stared at the woman. The woman smiled, a broad, bright smile. She stood up, her naked torso bright pink from being in the hot water. Her hair, long and dark blonde, cascaded down her shoulders, like sea kelp. Wide set eyes, skin the color of burnished copper, she looked as though she had stepped out of a solution of paint, still dripping, shiny and metallic.

'We're the selkies now,' she said, beginning to walk up the steps, out of the tub.

Clair felt an electric pulse race through her, causing her heart to beat fast. She took in a quick breath.

'He's gone now, but he was there. Right there. With you. Is he yours? Don't be afraid. You have the sign too. The spirits are using you. Don't be afraid.'

The woman walked up the steps, out of the tub, and across the tiled floor to the showers. Clair's heart was pounding. Looking around the locker space, she could see no signs of another person. There were no gym bags, towels, clothes either neatly folded on the benches or hanging from the hooks along the walls.

The room was quiet, no shower running, toilet flushing. Nothing but the sound of the radio softly playing nineties music through the overhead speakers. She recognized Stevie Nicks's 'Wild Heart' and smiled, remembering for just a moment how she had loved that song. How she had yearned to act wildly, just once. But she had been too reticent, too fearful of the reprimands that would follow. The shame piled on from her mother; the cold icy stares from her father, or worse, complete disdain and dismissal.

She sat still, waiting for what, she wasn't sure. She thought about her walk in this morning. Her new life, with its unfamiliar routines. Suddenly, like a traffic jam opening up on a multi-lane interstate highway, women began flooding into the space. Chattering like early birds, eager for the new day, they stripped off sweat suits and jeans, pulling on bathing suits. One woman, walking by towards the toilets, noticed Clair.

'Oh hey, are you new to class?'

Jolted out of her reverie, Clair self-consciously touched her right upper chest where the infusion portal sat under her skin, saying, 'No, not really. I was going to swim laps but it looks like you're all getting ready for a class.' No sign of the wet woman, anywhere. Had she imagined her?

'Come join us,' the woman said. 'I'm Pat. You'll love it. Great workout.'

She had been skeptical at first, not believing for a minute that she would achieve anything like her runner's high bobbing up and down in water. Mary, the teacher, drove them hard, and Clair was surprised. She enjoyed it. The youngest member of the group, she nonetheless found a deep companionship with these people, mostly women, many of whom had been coming for years. Mary was the reason. Perpetually cheerful, she sang tunes from musicals, while, even at seventy-five, she set the pace for the entire class. She learned they had parties for any reason: a birthday, anniversary, new house, and sometimes, a memorial for one of their group who died. Standing around in their Speedos, looking like a group of friends from for ever, who had wandered into a parallel universe where time stood still. Other than the gray hair and wrinkled skin, they were fit and engaged in life. Claire loved them.

Fatigue hit her like a train towards the end of class. She had been warned about this side effect of chemotherapy, unlike any normal tiredness. This must be it, she thought. Several people had already left the pool, sitting in the adjacent hot tub. Clair waved at them, as she left, feeling as though she had found a group of friends. As she walked down the long, darkened, empty hall towards the women's locker room, that tiny flutter in her chest, a lightness to her step, a momentary feeling of happiness startled her. At first, pushing it away, then allowing the warmth to spread through her bones. As she entered the locker room, Clair felt herself hit the wall, sliding down, until the rough brown carpet met her cheek.

Time drifted past. She heard voices, like birds warbling in the morning dew, trilling and light. Hands were on her, lifting her up. Sitting her on the bench, telling her to take sips of orange juice the receptionist had brought down, after being alerted by one of the ladies.

'Here, Clair, take this,' Pat said. 'You probably have low blood sugar. A collection of voices, all talking at once, brought her back.

'Are you OK now? Do you need to go to the hospital?' JoJo asked.

'Oh no, not the hospital,' Clair said, standing up. 'I'm OK. I got really dizzy. Thanks for the juice. I didn't eat before coming in this morning.'

'You can't do that, you know. Even just a bite of something, or keep some juice or candy with you. But do eat some protein and a carbohydrate, at least first thing. You know why it's called breakfast don't you? Because we break our fast. That means you are on empty, girl.' Nell, the retired nurse in the group spoke with authority.

'I know, I know. I promise, I will from now on. Ah, did any of you see a woman leaving just now? Or before?'

The women looked at each other, then back at Clair, shaking their collective heads, no.

On her walk back to the housing, Clair couldn't forget the odd woman who reminded her of a selkie. Wondering if it had in fact happened or if it was all a hallucination brought on by low blood sugar. And there was the water; it had felt different to her, like a second skin. The lights illuminating the bottom of the pool had danced like strobes, like the rays of sunshine cutting through the dense darkness of the Pacific, that morning when she had walked into the ocean, the last time she had seen Devon.

The realization that she had seen him hit her like a thunderclap. She had forgotten that. The memory emerged like a diver coming up for air, too fast, leaving her dizzy and disoriented. The woman in the locker room. She hadn't imagined that. Clair felt swallowed up by these images and feelings. She longed to be home, to lie in her bed, and sleep. Not the sleep of restoration, but the sleep of dreams. Lucid dreaming, she knew it was called, and she had found the way in. She would find Devon again, in her sleep, and through the uniting of their energies. The early morning mist was drifting down through the rising fog off the ocean, a wind picking up, mixing the two, creating sea smoke, a nearly impenetrable curtain of dense moisture, sky and cloud come to earth, as Clair hurried to her new, temporary home at the cancer center, using dead-reckoning as her compass.

Chapter 21

Clair

The black Mercedes was parked in front of the cancer center, adjacent to the apartment complex for residential patients. The sight of it caused her stomach to tighten, her throat to constrict. She felt dizzy again. Seeing Adam's car parked so close to her home, this safe place where she could focus on healing, felt like an invasion. *Breathing in, I am calm,* she said to herself. *Breathing out, I smile.* Over and over, she practiced the techniques Naomi had taught her as ways to ride the waves of change her body, mind, and it seemed, spirit were passing through. Slowly lifting her head, she leaned against the outside of the building, eyes closed, waiting for the light-headedness to pass. Waiting for her heart rate to slow, and a normal beat to emerge. Not flight, not fight, not freeze she said to herself. Just ride it out. It will pass. Breathe in, breathe out. Eventually she was able to open her eyes, look through the rain, now falling hard, towards the door of the cancer center. He was probably in there, asking about her.

She knew they wouldn't tell him anything, patient privacy laws protecting her. She hadn't signed a release for any information to be shared, not with Adam. She had allowed Ben and Jodie to receive information, in case she died or got sicker, and couldn't speak for herself. They were her health care representatives. Adam, he was nothing to her now. And her earlier hope for some form of reconciliation or new beginning felt like an adolescent daydream.

Rain was coming down now, a soft blanket. Its sound drumming on the parking lot transfixed her, freeing thoughts back to the water. Like a tidal surge, the desire to return pulled her out further and further, before sounds, a door slamming, voices, laughter, a dog barking, cast her upon the beach of now, here. Deep fatigue settling in again, she knew she had to get into her apartment and lay down. She had another chemotherapy treatment and then support group later that morning, and she needed to be rested for that. Clair fought against the urge to keep moving, like a shark, or fear dying, surrendering. She knew in her every cell that for her, death wouldn't be the end, but a beginning, a reuniting with Devon. Still, she wasn't ready for it yet. She had first to find him, the world of spirit was so vast, she wanted to be able to pinpoint his location. She had to beat this cancer, get stronger, and connect with him across the light years of space and time. The woman at the club was one of her guides, she knew that now. There would be others out there. But first, Adam.

Clair stood at the car, arms crossed, jacket hood pulled up to protect her head. She didn't want him knowing which of the small apartments in the housing unit was hers. Anger filling her chest, causing breaths to come in short, staccato puffs, she stared at the double doors leading into and out of the cancer center. As she watched people coming and going, some walking on their own two feet, others with walkers or wheelchairs, and one arriving in an ambulance, she marveled at the sheer number of men, women, children, walking, dying, living with cancer.

When she saw him, her breath stopped, catching in her throat. He was so beautiful, still capturing her senses the way he had that first night she had met him. More stooped now, weary lines around his eyes and down his cheeks, giving him a hero's persona. His eyes turned towards his car as he opened his large, black umbrella. When he saw her standing there, rain falling down on her, eyes large and fearless beneath the jacket's hood, he smiled, large and bright. He hurried to her, holding the umbrella over them both with one hand, wrapping the other arm around her, pulling her to him. She leaned into him, his heat the sedative she needed. He felt like a warm blanket, easing her stiffness. She wanted so much to give up, let him reel her back in but she knew deeply in her heart, it would be a mistake. That past was gone. There was no going back. The future was unknown, not even a suspicion of possibility. Live or die? There was only now, and this now, she had to do alone. She pulled back and looked up at him, his head bumping the metal braces at the top of the umbrella. She felt a smile break her face.

'You're going to get your hair tangled in that thing,' she said. 'Come on, you can come out of the rain.'

She took his hand, running towards the main doors leading into the apartment building. She was grateful that the shared communal room was empty. She decided she would rather talk with him out here, keeping her own space inviolate.

'Sit. I'll make us some tea. Or would you rather have coffee? We have one of those pod things,' she said, startled at her nervousness, her uncertainty.

Adam shrugged off his coat, turning it outside in, and laying it across the back of the couch. He sat, his long legs almost touching his chest as he sank down into the soft, fabric chair, designed for comfort, not style. She could feel his eyes following her movements. She consciously stood straighter, pulling her shoulders back, still feeling the tug on nerve and muscle fibers severed, searching for some memory of wholeness. At times, she felt phantom pleasure, as though her breasts recalled their purpose. Making love, feeding Devon, the first buds when she was a girl, proud and embarrassed, wearing tight sport bras to cover and hold them back. Always small, her breasts never defined her as with so many women. Yet, through giving of her love, to Adam and Devon, she had come to love them, as an extension of her nurturing nature. Now, they were killing her. Even gone, their power of giving life and taking life remained. The language of cancer was the language of war. Remembering the woman's words, there is no peaceful war. There is no friendly fire. Cancer was a battleground and she couldn't weaken. This was war, not peace; this was fire, and it was raging. She turned to Adam.

'Earl Gray or herbal? I have some green too,' she said, waving her arm over the collection of tea boxes on the cluttered counter.

'Earl is good. Thank you, Clair, what's wrong? I've never seen you on the defensive. You don't have to fuss, you know. I just wanted to see you to explain.'

Adam had begun to stand, and she shushed him, waving him back into his seat.

Bringing the tea over in two chipped mugs, one with a picture of Santa on it, she sat opposite him, on the edge of a rocking chair, careful not to set it moving. Her hands trembled. She tucked them between her legs, pressed together.

Adam, picking up the Santa mug, blowing on the steam rising from the cup, asked, 'Clair, why are you here? Why won't you come home?'

Looking around, seeing the room through his eyes, she saw its lived-in shabbiness. The old brown sofa, tattered, worn in places by grieving hands. Crocheted Afghans, needlepoint framed affirmations of hope, courage, tenacity. She noticed the many different body smells. Like a college dormitory, except instead of jubilant youth, this home was filled with terrified adults, fighting for time and comfort.

'I like it here. I have a small apartment. I don't have to share. I'm close to treatment, my group, others going through this. I feel safe.'

She wasn't sure why she said that but, for some reason, thought it was important that he know.

'I see. And you would rather be here than at home? I don't understand that, Clair. I need to explain…' he began to say, but she interrupted him.

Pulling her hands out from between her legs, unzipping her jacket. It was warm and she felt a surge of hormone heat rising up through her core. She ripped her head wrap off, tossing it onto the table. Picking up a pamphlet laying on the table, she began vigorously fanning herself. She could feel her face and neck turning red.

'I really don't want to hear any explanations, Adam. I saw what I saw,' she said shrugging. 'And, you know, it's OK. I don't care. I realize you and Claudia have been together all along. Thinking back to the very first night, it was she that was looking for you. My eyes had followed hers, and found you. My God, no wonder she's hated me all these years, but acted like she was my friend. What a fool I have been.'

As she spoke, she looked first at Adam then away, out the window, into the woods beyond the parking lot. Birdsong broke through, and she marveled at this, at how birds could sing in the rain. Their simple faith in the end of storm and the return of sun and worm was abiding. She found strength and comfort in this, enough to face Adam again. Her face had cooled. She felt more in control. She glanced at the pamphlet still in her hand. Living Beyond Breast Cancer Support Group. Her group, her new family.

'Tell me I'm wrong.'

'You are wrong, Clair, completely,' Adam said, softly, without force. He leaned forward, clasping his hands together.

'What you saw was a final goodbye. I had told Claudia I was taking a leave of absence, so I could take care of you. She finally got it that I would never be with her, not in that way.'

Adam stood, walked around the couch, too distraught to sit. He hadn't slept the night before, missing her, afraid for her, and for himself now that he had imagined a life for them together again. Everything was happening too fast. He had to find a way back.

'I have never, not once, been intimate with Claudia since you and I have been together. She's a colleague, friend, and yes, I do admit, she made it clear that she has been infatuated with me, but that's all it ever was. Maybe I encouraged it, especially in the later years when you were so wrapped up with Devon. And before, it was a silly game. A flirtation. I could always count on her to be my date for faculty events and yes, occasionally sex. But once I met you, and we married, had Devon, all that changed. At least, in my world. Not to her, I realize now. I should have been more honest, forthright with her. But I didn't want to hurt her and then, she became department chair and things got even more complicated. So, I let it all slide. When you saw us together, in my office, I had told her. She was saying goodbye to me, to her fantasy of me.'

Clair leaned back in the rocker, flashbacks to those early morning feedings with Devon, gently rocking him while he nursed, feeling the tingle of nerves under the taught skin, the erotic pull of milk as it let down, and filled his rosebud mouth with warmth and succor. When she looked at Adam, she could see Devon in his broad forehead, ears that slightly stood out, giving him a perpetual schoolboy appearance. His eyes, so clear and bright, luminous in the rain-shadowed darkness of this retreat, bore into hers, seeking answers to his pain, his fear. She felt her anger release in a flood of compassion. For the first time, she could connect with his suffering. Like quantum entanglement, they had been opposites of each other for so long, his death, her life, his joy, her sorrow. And now, she had to shift again, focus on her path to survival.

'It may be true, what you say,' she said, smiling gently at him. 'It may not. I can't care about that now, Adam. My life is on the line here. I can't handle the distraction. All bullshit aside, this is the fucking reality.'

She held out her hands for him to see. Her third round of chemotherapy had been tortuous. The skin was bright red, like a third-degree sunburn.

'And it's on the inside too. The cancer is spreading, like a wildfire. I have to work on this every moment of every day, and I have to do it alone.'

'I knew you were different,' he said, standing and walking over to the window, hands deep in his pockets.

He turned to look at her, his smile crinkling his eyes for a moment, then the sadness returned. He turned, leaning back against the window ledge.

'I wanted, needed that difference. I had always been chosen by women, fitting myself into their lives. They needed me to complete them. You, so fearless and believing, in your science, the truth of mathematics. It resonated with you and made you whole. I chose you. And you had my baby. You took it to the limit. You completed me. Old ways and habits, those well-worn neuropathways default our best intentions. But Clair, I never once cheated on you. I felt left, diminished, and I acted poorly. I was weak. I'm sorry.'

Adam's eyes filled with tears. He dropped his head into his hands. She wanted to go to him, to hold him, to smell his hair, feel the roughness of his face, trace the paths of his tears with her lips.

He looked up, ran his hands across his face, through his hair, started to speak again. She waved him to silence.

'Quiet now. You will endure, and so will I. Go and live well. If we are meant to be together, we'll find each other again, after all of this.'

She walked to him, took hold of his hands where they hung limply by his side. He bent his head down, lifting her hands and cupping his face, kissing her palms. She shuddered. Then she stood, sliding her hands from his, folding her arms across her chest.

'Now?' he asked, tears forming in his eyes.

'Yes, please. I need to lie down. I'll see you on the other side, or, if we're among the favored few, somewhere along this life's sojourn, sometime in the future.'

Clair sat for a while, feeling the absence of his energy. His largeness. If he was acting, he did it well. If he was being truthful, well, she couldn't think about that now. Looking around, deciding what to do, she saw his coat laying across the couch, where he had left it. Forgotten in his rush to escape before he fell apart. She sighed, knowing how much the coat meant to him, and realizing that his leaving it was a sign of how upset he had been. That black wool coat that had been the focus of an argument, the last winter the three of them had been together. It had been a fissure in the tender veneer of their life as a family.

She walked to the couch, picked it up, and wrapped herself in it. His smell emanated from the damp wool. She sat in the rocker, and let her mind drift. One year ago, could it be. Last November.

Devon had been agitated all day. Winter break parties at his school, shopping with her after school, and coming home, his favorite TV show changed for a holiday special. Clair had tried all of her techniques for calming. A bath with favorite toys, toast, with butter, honey, and cinnamon. Stories told from memory, so he could see her eyes throughout the telling. They had practiced Mommy and Me yoga. It was raining but he wanted to go out, having been cooped up all day. She had let him. He had put on his Superman cape and ran around the yard, rain falling down like spirit from the sky in the evening dusk. When he had finally worn himself out, she dried him off, helping him put on his pajamas. Still wearing the kind with feet in them, he had waddled around the kitchen, calmer now, wanting to help her prepare dinner. They had been baking bread, he rolling the dough between his fingers, creating shapes, and getting flour all over himself and the counter top. Adam had come in, wet, tired, wearing his new black wool coat.

Devon had run to him, throwing himself at his father, hands sticky with flour, like glue. Adam, in his surprise and rash anger at getting his coat covered with flour, had shouted and shoved Devon away.

They had been being frugal, without her working. And Devon's treatments, counseling, school, and tutors cost money. Neither had bought anything not necessary for over a year. When Adam came home, wearing this expensive coat, she had been angry, accusatory, telling him he cared more about his appearance than his family. He had made excuses, how he had to look a certain way, uphold his stature, and anyway, he hadn't had a new coat or anything new since Devon was born and by God, he was the one earning the goddamn money here and if he wanted to buy a coat, he would. The coat was special and the mines laid.

Chapter 22

Adam

Somehow, he reached his car, eyes burning with unshed tears, breath held captive in his throat. He couldn't swallow to release the pressure, vertigo causing him to weave like a drunken man. Once inside the car, he punched the starter, sat for several moments, listening to the engine hum. Remembering a technique he had learned in scuba training years ago, he consciously exhaled what little breath he had left, relaxing the epiglottis, and allowing cool, nourishing air to flow in. This pause between breaths, momentary death, ignited visions, like lightning flashes against a dark sky.

Memories of a trip he and Clair had taken to La Paz before Devon was born. She had been goddess-like in her sixth month of pregnancy, wearing a deep red bikini, her belly like mother earth, holding all promise for life and abundance. He had rubbed baby oil on her back, belly, thighs until laughing, hands reaching, touching, they waded out into the crystal-clear water to make love in the gentle rock of the waves, her legs circling him, his face buried in her breasts. He had told her he loved her, as they swayed together, his face nuzzling her neck, tasting salty skin, catching long, auburn hair streaked with sunlight in his mouth.

So far from now, from this sad, gray day. Grateful for his breath, bringing much needed oxygen to his struggling brain, he sat, the flashback resonating, reminding him of who he once was, who they were. Windshield wipers slid across glass, misted with light rain, their back and forth refrain calming him, like the placental swish. Remembering the first time he had heard that, the first ultrasound. A boy, perfect, all his tiny parts present. A son. He would be a good father. He would be everything his father was not. Then the diagnosis, his perfect son, imperfect. Had he minded? Had he felt differently about Devon after? He tried so hard to remember. Clair was devastated. Did she blame him? One moment they were the perfect family. Husband, father a popular man, respected, maybe even loved by his students, admired by his colleagues, and yes, desired by some. Clair, a woman of stature, internationally known for her research on theoretical mathematics, probability, and models of infectious disease. Then, the spiral downward into a different Clair, locked into trying so hard to change what was unchangeable.

In his memory, he had loved and accepted Devon as he was. He knew there was no such thing as perfection. He saw his son as he was, a being divined in his own skin, worthy of his care and devotion. Not Clair. She couldn't accept it. That was when they had divided. But, oh, the memory of that trip to Baja. Clair was there all the time. Her beauty. Her passion. He had fought so hard against it. Damn himself.

How had he missed all of this for so long? It had been right in front of him. He loved her. And now he was losing her all over again. To this thing he had no control over, a viper hidden in the tall grass, striking without choice. A convergence of wind, water, the circling of the earth, gravity pulling everything down into a hurricane of destruction. Cells nesting, then finding purchase, spreading and invading soft tissue, feeding on the essential nutrients that sustained life. Clair's life. His life with her. And Devon, before. He laid his head on the steering wheel, grinding his forehead into the leather, needing the pain. 'If only I could go back,' he moaned. 'To when it all started. I would love them better. I would watch over, protect, harbor them from danger.'

He heard a car's engine revving behind him. Looking over his shoulder, he noticed a driver waiting to take his spot, others circling the lot. So many, he thought, reversing. How did I think I was unique, special and that nothing monstrous would ever touch me? That I had somehow paid my dues in childhood. And that my acting would cover up all that was real, human. I was, no am, a fool. So much time wasted playing a part. And all the while, time was diminishing me, lie by futile lie.

The car righted itself, moved forward. Stopped at the signal, reflexively looking right to left. Advancing. He didn't know where he was heading, he just drove, like a shark, the need for movement compelling. Images of Clair's hands, those beautiful hands that had touched him in intimate places, red and inflamed, colored his vision. Knowing the cancer was happening inside her, in her stomach lining, lungs, brain, made him feel like slamming his car into something solid. A moment of agony then over. Not like the drawn-out process of being eaten alive from the inside that Clair was suffering. Who would care, he thought? Or even notice. *I struggled so hard all my life to escape, to not become the kind of man I hated, the kind of man my mother loved, I became him. The kind of man who watches another woman's ass while sitting with his wife, and making sure she sees him doing it.*

The road took him west, across the wide four-lane road separating town from coast. Once on the two-lane road, formerly a wagon trail, named Seven Devils for the wicked turns that caused many to crash and die, his brain registered his location. Looking right, the ocean held center stage. Chugging into the narrow cut, waves breaking over the bow, a tug was leading a massive freighter from Japan into the harbor to load Douglas fir timber. Normally, he would begin a diatribe on the idiocy of this, of a ship from Japan, picking up timber grown and harvested in the Pacific Northwest, to take back to Japan to cut into logs, manufacture paper products, and then sell back to the United States. No wonder he would rail, the once booming timber industry here was nothing but a museum of times past, and not too long. One generation ago was all. Many of his students came from those families, first members of the family to attend college. Today, he didn't have it in him. He noticed, then thought, what the fuck does it matter? What does anything matter, really? He drove on. Knowing now where he was going.

When he arrived at the turn off, wind was blowing rain sideways in gusts that shook the car. He looked around for his coat. It wasn't in the front seat. It wasn't in the back seat. Could he have tossed it in the trunk? Clearing his mind, he went back through the afternoon. Fuck. He had left it at Clair's. Just saying that, thinking that, that Clair had a separate home from him, sent him into a paroxysm of emotion he couldn't name. His sense of loss, of harm, was so great, he felt like a child, bereft of all protection and care. Wrenching the door handle, he pushed against the wind. Leaning into it, he muscled out of the car, flailing as he shoved the door back closed. His hair, wet, stung as it whipped his eyes.

The walk through the woods was slippery, rain uprooting debris, causing puddles and small lakes to form. Light was fast fading, the sword ferns and bracken creating eerie shadows on the path. Struggling to remain upright, the realization that 'this is me' hit him like a boulder, like an avalanche of clarity. The wind and rain pelleted him. He was not prepared, had nothing between him and the elements except his shirt, vest, slacks, all designed for clean, dry inside work, not a wet forest. His fine leather shoes no match for the thousand years of mulch built up underfoot. Sounds like a freight train swirled through the last of the blue-gray space above the tree-line, a symphonic climax to the normal synchrony of tree talk. And still he walked, or fell forward. His gait like a mad man. When he reached the opening, where forest met sea, he knew why he had come. This was where it had all fallen finally, and fundamentally apart. This was where they lost not only Devon, but each other, and in the doing, themselves.

Adam stumbled across the small, rickety, handmade bridge, made of narrow timbers, slick now with rain and salt from ocean spray. Slipping, one foot hit the creek beneath, running strong with all the water flowing down from the coastal range. He managed to stay upright, holding onto the sides of the timber as he pulled his leg back up onto the bridge. Soaked through, shivering, he carried on.

As so often happens in the Pacific Northwest, a storm will come in from the sea, lashing and turbulent, moving rapidly across the coastline into the welcoming valley, thirsty for water and leaving a shimmering light, so crystalline that rainbows cascade, illuminating dark places. Through this light he glimpsed his way forward. His steps left prints in the sand, alongside patterns of sea-birds. How ridiculous he thought.

My pointy-toed prints, and their suited for purpose prints. How did I get so lost? Who am I, really? This pointy-toed man, standing on a beach, in a storm, looking for what? Absolution?

The rocks at the edge of the cove beckoned him. The tide was low, and one of the many caves carved out by centuries of waves, cutting in, sluicing out, offered shelter from the storm. He hovered in the opening. His gut clenched and he was afraid he would be sick. This was the place, the last place he had seen his son. Right here. Squatting down, looking into the tidal pools. And he, the father, the husband, the man he was or could have been, was on his goddamned phone. Devon, his beautiful son, right here, right here. If only there had been waves like these, thrashing and pulsating. Devil's stovepipes they were called, their rocket like projectiles throwing water and all the small living creatures in the sea up into the air. But it was calm that day, pacific, like its name. Nothing to indicate a killer was on the loose. Except, looking back, if he had been paying attention, perhaps there had been clues, not to the ocean's madness, but to their own, his and Clair's, and their slipping away from what mattered, towards mutually ensured destruction.

Adam hadn't wanted to go in the first place. The night before, his back tight between his shoulders, leaning against the kitchen counter, trying to block out another battle of wills between Clair and Devon. He had lost the effort.

'For God's sake, Clair, just let him sleep in his cape,' he had shouted up the stairs. 'What does it really matter?'

'Because, he's just a baby still, he could be strangled by the ties around his neck, in his sleep.'

She was always looking for the worst possible thing, the most unlikely event, the dark side of the situation. He had just wanted a few minutes of quiet in his home. Not this unending battering ram of an existence.

He had gone outside on the deck, the late fall evening cool, half a moon in the sky, flitting in and out between clouds. Inside, the bickering had subsided. Devon finally surrendering to sleep. Adam had slipped back into the kitchen, hoping he could make it to his study before another exchange with Clair. He had grabbed a beer from the fridge, twisting it open, taking that first welcome draw, feeling an immediate release of tension. Oh, if only he still smoked a pipe, he mused, not for the first time since quitting shortly after Devon's birth. Fear of oral and lung cancer, second-hand smoke, and a plethora of other maladies the maternity nurses had threatened him with had hit their target. But oh, the smell, the feel, the romance of it all, he missed. Especially the smoke screen it put up between him and the rest of the world. A screen he hadn't wanted between him and Devon. Back before they knew about Devon. Back before Clair had taken over. And he, the father, had been cast out of the inner circle of mother, son.

Adam knelt, then collapsed, lying face down on the sand. He beat at it, gripped it in his hands, rubbed it on his face. In his hair. Railed at the ruination of it all.

Birds cried in the distance and then closer. Carnage, he thought, they think I'm some sort of hulk to eat. Adam pushed himself up, his body moving like a heavy bag, weighted down with an eternity of grief. He stood. The storm was moving eastward, darkness falling. Soaked and forlorn, he hugged himself, his mouth closing, lips sucking in, his teeth chewing on his bottom lip. *What kind of man am I?* he thought. Lear came to him. Miserable man, father, husband. *If not Clair's husband, Devon's father, who am I? What is left? Claudia's fantasy? Who was I before? An imposter. That's what? A man for all women. And I had this one chance to be different. To matter, and I did. I mattered to him, to my son. As ineffectual as I was, he didn't know it. He thought I hung the moon. And I let him go. I didn't hold on.*

Adam threw his face upward into the storm, this coming to terms, this awakening too much for him. Again, he hugged himself, as though trying to capture some essence of his boy, holding, keeping, desperate.

Night now. Darkness pervaded his space. No stars, or moon. Calling of sea birds settling in on the rocks, wanting him to leave. He felt in his pocket and found his key fob. A curious feeling of comfort came over him. I have a key. I have a car. I can go. I can do something about this. A surge of purpose electrified him.

'Devon, I won't let go. I'll hold onto your mom, and I won't let go. I promise.'

With urgency, he began the tortuous climb back through the forest, to his car, using the light from his phone as illumination. He slipped, fell, his hands abraded by roots, and fallen branches. But his mantra, 'I won't let go,' echoed through his mind and body, energizing him. He would not let Clair go through this alone. Even if she didn't want him, he would be there for her.

Chapter 23

Adam

Morning broke, shattering storm clouds open with beams of colored light. Prisms embedded in the cut glass windows cast rainbows across the pale blue duvet and on the white walls of their bedroom. Raucous bird calls had awakened him, Steller's jays, demanding food, hit the bird feeder outside the bedroom window with a crash, flashes of cobalt as their spread wings caught the emerging light. He lay there watching the colors drift around the room, dust motes captured in the movement of air from the open skylight above the bed.

That was one thing he had loved most about this house, the way the windows were designed to be open during the long months of rain, so that even in a downpour, they could feel and see sky above. He and Clair would lay there at night, listening to raindrops hit the sides of the skylight, feeling safe and warm in their bed. When had they stopped reaching for each other, he wondered? Not during her pregnancy. He had loved her bulbous belly, and would lay his head against her protruding belly button, listening and feeling the sensation of life inside. And not immediately after. Her breasts, swollen with milk, would leak during their lovemaking, and he would lick the sweet liquid from her skin. Somewhere around Devon's second birthday, they began to notice how different he was from other toddlers and that he didn't seem to be meeting the developmental benchmarks Clair read about in her childcare books. When they took him to the park, instead of playing on the swings, slides, and jungle gym playset, he would sit alone, in a corner of the sand-box, lining up the cars and trucks in exact order, from large to small. If another child came to play in the space, he would ignore them, continuing with his solitary activity.

Clair had told him this was 'normal' toddler behavior, called parallel play. But soon other signs began manifesting. His lack of eye contact, dislike at being held. He wasn't as verbal as the other children at his pre-school. It was his teacher who suggested they take him to the pediatrician for an evaluation. Dr Chung had said that yes, it was difficult to make a definitive diagnosis at this early age, but it did very much look like autism. She administered a neurological screening tool, and the signs were impossible to dismiss. Their beautiful boy was on the spectrum, and only time would tell how severe his condition was. And that was when their connection with each other had changed. The more she focused on Devon, the more he distanced himself, from them both, Adam realized. Feeling his face reddening with shame at this revelation, he closed his eyes, soldering the memory deep into his consciousness so he would never forget.

There had not been any seeds in the feeder for months now but still the jays came, each morning, nagging and demanding. Adam thought, today, I'll replenish their birdseed. Eyes still crusted with sleep and residue of salt, from the ocean and his own tears, he eased out of bed, muscles stiff from his time in the forest and on the beach. His stomach twisted. He thought he might be sick. Stumbling his way to the bathroom, he kneeled next to the toilet, waiting for what would come. Not sick, hungry.

* * *

The waitress placed a large plate filled with over easy eggs, large slices of bacon, hash browns, and a stack of wheat toast, soggy with melted butter, in front of him. She held a coffee pot aloft like an offering. Eyebrows raised, she smiled a question.

'Keep it coming, Cookie. Today's a day for extra coffee,' he said, holding his cup up to her.

'Haven't seen you in for a while,' she said, her large hip resting on the edge of the table.

The diner was filling, but still quiet this early in the morning. The night shifters had left, day shifters just coming in. Adam had been a regular for years, before Clair. She had teased him about his southern style big breakfasts and, in deference to her tastes, he had gone with her to a coffee house offering gourmet drinks and eats. He would drop into the 101 Diner occasionally, to gorge on thick pancakes, bacon, eggs, biscuits, and all the trimmings. Reminding him of the meals at his grandmother's, memories of the times in his life when he felt safe and loved, the diner provided him a respite from his daily act. Here, he felt he could be himself.

Just before his twelfth birthday, his mother had dropped him off in a state-run foster home, deciding that the new man in her life only had time for her and his younger brother, Allen. Adam had been rescued by his grandmother, and remained with her until he completed high school. She had made sure he ate every day, and had a quiet place to study and do his homework.

Life with his mother had been noisy and chaotic. He missed his brother but thrived in the love and care of his grandmother. And he was hurt, to the core, that he had been the one who was not chosen. His mother had told him he was big enough to take care of himself. Tall and broad shouldered, he looked older than he was, and people often expected him to act in a certain way. He wasn't athletic, preferring to read, daydream, and even then, act out scenes from his favorite movies. His grandmother was a seamstress, and would make elaborate costumes for him.

Before she abandoned him, his mother would criticize his daydreaming, snapping her fingers in front of his face, telling him to snap out of it. Their housekeeper, Bertha, would tell her to leave the boy alone, he's just playing in his mind.

It was a working man's diner, and at first, the regulars ignored him, bantering with Cookie or Tom back in the kitchen, casting doubtful glances at the man dressed casually elegant, when they were in their longshoreman or timber workers' clothes. But when they did talk with him, at the counter or if seated at the same table due to crowding, his quiet presence, active listening, and non-judgmental attitude towards others won them over. The few women who frequented the diner watched him out of the corners of their eyes, his handsome face drawing them in. During the search for Devon, Cookie and Tom had closed the diner so everyone could help with the search. The men volunteered their boats, dogs, and sheer determination in the search and when the focus switched from rescue to recovery, they cried alongside Adam. Their wives sent casseroles and pies to the home. The small coastal community felt each loss to the ocean as a rip in the fabric of their lives.

He looked up from the book he had been reading, at her kind, soft, round face, hair cropped in a no-fuss cut. He noticed she had lost weight since he had seen her last. He didn't know if she knew about Clair and all that had happened over the past few months. It was a small town and people talked. He couldn't detect any pity or judgement on her face.

'I know, been busy. You're looking good, Cookie. Everything going well for you and Tom?'

'Oh yeah, I had to lose weight. Damn those doctors. Diabetic. Have to walk and exercise now. And quit eating my own doughnuts and pies. Tom too. He isn't diabetic but he joined me, out of sympathy, you know. We're both doing it. And quit smoking. It's about to kill me but if I can keep it up for another few months, we're going to celebrate and go to Hawaii again, like on our honeymoon.'

Her voice rang out across the diner, years of cigarette smoking and breathing bacon grease had coated her vocal cords so that she sounded like a fog horn blasting a warning to ships coming into harbor. Patrons were used to it and didn't bother to look up, unless she was aiming her blasts directly at them.

Adam sat back in the booth, smiling up at her.

'That's great, Cookie. Hawaii, huh? That will be a nice place to be around February.'

'Don't you know it,' she laughed, and sauntered off, stopping to fill coffee cups, chat up a table, and deposit checks.

Adam thought maybe he and Clair could take a trip like that, once her treatments were over. Hawaii would be good in the dark days of February. Or Mexico again, that would be good too. Anywhere sunny and warm. Shake off winter and bring in spring and all its newness and possibilities. *I won't say anything now,* he said to himself. *I'll wait. First, I have to win her trust back. Win her love back. And I will.*

With his new resolve, Adam drove back to the cancer center, to Clair's apartment, to get his coat, or that would be the reason he would give her. He still had a hard time referring to the residential housing as Clair's home. To him, it was a temporary placement, a way station on their journey back to their shared, real home. He could wait. He had showered and shaved that morning, dashing his face with the aftershave cologne she had given him on his birthday, back in March. Clair had surprised him with dinner out. Their first in years, since Devon's diagnosis. Dressed in a swirl of blues and greens, a shimmering fabric that had clung to her body like a second skin, she had been glowing, beautiful.

'How did you manage to do this?' he had asked, incredulously. 'Who's watching Devon?'

She had met him outside his office, with a dinner reservation and tickets to a film playing at the old, renovated Egyptian Theater. A black and white, with stars playing heroic roles.

'Shelly,' she said simply. 'I found Shelly.'

'OK, and who is this wonder woman Shelly?'

'More girl than woman, but she is a caregiver who specializes in children with autism. Devon's teacher gave me her contact information. And I called. She came over, met Devon, played with him for an hour or so, and I could tell he bonded with her. And she'll come every day now, for a few hours after his school. Oh Adam, it means I can return to work!'

He remembered how her eyes glowed with hope and joy at the prospect of returning to her classroom. Of being in the space where learning happens and students, faculty, staff are all engaged in the active process of seeking and finding new knowledge and ways to apply it. She had been trying to keep up using the online learning management system, and it worked, but she missed the smells, the sounds, and energy of the classroom.

'Just part-time you know, for now. But it's a start, and it is so good to see Devon happy again. He's doing much better now that he has a regular schedule, with his school, after school therapy sessions, and now structured play time with Shelly. I know it's busy and leaves him little time to just be a free-range kid but I think that is what he needs most right now. His therapist thinks so too. He told me children with high functioning autism need to be challenged and stimulated, highly structured, or they feel anxious.'

'Sounds like he thinks Devon's a problem to be solved, rather than a kid to love.' Adam said, frowning. 'He is just four years old.'

'Yes, but a very bright four-year-old with a neurological disorder. If he is going to have any chance of a normal life, he has to find ways to fit into mainstream education,' Clair said, her glow fading in this replay of an argument she and Adam had on a regular basis.

He had wanted Devon to have more time to play and be creative, use his imagination. He thought that Clair wanted him tucked away in a neat little box, where he would fit into society. It caused angry words, sometimes tears, and always regret. He didn't want that to happen tonight. He didn't want to spoil their night out, a simple thing but for them, a step towards normalcy. Going out together, as a man and woman, husband and wife. Since Devon, they had either been living in denial, fear, or blind faith.

He had reached across and taken her hand.

'And I am so glad to see you happy again. And if Devon is happy, then that's a perfect solution.'

Clair had let the argument go, giving his hand a squeeze, then handing him the small, beautifully wrapped package containing the cologne. When he splashed some on before climbing into bed, she had straddled him, her hair falling into her face. She had begun licking the cologne off, starting at his cheeks, then his neck, and carried on down until he reached for her, pulled her to him, holding her so tightly, their skin felt merged, their hearts one beating organ. His knees weakened at the memory. It has been just before their fateful trip to the coast. Before everything changed. He fretted about leaving the scent on or washing it off. In the end, he left it on, thinking it might bring happier memories to Clair too. When he saw her again? And he would, he believed, always see her one more time.

He parked outside the residential unit, building up his nerve to knock on the door. He knew the common room was locked so that only those staying in the apartments could go in and out. While he waited, he saw Jet coming across the parking lot, her yellow dog prancing at her side. A stunning woman, he thought, not for the first time, but terrifying. It was like she could read his mind, know his every thought, and found him lacking. At least, that had been his impression the few times he had met with her to talk about Clair, during her hospitalization. He felt guilty so he thought others thought him guilty also. Even though he had been the one to be poisoned. He shook off the memory. Ancient history, he said to himself, nothing but future thinking now.

He continued watching as Jet and the dog walked up to the residence door, knocked twice, and then pushed the door open. To his surprise, a woman with long, red hair, tied back with a bright purple hairband walked back out with her after a few moments. The woman was tall, slender, and walked like Clair, head high, shoulders back, but this couldn't be Clair. Then he noticed the coat, and knew it was. She was wearing his coat, the black cashmere falling to her ankles, the collar up shielding her face. The long red hair cascading down the back like a waterfall. A wig, of course. He felt a shiver of something, jealousy, at Jet's closeness to Clair. He had never believed in therapy, thinking it theater but without the intention. Following their movement as they hiked across the parking lot, weaving around puddles left by yesterday's storm, he wondered what stories Clair had shared, and what reality she had conveyed to Jet. Each person sees and knows only through their own personal lens. What visions of harm and affliction had Clair passed on, through her telling? And he felt something else, contrition perhaps, at being in a place to be misperceived. If in fact he was.

The dog walked between the two women, every few moments licking Clair's hand when she reached down to pet its head. They disappeared into the cancer center's main building. Adam wasn't sure what to do. Part of him wanted to follow Clair, to be with her, in whatever situation she was about to experience. But he held back. He was overjoyed at seeing her wearing his coat. To him, this meant everything; that she loved him, that she wanted him and his scent, his energy wrapped around her. That she hadn't given up on him, on them. It was enough. He started the car, backed out of the space, remembering how just yesterday he had made this same move, and how much had changed in so little time. Today, instead of hopeless and helpless, he felt magnetized, as though he could attract all he wanted to himself, just by being alive. He put the car in drive and, looking north, began the journey towards the rest of his life.

Chapter 24

Adam

Claudia was in the theater, working with lighting and stage crews for the upcoming winter showcase. Several young student actors were scattered about the audience seats, offering their feedback on set-ups. A few more lay about onstage, in dancer's stretch poses, or reading scripts. It was a typical scene and Adam knew he would miss it. Their youth and vitality. The promise of magic on opening night. The shift from the mundane to looking at the world through a new lens. This was his calling, and his craft. And maybe he would return, with his own new story to tell. For now, he had to leave this one place where he had developed as a person and actor, in order to continue growing.

He took a seat in the back row, watching Claudia direct the activities. She had been a good friend to him, and he had known she wanted more. Had he played her along? Yes, probably, because that was who he was then. Even after marrying Clair, their enduring flirtation was a distraction for him, and for her, he wasn't sure, but he thought it might have represented hope. Feeling bad about this, abashed at his insensitivity, he vowed to be straightforward from now on. Leaving acting for the stage, he would be fully present and honest in his actions in the real world. He laughed inwardly at this idea, knowing that Clair would have said, 'but there is no real world'. Still, in a world where he and any other person mutually agreed on a reality, he would be honest and authentic.

Acting on his epiphany, he stood and walked down the aisle, smiling and nodding to students as they called out to him, the buzz always there. His pleasure at being liked, respected, noticed. Claudia looked up, watched him advance towards the stage.

'Let's take a break,' she called out to the crews. 'We'll resume in an hour. It's lunchtime.'

Adam bounded up onto the stage, feeling his muscles twinge from their work in the woods and on the beach yesterday. A good reminder of his new resolve.

'The set's looking good,' he said, walking around the stage. 'It will be a great performance.' He turned to face her. 'I'm sorry I won't be there, Claudia. I need to take a leave.'

* * *

Two long hours later, he was locking the door to his office, not certain if or when he would return. He had been granted official family medical leave of absence, MLOA, for an indeterminate time, to care for his wife. As department chair, Claudia had to sign off on it. She had argued, offered him all the informal time he needed, and pleaded with him to remain on schedule. She just wanted, needed to know he was there, and that she could be with him, from time to time. Claudia had cried. Adam was appalled that he had brought this on. Easing his way out as best he could, he finally obtained her signature on the forms he had picked up at human resources. He felt like a prick. But that was that. It was done and now, he was free to be with Clair, if she would have him. No, he corrected himself. There was to be no if, he would be there, period.

The house was cold when he entered, smelling like old ashes. He opened windows, letting in sunlight and warmth. As he stood at the kitchen window, looking out on a rare spring-like day in late fall, the river running briskly through the fields next to the house, he could hear the neighbor's sheep calling out, and geese flying overhead. A deer and her fawns stood still, watchful for an intruder, then in a few majestic leaps, bounded the riverbank, disappearing into the forest.

Their home, he thought. *Our home.*

After cleaning out the fireplace, he laid a fresh fire. He wouldn't light it now, he decided. I'll wait until Clair is here. We'll light it together. It had been a favorite of Devon's, and he would lay the fire just so, mouth tight with concentration, tiny pink tongue poking through his rosebud mouth. First paper, rolled up in tight sticks, and crisscrossed over the grate. Then the kindling, cedar and pine. He would smell the cedar, closing his eyes, and saying, 'Smells like the forest, Daddy.' Finally, the thick fir logs, piled high. At first, Adam was fearful of Devon striking a match. But his son persisted. Not whining, but using reason to muster his points.

'The matches are long, see,' he said, holding the long, thin matchstick in front of him. 'My hands are big. I'll hold the very tail end. I won't look at the flame so smoke won't get in my eyes. I won't get hurt, Daddy.'

Looking over his shoulder to make sure Clair wasn't watching, he held Devon's tiny hands in his, helping him strike the match, put it to the paper, and then together, laughing, they jumped back as the flames took hold. Devon jumped up and down, so excited at his accomplishment.

'I made a fire, I made a fire,' he sang, leaping around the living room in his red cape. I'm the fire man.'

Clair had come in to see what the racket was all about, clapping her hands at Devon's joy.

'Let's get some marshmallows,' she said, hurrying back to the kitchen.

That had been one of their happier times, after the diagnosis. A time when they could forget for a while, roasting marshmallows on long straightened clothes hangers, that their beautiful boy was injured, that his brain was not normal, never would be, and that his life would be forever clouded by social expectations and barriers. But he and Clair had been together then. Parents devoted to the well-being of their son, unwilling to accept the limitations science and society placed on children with neurological disorders. Some of his new-found joy seeped out of him at this recollection, so he quickly stood, and began cleaning the house, vacuuming, dusting, clearing out the hungry ghosts of the past. He turned on music, playing his favorite arias from Puccini, singing along, gesticulating and posturing with dramatic flair.

The kitchen clean, living room orderly in the simple, elegant style Clair favored. Soft, welcoming couch and chairs, fluffy blankets available wherever one chose to sit, throw rugs and pillows scattered about, creating patterns of vibrant colors against the cool natural fibers. Everything accessible, nothing that was so dear a small child couldn't be at home on or in. Adam stood for a moment, reliving those hectic times, remembering how he would disappear, out to the deck, or leaving all together to drive to town. He shook his head, casting out the memory. Don't go back, he chanted to himself. We only go forward now.

Moving down the hall, he stopped outside Devon's room,

the door closed. The outside had been painted bright red, with the small boy's handprints sculpted into the drying paint. Specks scattered along the walls had left marks like spattered blood. He had ranted at this when he had come home, decrying the mess, demanding clean-up now, before it all dried. Devon had held up sticky fingers, smiled his gap-toothed grin, and told him that it was OK, Daddy, he would use his sharpest tool and scrape off every single speck of paint when he was done with his art activity. Clair had looked at him with a quizzical look, challenging him to respond to this logic. He had dropped onto his knees, hugging Devon to him, saying, 'That's great, buddy, let me help.'

He turned the door handle, slowly pushing it open. The cold air hit him like a force. His first reaction was that Devon would be freezing. Then thought took over. He swung the door wide open, feeling the warmer air from the hall sifting into the cooler space. The room was just as it had been those terrible months ago, the last morning of his son's life. No matter what Clair believed, her theories on multiple universes, non-linear time, energies transmogrifying from one being to another, he knew Devon was dead. And that was that. He would leave it for Clair to pack up, if she wanted to. And if she didn't, he would let it stand for as long as she wanted.

Feeling stronger with each decision, he walked over to the small table that held Devon's precious boy objects. Feathers, rocks, bright colored pieces of plastic worn smooth by the river. Adam saw Devon's hairbrush lying amongst the possessions, light brown strands of hair interwoven in the soft bristles. Hand shaking, Adam lifted the brush, gently pulling out a few strands, holding them to his nose. Inhaling the scent of his son, fresh as the day he was born. That first whiff of him, fresh from the womb, brought Adam to his knees. He folded, his head resting on his chest and breathed in his boy. He felt a sob rising up like lava from his gut but he pushed it back down. *Enough of that,* he said. *I can be, I will be, stronger than that.*

Leaving the door open for fresh warm air to circulate through, he walked on down the hall to their bedroom. This entire passage seemed as though it had been going on for years when, in fact, it was just a little under nine months since Devon had died. Nine months, to lose a son, a wife, a life. Like a pregnancy in reverse, he realized. And they could, would start new, reclaim their life together, and create a love so strong it would preserve all the best of them both and hold Devon for ever in their hearts. He would live on in their love.

Midday now. One shot of Scotch whisky for luck, another for courage. He was ready. A final look around, and then he walked out the door. He had showered again, dressed in his soft gray cords, a hand-knitted gray shawl-collared sweater over a black turtle-neck. Clair had made the sweater for him during her pregnancy. She had said she felt earthy and motherly and needed to do something with her hands. As in everything she touched, it came out perfect. His silver-blonde hair clean and softly falling over his forehead, he smiled, seeing her knitting while reading theoretical math dissertations on her computer, not even looking at the needles clicking in her skillful hands. Dabbing on a bit more of the cologne, he imagined how Clair would react, seeing him, feeling him. He would say he had come for his coat. Just that, so as not to rush her. They would sit together, calmly this time. That woman he saw, with the long red hair. She was new to him. And he would be new to her as well.

The drive back to the cancer center took him just under

thirty-five minutes. Not too long, he mused, for him to drive Clair back and forth for appointments. They could talk, listen to books on tape, music, or just savor the quiet time. Winter was approaching and soon the rains would come in earnest. Long nights, short days. He was on leave so he wouldn't be teaching. No reason to go anywhere without Clair. He would cook for her, bring her tea. They used to read aloud to each other, taking turns with their book of the week selections. She usually chose mysteries; he biographies or plays. So many paths back to where they started.

It was Friday afternoon, and judging from the parking lot, staff and patients took off early. A few cars were scattered around, glistening in the rain, which had just begun to fall. Lightly at first, then quickly gaining momentum. *A good excuse for coming back for my coat,* he relished the thought. *I don't have to make it up.* Heart racing, he maneuvered his car into a spot in front of the residential unit. Lights were burning brightly inside, and someone had already begun placing Christmas decorations around the walkway and door. Taking a deep breath, he turned off the engine, opened the door and rushed up to the entrance, huddling under a small overhang. There was a doorbell, decorated with a Santa face. He smiled inwardly, imagining how they would spend the time together. Maybe they would drive up to the Crater Lake Lodge, bring in the holiday in a new way. Start a fresh tradition, for themselves. Not forgetting, no never, but bringing the best of the past with them into a preferred future.

He pushed the bell; a series of ascending chimes rang out. The wind began sweeping rain against him. He leaned against the side of the building. Footsteps sounded inside. A tightness clenched his chest. He thought he might have a heart attack standing there. Expecting Clair to open the door, he stopped breathing when the face at the opening was not Clair's but an older woman, wearing the tell-tale scarf wrapped around her head. The woman smiled, her eyes friendly but wary.

'May I help you?' she asked.

'Yes, thanks, ah, can I come in? I'm getting drenched out here. I'm looking for Clair Mercer. Is she in, do you know?' Adam said, his words running together in his excitement.

'Do come in. Sorry. Clair, ah, no, she's not here. I saw her leave about an hour ago.'

'Oh, did she say when she'd be coming back?' he asked, his disappointment ringing in his words.

'Well, I don't think she's coming back. She had a large tote bag with her. And I heard her call a cab to take her to the airport.'

Adam, feeling like he was plunging down twenty floors in an out of control elevator, his heart detaching from the rest of his body, too stunned to speak, heard a soft burring noise and looked up to see the 1.55 p.m. Alaska Flight to Seattle banking north. It wouldn't have taken Clair long to get through security given it was such a small airport, and the flights were as regular as clockwork.

PART THREE

Chapter 25

'Walker, there is no path. You make the path as you walk.'

Antonio Machado

Clair

The roaring of the jet engine spooling up, vibrations rattling the inner panels next to her seat, cast Clair back into that subterranean depth, when the wave captured her, ripping awareness and memory open. Clair was there, in that deep, cold watery place, rich and murky, all light lost to seeing eyes. And yet, she had seen. The whirring and thumping of the plane's landing gear lifting, the intense sinking feeling during lift-off, triggered flashbacks. Like the Moken children of Thailand who, like seals and dolphins, are able to adapt their pupils and lens shape in order to see clearly in the blurry underwater, Clair recalled vividly everything she had seen during her near drowning. As the plane shot through space and time, she relived her tumble through the roiling surf, being pulled down, a reversal through the birth canal, the sense of soaring through canyons of rock and forests of kelp. Giant tentacled moon jellyfish hovered over her. An octopus, latent and quiescent, had studied her with indifference. A voice, tinny and glib, announced that they had reached cruising altitude and passengers could now move about the cabin and resume electronic device activities. Resisting abandoning the reliving, wanting desperately to see Devon again, as she had seen him during her descent, she held on, clutching the seat arms, eyes tightly closed, willing the memory or dream or whatever it had been to return. She had been so close. Clair tentatively opened her eyes. It was gone. He was gone. And she was here. Now. That was that.

As her gaze settled, like white water clearing to calm, Clair's reflection in the window emerged. Her breath steamed the glass so that she appeared as in a cloud. Is this me? This gaunt woman, strange wig slightly askew, eyes darkened and dim. She watched her breath on the glass widen then turn to condensation. Such a simple thing, breathing, she mused, watching the oval of mist wax and wane. A baby cried, the man in the seat next to her coughed. She could feel pressure of his arm against her own. She subtly shifted her weight to lean heavily against the side of the plane, head resting against the window glass. Dark had fallen fast. As lights below dissipated, Clair considered the haste in which she had rushed out of the residence, into the cab. She hadn't even packed a bag. Just this tote, with a change of underwear, toothbrush, and jacket. And Devon's shiny red truck.

Thinking back, so much had changed since morning. She remembered waking with something other than dread at the fact she was alive. A spark of something, not quite hope, but a willingness to feel, her heart not clenching, a moment even of wonder at the bold blue sky after a night of storm. As the plane banked south then righted itself, flying north-west along the coastline, she recalled dressing. First, a flowing top that concealed her flat chest under folds of silky fabric. A skirt, not jeans, this morning. She wanted to feel alive, feminine, a woman. She had even put on a small amount of make-up. Her eyelashes were gone, but she added eyeshadow, liner, and a faint blush to conceal her pallor.

She had planned her day the night before, as she readied for bed. First, she would join the breast cancer support group, then coffee with Jet, then she would see Ellerby. He wanted to go over her most recent PET scan. She felt good. No pain. Her fatigue had lifted. The swimming helped, as did the talks with the other patients and families. Nothing like another's suffering to put our own in perspective, she often mused now. And she looked forward to seeing the women in the support group. This surprised her, always being such a private person. Naomi was kind, the women gracious, and welcoming, but for her, talking about such personal things had always been abhorrent. Unlike Rosemary, she smiled, remembering, who described her phantom pleasure when she made love with her husband. 'My breasts might be gone', she had exclaimed, 'and they were double Ds, naturally, but the sensations remain,' she had told them, laughing at herself. Thinking back, Clair realized she was envious, that this woman still had a sexual relationship with her husband. Then, she remembered the time with Adam, when they had first come home from the hospital, her drains, the shower. His visit, just yesterday. He had seemed open, genuine. Caring. *I can't think about that,* she chanted to herself. *No doubts now. I can't think about Adam. I'll lose my direction. Think about today. Think about how you got here; where you're going. Find a trajectory.*

The flight attendant came through with offers of water,

beer, wine. Clair chose wine, a white burgundy. Drink, eat, she thought. Maslow's hierarchy of needs. She had catapulted to the top. Self-actualization. So, wine first, water and food second.

Sipping the wine, cold and sharp, savoring the ease with which it slid down her throat, she closed her eyes, recalling the earlier events of the day. Group had been energizing. There had been upbeat chatter, laughter, talk of the coming holidays. The room was decorated with fall leaves, wreaths, scented with apple and cinnamon pot-pourri. As they went around the circle, checking in with themselves and each other, Clair had felt a unity uncommon to her. Their one man had graduated as they called it, once treatments ended. He told them he felt like he was ready to let go of this whole experience and move on with his life. They had all shared hugs and tears, best wishes, and a 'hope I never see you again' farewell. Noticing she wasn't the only one who had dressed up for the meeting, she smiled and sat up straighter in her chair.

A few of the women had left their heads bare, revealing newborn-like tufts of hair covering their bald crowns. Several had scarves, intricately wound around their heads, jewelry and make-up on. Clair felt overcome with love for these women, whom she had come to know intimately. She knew about their hopes, and fears, their anger, heartbreaks and self-doubts. Their pain, physical and emotional, was her pain. The ones whose husbands no longer touched them, who sat curled up, hiding their flat chests, made her want to reach out and hold them, tell them that they were more than their husband's, or anyone's desire. Some had turned to religion, alcohol, or drugs to see them through. Retail therapy had caused more than one to max out several credit cards. Jenny had given up on life, the lymphedema in her arms disabling, sinking her into a deep depression. She came to group, sitting quietly, arms at her sides, covered in the tight ace wraps to palliate the swelling. Margaret was in that terrifying period of frequent follow-up tests and scans, when active treatment ended and she was waiting to see if it would come back, hoping and praying for remission. Deborah, like Clair, was stage IV, metastatic, and remission was not an option for her. She had a new grandbaby and was determined to see her grow to her first birthday.

Their stories changed each week as their self-identities reconfigured. Bits and pieces of biographies morphed into brighter, more capable, happier selves. Or if unable to assimilate their realities into new visions of themselves, they dissembled, as Jenny had done, preferring the rapid slide into merciful oblivion through psychoactive drugs, fragments of her former self drifting away like tufts from a dandelion seed pod. As they sat in a circle, sharing their newly emerging selves, each like a chrysalis, Clair recognized in them a little of herself.

Naomi had started the sharing circle with a parable about how monkeys were trapped in China, by cutting a hole in a coconut, and putting rice into the hole. It was just large enough for the monkey to push his fist in, grab a handful of rice, but he would then be unable to pull out his fist. The only way to free himself was to let go of the rice.

'What is your rice?' she asked. 'And what is stopping you from letting go?'

After group, Jet had met her at the hospital coffee shop. Upbeat, feeling like she might actually be able to manage all of this: cancer, treatment, being in a chronic state of treatment. That was what it was for women like her, with metastasis. They learned to live with their cancer, gathering the best moments of each day and holding them front and center in every waking moment. When panic hit like a taser, shattering any sense of safety, causing heart to race, veins and arteries turn to ice, affirmations, prayer, alcohol, or drugs were grasped.

'Everyone's dying,' Ellerby had told her that first time they had talked. 'The train is coming for each of us. The difference with people like you is that you can see its light shining through the dark tunnel. Most of us can deny our ultimate death, live as though we have for ever. We waste what we have. You see the train; you can time its arrival. You have a chance to live a purposeful life.'

She had thought that a strange thing for a doctor to say, but it made sense. She thought she had more time then. She had fretted about how best to spend it. Now, that time was gone.

This last visit, the news had been bad. Curiously, she thought back now, she hadn't been expecting that. She had deceived herself into believing that she would be able to continue on indefinitely. The clinic staff were always so positive. Offering this clinical trial, a new drug, hope for a future that wasn't hers. She knew they did this out of some sort of misdirected kindness, not deceit, but it would have been kinder to not let her have false hope.

'Clair, I'm so sorry,' Ellerby had said, his gracious expression conveying such compassion she felt she needed to comfort him.

'You're not responding to the treatment, the tumors are proliferating, in your liver, and lungs now. I've consulted with our treatment team, and we have nothing else to offer you. I think it's time to gather your loved ones around you and say your goodbyes. I can make a hospice referral for you, if you like.'

Jet had been with her, asking all the right questions. How long? What if they went up to Portland? Seattle? Alternative treatments?

'Thank you, Dr Ellerby,' Clair had said, reaching her hand out to grasp his. You have been very kind.'

Up until that moment, Clair hadn't been uncertain what she was going to do. His mention of hospice, dying, lying in some bed somewhere, helpless. Having her basic needs met and by whom, Adam? Ben and Jodie giving up their work, their mission to come take care of her? A stranger? Paid caregiver? That wasn't going to happen, she decided, certain now. Standing, she hugged Jet.

'You have been a good friend, even though I resisted you in the beginning. If I never see you again, know that you have helped me, and I am grateful.'

'Clair, wait, what do you mean? What are you going to do?' Jet asked.

'I'm not going to wait for death. I'm going to make death find me.' Clair said, walking out the door, into the shimmering golden light of noon.

The plane was circling the airport now, waiting for clearance to land. It had been a short flight to Seattle. A switch from Alaska to Iberia, the overnight to Porto. From there, she would begin walking. She was thinking about having to shop somewhere. She couldn't walk to Finisterre in these few clothes, without even a toothbrush. That was no way to start a new life, the rest of her life. The end of her life. Gazing out the window, a field of sparkling lights covering the horizon, she watched as wisps of horsetail clouds caught in the landing lights created fantastical creatures in the sky. *I'm a dead woman walking, like these formless shapes,* she said silently to the face in the window. Coming and going, identity shifting. Things that used to matter, disappearing with the miles.

Clair thought about the simple story of letting go of the rice, of attachment and greed, of holding on so strongly that your very being was taken. Was her rice Adam? Devon? Life itself? Certainly, her hope, some would say, delusion, of finding Devon, or reconnecting with Devon, somewhere in the universe, might be a futile way of clinging to the impossible. Her rice. Had Adam been misplaced remorse, a target that was safe, risk-free? She couldn't let him go, and wouldn't allow him in. What kind of person does that? And now, it was over for her. Time had run out. Feelings of deep remorse and shame at her past behaviors caused her to moan out loud. The man next to her leaned towards her.

'Are you OK?' he asked, in a soft, quiet voice.

Night was thick, the lights of the city below spanning across hundreds of miles, into the valley and along the coastline. People were shuffling around the plane, preparing for their landing, next directions, new experiences.

'Sorry,' Clair said, glancing at him. 'I must have been dreaming.'

'I always fall asleep on planes too,' he said. She noticed his eyes were deep brown, almost black, with specks of amber light flitting about in irises, opaque and clear.

'Where are you off to? Or, is Seattle your home?'

A simple question, Clair thought. I could lie and tell him some story about going to visit a family member, or a conference, or a million other ways to create a life in the moment that would make sense. But something about him, his kind eyes, his gentle face, not young, with smile lines at the corners of his mouth and eyes. He looked so eager to hear what she had to say. His hands gave his age away. Spotted and wrinkled, as though having spent a long time in the sun. They rested quietly on his upper thighs, covered in soft, gray corduroy.

'I'm going to Spain,' she said. 'Finisterre.'

'Ah, a peregrina?' he said. 'Walking the Camino, to the End of the Earth?'

Clair smiled, broadly. 'Something like that,' she said, laughing softly. 'How did you know?'

He shrugged, cocking his head to one side, a smile playing on his lips. 'And what do you expect to find there?' he asked, his eyes searching.

Shocked by his frankness, she sat quietly for a few moments, as the plane began its descent. Announcements overhead cautioned passengers to secure their seatbelts, return trays to the upright position, and other safety compliance instructions. Clair looked out the window as the ground rose up to meet them, runway lights like signal fires in the near distance.

Looking at the man, whose name she hadn't bothered to ask, she smiled as he tightened his seatbelt. He seemed deep in thought, so she returned her gaze to the approaching tarmac. She didn't know what she hoped to find. Wasn't that the point of a journey? She had spent her life in a state of perpetual being; the perfect daughter, student, professor, wife, mother. Each of these roles had a set of rules, and she had been a rule follower. Set the formula, follow the equation to its end, and all will work out, had been her philosophy. Until Devon. Since his loss, Clair realized, feeling the plane bumping along, big engines pulling back, that now, she was in a state of becoming. And that like a chrysalis, her unfolding would come through her, not to her. She turned, laying her hand on his arm.

'I don't have any expectations,' she said softly, as the plane touched down, causing her to grip the arm rest. Looking into his eyes, dancing now with curiosity. 'I'm just taking things as they come, or trying to.'

'I can tell you that whatever you think you might find, you will be wrong. And whatever you fear, you will be comforted. And whatever you need, the Camino will provide.' He had lain his hand over hers. He gave a gentle squeeze, as people began standing and removing bags from overhead bins.

'*Buen Camino*,' he said as he began the shuffle towards the front of the plane.

'Wait, I didn't ask your name,' Clair called out to his back.

But he was several passengers ahead of her now. She had remained seated, wanting to be last off the plane. Taking time to gather her courage for the next or first, she didn't know, steps toward her becoming.

Perhaps it was like Jet had said, a process of cumulative trauma, this one last thing that tipped her balance. She realized she had been living in a sort of placebo effect, the treatments giving her false hope of survival. Thinking back to her first encounter with Dr Ellerby, she remembered him telling her that metastatic breast cancer could not be cured, but that they could hold it at bay for a while, possibly years. There were clinical trials, new treatments being developed every year. But this morning, reviewing her latest PET scans, and blood work, he said they had reached their limit. Her specific oncotype was not responsive to treatment. She had been so hopeful going into the appointment. Ellerby had said any further treatment would be like tweaking a jet plane as it was crashing. If she was going to crash, it would be on her own terms, in her own way. If she couldn't be cured, then she would find a way to be healed.

Chapter 26

Clair

Sounds and lights assaulted her as she made her way through the airport, following signage towards the international terminal. Thoughts of Devon, Adam, their home, flashed through her mind, like spikes of sunshine through a dense cloud, illuminating her situation. Clair remembered a photo she had seen in a travel magazine, somewhere in Spain, of a house, standing on its own, on top of a gentle hill. All around it was space and light. In the distance, a hammock of wind-shaped trees leaned into each other, offering solace, but the house stood alone. She felt like that house. Except that she was on the move. She would hold her trees, Adam, Devon, close to her and open space for knowing and remembering them, and how they were. As she moved further away from the physical place where they were last together, she experienced a feeling of joy, almost as resistance to the expectation of sorrow, loneliness, and grief. It felt good to be here, alone, but holding their images and energy in her heart. In a place where she could not lose them again. Safe now. Whole.

To her surprise, the man from the plane was at the ticket counter for Iberia when she arrived at the terminal. She recognized his broad back, slightly hunched as though having spent a lifetime ducking under low ceilings. Taking her place in line for pre-flight check-in, she noticed a shell hanging from his backpack. When he turned away from the counter, he caught her eye, and smiled broadly, as though enjoying having played a trick on her.

The waiting area was packed with travelers, many animated, excited to be on their way. Families with small children clustered around a play area. Clair joined them, sitting off to the side but close enough to be able to see and hear their laughter and delight, some tears and cries of fatigue and weariness.

'To be happy as a child, for no reason other than being alive in this moment, that is a gift, yes?'

Clair turned to see the man, she must learn his name, taking the seat beside her, that playful smile on his face, eyes shining with delight.

'You,' she said, shaking her head in surprise. 'Are you on this flight to Porto as well?'

'Yes, apparently I am. My original ticket was for Lisbon but seems I have been re-routed. Maybe it is kismet, or fate, that we travel together. You can tell me your story. We are bound together now for a few hours while we wait. Let's enjoy our time.'

Clair laughed at his eagerness to befriend her. She thought she must look a mess but he was so much older, she didn't think he was coming on to her in a sexual way. He seemed genuine in his simple human desire for company.

'First, tell me about the shell hanging from your backpack. Is it a clam shell?'

'No,' he smiled. 'A scallop. The symbol for the Camino de Santiago. Pilgrims wear the shell to identify themselves when walking.'

'Why?' Clair asked, her head tilted to the side to better see the shell dangling from his pack, on the floor in front of him. There was a symbol of a stylized cross painted in red on its curved outside.

'A long story and one you will learn as you go. It means different things to different people.'

'So, are you going on to Spain too now, or are you getting off when we land in Porto?' Clair asked, feeling like she was grilling him, as she did her doctoral students taking their oral exams. She didn't care, she wanted to know. And he seemed unbothered, even eager for her questions.

'I haven't decided.'

Clair looked at him with skepticism. 'So, you just fly around the world, changing your destination en route?'

'Sometimes, yes, that is what I do.'

'I think there is a good story here, Mr. And what is your name?' she asked, leaning forward in her seat.

The play area had cleared out, parents shepherding children towards seats, food stalls, and gathering in corners with blankets and sleeping bags laid out for sleep.

'My name is Michael Kraft and I am going to get a coffee. May I bring you one, Miss, Mrs?' he asked in return.

'Clair Mercer,' she said simply. 'And yes, I would love a coffee, black please. Thanks so much. I will tend your pack.'

She watched him walk away, that slight hunch but head held high. He moved through the crowds easily, like a breeze passing through a field of wheat. People turned and shifted to make room, or looked up if he brushed them as he passed. Returning with the coffees, earnest in his purpose, his stride long and direct, she felt a tremble in her heart. Wondering if it was the chemotoxicity she had been warned about causing heart dysrhythmias. Maybe it was hunger, fatigue, all of these or an anticipation at hearing his story and spending time with this man. She took a deep breath and wrapped her arms around herself, settling in for a long night's passage.

'What would you like to know?' he asked, crossing one long leg over the other. She noticed his shoes, well-made leather, scuffed, and worn but with a good sole.

'When did you walk your first Camino?' she asked. 'And why?'

Michael squinted his eyes, looking into the distance, past the crowds, the overhead signs, the vendors, and shops.

'My first official Camino de Santiago began in 1972, when I was twenty years old, but I guess you could say my real journey began the year before. When I first learned about and experienced the mysteries of mescaline. I was a seeker and in the practice of sacred peyote, found a way to explore my inner consciousness. I found too much, too soon, and was not able to contain the power, to make the alchemical shift from base corporal elements to gold, or pure transmutation. I imagined I was transcending reality but in truth, I was distorting it. And it distorted me. That wouldn't have been so bad except I took another with me. My girlfriend, a slight girl, easily deceived. She believed she could fly off the top of a rock cliff in the City of Rocks, near Santa Fe. We had been camping there for a month, eating little, holding our ceremonies, a few others joining us from time to time. One morning, Suzanne woke early, before me or any others. She took a button, climbed the rock, and just as I opened the flap on my tent, welcoming the new day's dazzling sunlight, I caught her shadow lengthening along the dry earth before me. I looked up in time to see her face as she fell to land, and heard a sound that still echoes in my ears, and I feel it again and again. The impact of the sound. The sheer terror on her face.'

He hadn't moved once through this telling. Neither had Clair. Based on his age at the time, she now knew he was in his late sixties. She could see it in the furrows along his broad forehead, and his hands, weathered from time outdoors. But his voice, his carriage, his presence were those of a much younger or ageless person. She thought again about being and becoming. How when we tell our stories, we become new, through each telling. Seeing ourselves through the eyes of another, recreates us.

Michael sipped from his coffee. Clair sat still, not wanting to disrupt his memory or influence how the rest of the story unfolded.

'My family hid me away in a private rehabilitation facility in upper New York state, as far away from New Mexico and peyote as possible. Lawyers settled. Newspapers were paid off. Promises for generous donations to worthy causes stilled rumors and scandals. You see, the Kraft family was old money. Very old, and very rich. There were appearances to keep. Funds were distributed and I was enrolled in an ivy league college. But instead, as soon as I was released from the facility, I began walking. And have been walking ever since. I would stop and work, earn enough for the next few months, and carry on. The sound of Suzanne's landfall always in my head. Like a siren sound, warning me off any sort of relationship with another, or any happiness in life. I donated most of the money my parents sent me. And I still do. I keep just enough of my inheritance to stay in motion and contribute where I find need. I was not found to be legally culpable but in every other way, I am guilty. I do penance with each step.'

Clair looked down where her hands entwined in her lap. His story, his feelings of guilt, remorse, and the need to pay, someone for something, resonated with her. He was treading close to her own heart's intent.

'Where have you walked?' Clair asked, wanting to keep the conversation away from the pain. For now.

'This is my fifth Camino. I have also walked others, the Muslim and Jewish pilgrimages. Hadrian's Way in England, the Missions Trail in California. Across Germany, through Scandinavia. So many. The only formal long-distance hike I haven't and won't do is the Pacific Crest Trail because I have a near phobic fear of bears, and I know my fear will bring one to me.'

She saw his face break into a grin at this confession and laughed with him.

'I would be too,' she said. 'So, the Camino, why do you keep coming back?'

'That question you will answer for yourself. It is different for everyone. Walking helps me keep my head in place. Spain is a beautiful country; the people are kind and generous. The food, wine, ah. That is enough for me, now. And you? What brings you to the Camino?'

Clair felt her breath catch in her chest. What to say? How to frame her story so that it made sense to another when it hadn't, it didn't, make sense to her. When did her journey start? When Devon went missing? When she tried to kill Adam and herself? Earlier today, after learning she was imminently dying? Or now, just now, as she shifted from becoming a person unfinished, to being here, in this moment, as she told her story, making it real. She could tell any story, she realized. And so, she did.

'I'm meeting my family here for a reunion of sorts. My brother and sister-in-law are both physicians for Doctors Without Borders, and we have rented a house on the coast of Galicia, A Coruña. My husband and son will be joining us next week. After they visit with his family in...' Clair hesitated here, blocking on a place or reason that made sense. 'Um, they're meeting his family in San Francisco first. So, they flew south. I flew north.' Realizing she was rambling she stopped, removed the lid from her coffee, blew gently across the top. Taking a tentative sip and then another, she began to live her story.

'My son is just five, you see, and the long flight is very hard for him. Adam, that's my husband, will break it up for him. they'll stop in New York, and also, stay a few days in Amsterdam, cycling and exploring the waterways. Devon, my son, loves water and boats. They might take a boat ride. They'll meet us in A Coruña.'

'Ah, sounds wonderful, for all of you,' Michael said, looking up at the flight monitor on the wall opposite.

'Our flight is on time, and we should begin boarding soon. I think I'll stretch my legs.'

Clair could sense a disappointment in him. She felt that he knew she was making it all up. He had shared his truth with her, a complete stranger, and she had not.

'Wait,' she called to him, as he began walking away. 'I lied. That isn't my story. May I walk with you?'

He smiled at her, adjusting the straps on his pack.

'I thought so,' he said. 'And I'm sure you have your reasons. I don't mind, really. It was a good story. If that is what you need to get through this day, then it's yours to own.'

'But it isn't mine to own. It's no one's. And I am someone. I need to own my real story. That's why I'm here. To find out who I am and what my true story is. I will try again, see if I can get it closer to the truth this time.'

'Then, let's begin. And continue,' he said, offering her his arm. Together, they walked down the concourse, slowly, easily as though they had been sharing time and space for years, their steps rhyming in rhythm and pace. She felt her heart slowing, her breath calming. Swallowing, she looked up at him, and then as they passed a women's restroom, she said, 'Wait here. I'll be right back.'

Hurrying in, she went to the counter, looked in the mirror, removed the wig. The feeling of cold air on her bald head was exhilarating. She rubbed her stubble, causing small tufts of feathery white hair to stand on end. Wetting her hands in the water from the faucet, she patted her head down, rubbed her cheeks vigorously, trying to bring color into her pale complexion. Satisfied it was as good as it was going to get, she exited, waiting for his expression to show shock or repulsion. What she saw was surprise, yes, but also, admiration.

'Thank you for sharing yourself with me,' he said, taking her arm and tucking it under his.

As they walked, she talked, about her life as a professor, her music, her brother and his wife, their work in the world. She talked about everything she could think of except Devon, Adam, and her cancer. When she had run out of words, he nodded his head.

'And you have set off on this Camino, because your life at home was so perfect?' he asked, stopping in front of an Elliot Bay Book Company.

'You didn't mention Devon or Adam, from your first story. Do they exist?'

'Yes,' Clair said, her eyes tearing as she saw a display of children's books in the store window.

'Adam is back at home in Harbor, Oregon and Devon, my son, he is in the world. Somewhere I think, maybe Finisterre. He was taken, by a wave. And I know that he is there, not in his physical form, of course, I know that isn't possible. But his energy, his atoms, his enduring self, exists and is pulling me to him. Like coagulation, our cells are being drawn together, to complete us, again. I know this. And yes, I am dying, or so I have been told. I am dissolving. So, I have more clarity about these types of things, don't you see? I'm not burdened by heavy desires and fears. I have forgiven others and most importantly, myself, and let go of all my attachments. I am free.'

Clair had stepped in front of Michael, taking hold of both of his arms.

'And I just realized this as I said it,' she said, almost bouncing on her feet, the epiphany lifting her up like a cloud of joy.

Michael took hold of her hands, pressing them between his larger ones. 'I am happy for you, Clair, to have found this release. May it sustain you along your Camino.'

Overhead they heard their flight being called. Looking into each other's eyes, they knew they might not see each other again, but in this short time, this passing time together, they had reached a level of deep friendship. Clair would remember him. This kind stranger who had opened her eyes and heart to seeing and telling her truth. Now her challenge was to follow it.

'*Buen Camino*, Clair Mercer,' he said as he turned to leave. 'Perhaps we will cross paths again someday, on the road to Santiago.'

'And to you, Michael Kraft, *Buen Camino*. Thank you for the moments.'

213

Chapter 27

Clair

Clair was awakened by the sounds of cutlery, metal against metal, plastics rustling, soft words in many languages. Eyes easing open, she saw daylight peeking in through the crack in her window shade. The flight attendants were passing out breakfast trays, hot towels, coffee, tea, water. Her head was twisted to the side, and she could feel her mouth wet where she had drooled while sleeping. The wine, food, warm cabin, studied ministrations by the attendants had lulled her fight, flight or freeze into submission, and allowed a deep relaxation response or perhaps just pure exhaustion to take over. Stiff but rested, she accepted the warm towel, running it gingerly over her face, then hands. It felt good. The flight path monitors on the screen in front of her showed they were eight hours out. They would be landing in Porto at noon, which meant it would be 4 a.m. for her biological clock. The deepest hour for circadian rhythms. The hour of sudden death, heart attacks, and stroke. Staring at her reflection in the glass, eyes bleary with sleep and disorientation, she felt a growing sense of exhilaration, and wonder at what she had done. Was doing right now.

Her gaze returned to the screen in front of her. The tiny icon showing the space between her past and future expanding second by second. Between what had been and would be. How simple, she thought, to just sit here, allowing this to happen. All of her previous striving, gone, dissipating like rolling thunder after a lightning flash. Efforts to please her exacting mother, absorbing her daily carping and criticism. Futile attempts to connect in any way with her brilliant, distant father. She had excelled in her work, gaining recognition and acclaim, but it wasn't until she became a mother that she began to believe she mattered. Devon, with his bright eyes and crooked smile, hair dancing with light, always a bit too long. He hated haircuts. She smiled to herself at the memory of her sneaking up on him while he was sleeping to snip away at the rampant curls. Clair felt her eyes sting with tears, unwanted and quickly wiped away with her now cool washcloth, remembering how she had carelessly tossed them into the trash, never imagining a time when she would have done anything to be able to hold one of those precious locks in her hands, feel the silkiness slide between her fingers again.

It was Devon who had launched her on this path, she realized, watching the flight map. He used to play a game at the beach, digging a hole and calling out, 'I'm going to dig a hole to the end of the earth.' Once, when Devon had just turned three and all things were still possible, Clair had pointed out on his illuminated globe the peninsula jutting out into the western Atlantic. Finisterre, she had told him. This is where it was once believed the earth ended. Finis Terrae. He loved the sound of it and would recite it over and over, 'Finisterre, the end of the world'. 'We'll go there one day,' she had told him. And so, now, she was. And in the way of energy, neither created or destroyed, always changing, she knew Devon would be there also. In some form. And she would know him.

Flight attendants were preparing for yet another meal. She needed exercise more than food so she asked the attendant to hold hers for a few minutes, while she walked around the cabin. Curious about where Michael might be sitting, she cautiously scanned the passengers. She was sure he hadn't flown first class, and even if he had, she would have seen him when she walked through that cabin on her entrance. She didn't find him anywhere. Maybe he was in the bathroom. She made a second round. No Michael. And no backpack with a scallop shell leaning up against a seat.

An announcement directed passengers to return to seats and fasten their seat belts, they were expecting turbulence. Reluctantly, Clair did so, curling her legs up on the empty seat next to her. Twinges of tingling ran through her legs, both feet suddenly becoming numb from her ankles to her toes. The neuropathies that often accompanied chemotherapy, she realized, looking at her ankles, swollen and stiff. Gingerly, she stretched first one leg and then the other out towards the aisle, rotating each ankle, flexing and extending each foot. Shockwaves of feeling returned, heat and waves of ice. Good shoes will be the first thing to buy, Clair determined. With a slight moan, she promised herself that she would get back to the daily stretching and self-massage for the lymphatic system Naomi had shown her and the other members of the support group. This final quest mustn't be undone by side effects. Only head-on actions now.

Watching the morning clouds lift to reveal a carpet of green, a wide ribbon of blue, and areas of cultivation that looked like ancient markings in the fields, Clair felt overwhelmed with gratitude for her life, this chance to regain, or perhaps discover, her true self. Yes, Devon may have launched her on this course but as she felt her body begin to awaken from the deadening grips of toxicity, her spirit also felt a kindling, a stirring of feelings she hadn't experienced in a long time. The first time she had drawn bow across cello strings and felt the vibrations deep in her bones, wind in her veins. Making love to Adam, without self-consciousness, joy stirring in her belly with the first signs of life.

Each step of this pilgrimage will be both a penance and a homage, to all that has gone and all that is to come. I will join that sea of humanity that has loved, becoming love itself.

As the plane began its descent, she thought about Michael and what had happened before. Had she dreamed the whole thing? Did he exist or was the experience one of the hallucinations she had been cautioned about, another side effect of chemotherapy? But he seemed real, and his story? How could she have dreamt that up? She didn't know anything about peyote or the mountains in New Mexico. But his story, it did speak to her. And his living each day, making penance, finding joy and comfort in whatever the present presents. Michael had talked to her about simplicity; waking each day, eating, walking, sleeping. Each step a prayer. That also made sense to her. What if he wasn't real? She might never know, so she would keep his story in her heart. A remembrance of a time when a friend found her when she needed one. She looked at her hands, feeling his large, rough, but gentle hands enfolding hers. His touch remained on her skin. How could that be imagined?

At the first vendor she passed after disembarking, she purchased a small day pack, toothbrush, toothpaste, phone charger with adapter, lip gloss, and hand cream. Michael had told her the Camino would provide whatever she needed.

But she wasn't sure about good walking shoes, a change of underwear, and a warm jacket. From her research on her phone during the flight, she knew the walk along the coast would be wet, cold. Shuffled through all of the checkpoints, she finally found the main doors opening up to brilliant sunshine. She waved down a taxi, to take her into the city center. Clair knew she needed to get properly outfitted. She also had to charge her phone. Reluctant to speak with anyone, she mentally drafted a message, telling Ben, Jodie, Adam and Jet that she was fine, would be out of touch for a while, and not to worry. She would reconnect once she felt more stable. For now, she needed time, to find a way to be in the world with this knowledge, that she only had a few months, maybe weeks, left. 'I'm OK,' she said to herself. *Weak from the effects of chemotherapy, but so far, no pain. So, I'm going to walk.*

Clair felt, for the first time since hearing her diagnosis of terminal cancer, that she was living, not dying. She hadn't done any of the right things one is supposed to do when facing certain, imminent death. Ladies from the support group had talked about the list, as they called it. The 'to dos' for those last days.

Molly had described rushing all over town buying Christmas presents even though it was still before Thanksgiving. Vicki had said she refused to think about it or talk about it. She and her husband were going to Mexico for a month in their casita. 'After the girls finish their volleyball season,' she had said, 'like always.' Naomi had counseled them all that there wasn't a right or wrong way to feel. Clair hadn't paid much attention at the time, certain that she would not fall into the category of being one of them, the terminal ones.

And now, thinking back to the previous twenty-four hours,

her reaction was so unlike herself, that she felt uninhabited. As though some extraterrestrial being had taken over her mind and body. Normal Clair would have recorded a final lecture for her students. Would have signed off on her students' theses, handing them off to another professor to continue on with. Before Clair needed to have all of her affairs in order, lists made, details checked off. This Clair, she smiled to herself, couldn't give a damn. Let the world slip by. Like a thought, a wisp of daylight breaking through the early dawn, she felt insubstantial and porous. And it was OK.

As the Porto scenery flashed past, the broad river running through the center, the vast ocean to the west, excitement began filling her senses, replacing the fear and dread she had felt earlier. Letting go of the anger and blame, in her dream or in reality with Michael, had lifted a heavy weight from her heart. Clair felt her phone vibrate, again. It had been almost non-stop since she took it off airplane mode at landing. Adam. Jet. Ben. Jodie. Even Naomi, the oncology social worker. They had all been calling. Mostly Adam. Later, she would text, let them know she was safe. For now, she wanted this time just to herself. She turned the phone off, watched the landscape take shape around her.

As she stepped from the taxi in front of a city park, Clair had no idea what to do next. She had asked the taxi driver to take her to the Albergue de Peregrinos Porto, a place she had learned about from a pilgrimage app she had downloaded onto her phone. There, she could rest, eat, and receive guidance on the Camino.

He had pulled over and pointed her into the maze of old buildings, cafés with gardens flowing out onto the sidewalks. Feeling a sense of overwhelming disorientation and dizziness, she leaned against a wall, feeling the cool, ancient stone beneath her palm. Standing still, pressing her back up against the wall, she watched as groups and singles walked purposefully down the street. They seemed to know where they were going, so she joined them, following the human compass through the narrow, twisting, cobbled streets, learning to be at home in this journey, trusting others and herself to find the way to wherever she needed to go. Sensing a presence to her side, she looked, but saw only shadows. Ahead, a man's shoulders, a turn of head. Michael? Her heart quickened.

A pair of large wooden doors opened into a small office, staffed by a single woman, her age unknowable. Clair filed in behind a line of people. Pilgrims, like herself, she concluded, feeling a connection. Uncertain what was going to happen when she reached the destination, but as in elementary school, knowing the best thing was just to keep her place in line, a few inches distant from the body in front of her. It was a large male body, the backpack reaching over the man's head. Looking around, she noticed everyone carried some sort of pack, many with tightly rolled up sleeping mats tied beneath.

Realizing how completely unprepared she was, she decided her first action in the morning would be to get outfitted. When she arrived at the counter, she answered a few questions, was given a Pilgrim Passport, and invited to select a shell from the tray of scallops next to the counter. They were all similar in size and shape, some slightly more battered and scarred. She found one that had marks where tiny sea creatures had made their homes in the shell, feeling close to it, close to its watery life, both in and out of the sea. Her eyes filled with gratitude at this kindness. It was as though she had stepped through an opening into another universe, where being human fulfilled the original meaning of the word, humanitas, and to be civilized meant to be kind.

A group of five women, traveling together from Wisconsin she learned, adopted Clair, shepherded her through the hostel to a dormitory type room with six bunks, metal frames, thin mattresses. The women chattered all at once, their voices like starlings circling the sky at the end of a long day. Clair relaxed into the sounds, feeling at home, like an orchestra tuning up before a concert. She was content to listen, not trying to discern any specific voice or story. Just simply being. Once settled in, the women rummaged through their collective bags and offered her an assortment of warm clothes, including socks and underwear. Shoes, they had told her, would have to be purchased first thing in the morning. They were most important because a blister could cause infection and rot. A rainproof parka would also be a requirement, one of the women, Maggie, read from her guide-book.

After dinner, served family-style in the *albergue's* dining room, they all settled in for the night, friendly jostling, games of rock paper scissors to see who claimed the top bunks. Clair was content to be on a bottom bunk, her belly filled with hot soup, wine, and bread, her heart warm with friendship. She turned her body away from the group to slip into a soft T-shirt for sleep. Her body would shock and horrify anyone, she felt, scarred, the infusion port poking out of her upper right chest.

When she turned around, she was met with the women, standing together, tops off and breast-less bodies displayed. Two were missing one breast, the other three both, like Clair. Each had a unique tattoo covering their old scars. Maggie, the tallest of the group had a vine stretching across her chest; Andrea, a rose over her left breast; Celia's bilateral scars were covered in

Celtic swirls, with the tree of life in the center of her chest. Sandy, the oldest member of the group, had written across her chest, 'Do Not Resuscitate'. And Robin, the newest and youngest member of this elite club, as they called themselves, had a butterfly on one side, a dragonfly on the other.

'To transport me to the other side when it's time,' she said, as Clair admired the artwork.

Sandy told Clair they had all met and become friends in a breast cancer support group in Madison. This pilgrimage had been their goal for a few years. When Robin joined them, they decided it was time. She was getting married in four months. They had their tattoos done a month before, Sandy told Clair.

'It's a must do,' she said. 'It will transform your perception of your body. Decorate yourself instead of being scarred up.'

As she fell into sleep, images of her shell, nestled into a grassy floor, fish swimming above, its mouth opening and shutting to let in tiny creatures for substance. A swirl of filament, iridescent and inviting, called her to follow. Wrapping her arms around her body, she allowed herself to be carried along, until voices, footfalls, and doors opening and closing released her from the current, tossing her back onto the ground of her reality. She clasped the scallop shell in her hand, tucking it deep inside the pocket of her jacket, feeling its heat. *You're here with me, I know,* she said to the shell, to the world around her. *We are all here together.*

Chapter 28

Adam

Adam grasped the phone in his hand, holding it like it was his lifeline, salvation.

'Where is she?' he shouted into Jet's voicemail, his grip on the thing causing tiny bleeps to interrupt his message.

He was walking as he talked, the wind stirring up leaves. Small birds, drinking from puddles forming on the parking lot, skittered out of his way. He looked up to the third floor of the main hospital building, across the lot. He imagined Clair there, in Jet's office. They would be talking about him. He hoped that was where she was. The idea of her anywhere else, on a plane to God knows where, was unfathomable.

As he strode up the wheelchair access ramp, through the automatic double doors, he noticed people stopping to look at him. He clicked off the phone, shoving it into his coat pocket. Smoothing his hair back with his hands, he forced an expression of calm demeanor.

Once past the elevator stand, he bolted up the stairs, causing staff to turn sideways to avoid being jostled by him. Many were holding their lunch trays, eating as they climbed. No one commented. It was a hospital and strong emotional responses were familiar.

Adam called behind him, 'Sorry, in a rush.'

Once through the door onto the third floor, home of the psychiatric unit, a quiet permeated the hallway. Adam knew this place well, and yet it still seemed like a strange land, alien and separate from humanity. A place apart, where broken minds, hearts, and spirits were medicated into compliance, counseled into normality. A momentary sense of outrage infused him, turning his face hot, his hands cold. *Oh Clair,* he moaned inwardly, *what happened to us? How, why did I allow this to happen?*

Jet's door was closed. He knocked quietly at first, then strongly when there was no response. A voice from an intercom asked him, 'Sir, how can we help you?' The voice came from the door to the locked unit, where staff monitored the hallway and entrance twenty-four-seven.

'I'm here to see Dr Taylor,' he said. 'Please, it's an emergency.'

'Dr Taylor's with a patient right now. If you have a seat there in the waiting area, I'll let her know you're here. It's Dr Gage, right?'

'Yes,' he said into the intercom. Recognizing the voice of Belinda, the day shift unit secretary he immediately felt better, grateful not to have to engage in verbal judo. 'It's Adam Gage. Thank you.'

A row of stiff, wooden framed chairs lined the hallway to his right. He sat, the chair uninviting and institutional, upholstered in a geometric patterned vinyl made to withstand body fluid assaults. As he waited, he watched people coming and going through the double locked doors, the clicks and clacks causing him to twinge inside each time someone passed in or out.

He stopped glancing up each time he heard the lock from inside the unit click, hoping to see Jet. Instead, he stared at the door, willing her tall, slender shape to appear. After what seemed to him like hours, she did. Walking quickly, she glided past him, motioning with her hand for him to follow her. She held an electronic tablet in one hand, opening the door to her office with the other. He noticed her normally straight, almost haughty posture was softened today, even slumped.

Adam followed Jet into her office. It was familiar to him, having spent countless hours there in family counseling with Clair. Jet knew all their innermost feelings, fears, doubts, hopes, dreams. What had brought them together and torn them apart. He felt like an adolescent in her presence, one that never quite reached that grown up bar, couldn't make it over the hurdle into adulthood. Her white hair gave her the look of an old crone, even though her face and body were those of a much younger woman. He was both drawn and repelled by her. Afraid of her, if he was honest, and her ability to see him. Know him without judging or wanting to change him.

'Adam, come in please,' she said, waving him towards a chair. She sat in its opposite, a small round table between them. A vase of white hydrangeas sat in the center of the table. She moved the vase, placing it carefully on her desk, behind the table and their chairs. Sitting back, she looked at him. He felt a spark, an arc like a welder's fire, linking his world now and the next to come, after he heard her words.

'Where is she?' he asked, his hands clenched in his lap. 'Where's Clair?'

He felt her studying him, her expression changing from concern to curiosity. She cocked her head to one side, as though looking through her side vision, like a bird, scanning the ground for a worm.

'I don't understand your question, Adam. Do you mean where is she right now physically or are you asking where she is mentally? You know I can't talk about her with you. Her trial visit is over, you are no longer her legal guardian, and I don't have a current release of information.'

Adam was momentarily transported back to the early days of Clair's commitment and institutionalization. The line between criminality and mental illness; the criminal justice system and medicine blurred. He had changed from being her victim, to her keeper. All of that had flowed away down the river of time, and like flotsam left behind, he was without purpose or movement. Until now. He felt purpose. Find Clair.

'I mean, Jet, where the fuck is my wife? You went to her appointment with her and then she just disappeared. What happened?'

Jet leaned forward towards Adam. 'She did receive a poor report, and said she needed time to process. She said she wanted to be alone. Why? What's happened, Adam?'

'I went to see her. One of the other residents said Clair had left in a taxi, carrying her large bag. The woman said she heard Clair tell the taxi driver to take her to the airport. I've been calling her cell but she won't answer. I'm afraid for her, Jet. Did she say anything to you? Tell you where she was going?'

Jet stood up, walked to the window, looking out over the neighboring woods. A trio of deer were grazing in a clearing, next to the Life Flight Helipad. She turned to look at Adam.

'She did not, Adam. I've never seen her so shut down. When she heard the report…'

Adam broke in. 'What did Ellerby tell her?'

Jet sighed heavily, returning to her chair. 'That her cancer had spread, to her lungs, liver, spine up along her cervical vertebrae. That was what was causing that pain she thought was just a tension headache or muscle spasm.'

Adam sat, stunned. 'What else?'

Jet leaned forward. Her hands clasped in front of her, like a penitent. 'That there were no further treatment options for her. She had maybe three to six months to live. He recommended hospice. Clair said no to that, that she would deal with her death in her own way. She left the cancer center, telling me not to worry, that she would be OK. That was the last I saw or heard from her. Adam, I am so sorry. I thought for sure she would call you, Ben, and Jodie.'

Adam dropped his head into his hands, his shoulders shaking with the effort not to cry. Unable to hold in his emotions, a guttural sound, like having the breath knocked out, escaped his mouth. Jet stood up, came beside him, laying a hand on his shoulder.

'I have to find her, Jet. I can't let her go through this alone, even if that is what she wants, or thinks she wants.'

'I understand. But it is her choice, you know. She is of sound mind now, no longer considered mentally ill.'

'Oh Christ, you know that's the legal term. We both know the emotional reality is different. Look at all she's gone through. Losing a child. Trying to kill me and herself, and then, just when there was a glimmer of hope, that she and I might find a way to create a life together without Devon, she learns she has this breast cancer, already spreading. And now, no more treatments? Yes, she may have free choice but her options are limited. How far can she go without becoming really ill? And where would she go? I'm all she has now. And she's all I have.'

He broke down, openly sobbing, laying his head on his folded arms.

'Adam, no, you are not alone. You know I'll help, do what I can. And Clair's brother and sister-in-law, they'll help too, I'm sure.'

'She's so damn private. That's the thing,' Adam said, rubbing his eyes with his hands.

He accepted the box of tissues Jet handed him, standing up and walking around the small space, embarrassed now for his show of emotions. On stage was one thing, for real, in person, his own true self revealed, was not something he did, or hadn't until now, until life with Clair and Devon had opened him up like an oyster, offering not pearls but tears. Tears of futility, shame, and deep sorrow at all that had been possible then, like a river flowing into an ocean, had been subsumed by the wide world of work, Devon's therapy, Clair's total absorption in Devon's care and everything that went with that. They, the two of them, had never been an us, always it was Clair and Devon, and then Adam added on as an afterthought. At least, he had felt that way. Maybe all he had felt, experienced, imagined, was just that – a delusion fed by jealousy at their closeness. He had loved them both. And it wasn't enough. He had lost Devon; he wouldn't lose Clair. At least, not without an appeal.

'I'm going to find her, Jet. Will you let me know if she contacts you first? Please?'

'If she says yes, Adam. I won't go against her wishes.'

'I understand,' he said. 'I do, but still, please, even to let me know she's OK?'

'Yes, I can do that.'

Adam turned to walk out the door, glancing back at Jet, and around her office.

'You know, we learned a lot here with you, about ourselves, each other, and how we fit in the world. It wasn't all bad. Could have been worse. I thank you for that.'

'It's my job,' Jet replied.

'Oh, your connection with Clair, and through her, me, goes far beyond your job description,' Adam said. 'I think you really care.' He walked through the door, pulling it shut quietly behind him.

Walking back to his car felt like an eternity. Hospitals were tiny microcosms of the world, in life, death, and all that lay in-between. Codes were called overhead, people rushing to the bedsides of others dying. New mothers, their laps piled high with balloons, flowers and gifts, a nurse carrying the newborn, nervous dad rushing behind, holding the car seat, looking like he had just been catapulted into a new solar system.

Adam remembered he and Clair bringing Devon home. He had felt like these dads looked. So in love and terrified of making a mistake. This tiny, helpless human being. His responsibility. And he had failed so monumentally. Both his boy, and now his wife. Good God! How had he missed this basic building block of the human system? Being a man, a father, a husband, someone others can depend upon.

Determined to find Clair, he rushed back to the housing residence. The rain had abated, small rainbows dancing in the motor oil surfaced puddles. The air was cool to his face, and he compelled himself to gather his energy, feeling the freshness on his face, then feeling the descending darkness, November in the north-west. His anxiety grew as he increased his knocking to a pounding rhythm. The door opened. An elderly man stood at the door, his expression open and friendly.

'Good evening,' the man said, holding the door open. 'Come in.'

Adam was taken back by this man's uninhibited fearlessness, opening the door to a stranger. Part of him wanted to say, 'Wait a minute. You don't know me.' But instead, he did walk in. The older man stood aside, making room for Adam to pass through, a smile on his face. Adam wondered if maybe he had dementia.

'Robert Hall, how can I help you?' the man said, holding out his hand.

'Robert, Adam Gage,' Adam replied, taking Robert's hand. 'I'm looking for my wife, Clair. She was a resident here. I heard she took a taxi from here and I want, need, to talk to the woman who saw her leave. I don't know the woman's name. But she had gray hair, worn in a bun at her neck, and was wearing a shawl, made of soft pink wool I think.'

'Ah yes, that would be Audrey. My wife. I'll get her for you. Please sit down. We were just getting ready to have a cocktail. Would you like one? There's sherry, martinis, whisky, wine and, of course, our own Seven Devil's craft beer?'

'No, but thanks, so much. Just Audrey please, if she's available.'

'Yes, she had her last treatment today. She's celebrating but tired too. That chemo builds up, you know. Toxic.'

Adam had an image of Clair, weak, sick, wandering somewhere, without roots or destination. His heart hammered in his chest.'

'Sit,' Robert said, more like ordered.

Adam did, and felt a momentary relief as his muscles, fatigued from all that had gone before, relaxed the moment he removed gravity from their grasp. He almost wept with relief. Sinking back into the deep, shabby, worn sofa, he felt the energy of all the bodies and souls who had sat or lain there, an island in the constant stream of treatment induced semi-consciousness. Unlike drug induced states that seemed to generate feelings of bliss, or hysteria, the state induced by treatment was different, terrifying in its magnitude, implications for failure, and yet, somehow, the taste of it, the feel of it coursing through your veins, in your skin, brought solace. Fighting the cancer. A war in your small, vulnerable body.

Adam felt this, from all of the bodies that had sunk into the depths of this sofa, its fabric thin where hips had turned from side to side, seeking comfort. Pillows where heads had rested, holding back nausea, sipping on ginger ale and crunching saltine crackers. Clair had been here. He leaned back, closed his eyes momentarily, sensing her being, smelling her hair, her body, mixed with all others.

'Hello, Adam is it?' Adam heard the melodious voice, standing before him. He opened his eyes. Yes, it was the same woman. Sitting bolt upright, he shook, as though repelling images of others from his vision. Only Clair now.

'Yes, hi, I'm sorry to barge in,' Adam stood, embarrassed to be sitting. 'I'm looking for Clair. You told me she left in a taxi for the airport. Do you know where she was going? Did she give any indication at all?'

They stood, facing each other, Audrey's hand resting on the sofa. The older woman looked so frail; Adam felt terrible for having disturbed her rest. Then Robert brought her a drink, a martini. She took a sip, smiled up at him, and their eyes locked. Adam thought this was a ritual that had probably been reoccurring for many years.

'No, not really. I'm sorry. But she turned and looked at me and said, "*Buen Camino*".'

'*Buen Camino*?' Adam repeated, his expression confused. 'What does that mean?'

'Well, I have a great niece, Becca, who went on a long walk. It was called the Camino de Santiago. And her photos all had a yellow arrow pointing one way or the other, and the words *Buen Camino* written on stones, walls, store fronts. It was in Spain; I do remember that.'

'Spain? Clair has gone to Spain? Why on earth would she do that?'

'People do strange things when they're dying,' Audrey said, casting a loving look at Robert. 'I just married this fool, crazy to be in love with a walking dead woman.'

Robert grinned and, in that moment, looked like he had won the lottery. 'A year or two with Audrey is better for me than a lifetime with any other woman. I hope you find your Clair.'

Chapter 29

Clair

The cluster of women stood outside the café, where they had gathered for coffee and pastries. It was cold, a light rain falling. All were wearing their ponchos, their packs underneath making them look like human camels. They had taken Clair shopping, helping her purchase boots, a waterproof hat and poncho, and other necessities for walking the long coastal Camino from Porto to Santiago.

'Come with us, Clair,' Sandy implored, reaching out to give Clair a final goodbye hug. 'We won't talk the entire walk, promise. And we're just going to spend one day here exploring Porto, then we'll begin our walk. A river cruise, wineries, museums. How can you refuse?'

'You all go on, I'll be fine. I need to walk alone, Sandy. For now. Maybe we'll meet up along the way.'

'All right, but if you get sick or need anything, you can text me via the WhatsApp I installed on your phone, remember?'

'Yes Mom, I remember,' Clair chided.

Sandy pulled a long face, then a smile. '*Buen Camino*, Clair,' she said, her eyes filling softly with tears. 'We all walk the long road alone, after all.'

Clair watched as Sandy joined her group, and they began

their morning walk, their singsong chatter filling the spaces between them. This is a time of beginnings and endings, Clair thought. First times and last times. She wiggled her toes, now encased in a pair of toe socks, feeling oddly comforted by the tightness, like having her feet massaged. Shoes, backpack, walking stick, she was ready. 'Let the rumpus begin,' she said to herself, smiling at the memory of Devon's favorite story about the Wild Things. One foot, one breath, she chanted to herself, stepping onto the path, locating a yellow scallop shell and arrow on the side of a stone wall pointing the way.

Porto was a busy city, hustling and bustling. The rain had stopped, and a cool golden sepia light shone over the city. Clair pulled off the poncho, reveling in the feeling of the cool air against her scalp. She adjusted her pack, shifting the weight so that it rode higher on her narrow hips. The one strap on her right side pulled across the infusion port site. Stopping at a traffic circle, at the edge of a large municipal park, she offloaded the pack onto a nearby bench.

An older woman, dressed all in black, walked across the roundabout, cars racing to gain leader of the pack status at the turns. Once by Clair's side, she sat down on the bench still damp from the morning rain. She perched her cane between her knees, her long dress reaching her ankles enclosed in thick rubber boots. The only color adorning her small, corpulent body was a richly flowered scarf, which she draped around her head and neck. Her deep blue eyes had a slight film over them, as though she was looking through glass.

'Peregrina,' she said, looking Clair up and down. Not a question. A fact.

Clair wasn't sure how to respond. She knew a little Spanish but also knew Portuguese was not the same thing. She tried a universal head nod along with a smile. She wanted to get on her way, not stop and struggle to communicate with this woman.

'Sit,' she said, surprising Clair with the clarity of her word. And Clair did sit, first laying her poncho down as a barrier to the cold wet bench. The woman reached across Clair's body, taking the backpack, adjusting straps, burrowing into the depths of the pack, moving her few belongings around. Then bouncing the pack on her knees, feeling its weight and balance.

'Now, you try.' Holding the pack to Clair, the woman nodded her head, shaking the pack a bit.

Clair stood, amused at both the woman and her own compliance with these orders. She slipped the pack on her shoulders, astounded at the different feeling, of lightness, and fit. It was as though the pack now was a part of her body, not a thing apart.

'Good, yes?' the woman asked.

'Thank you,' Clair said, sitting down, leaving the pack on her back. 'How did you know?'

'Many Caminos,' she said, pointing at her heart. 'I have walked many kilometers to Santiago de Compostela. These feet won't walk that far today so I sit here, in the park, enjoying seeing peregrinas and peregrinos begin their journeys. None the same. Each different. And you will be different each day.'

'I do feel different just being here now, with you,' Clair said. 'Like I'm waking up.'

She gestured with her hands, trying to communicate a coming alive, brightening feeling. The old woman smiled, nodding her head.

'Yes, yes, I remember. Feeling affinity for all, everything together. But you are troubled. You must leave the trouble here on this bench, not take it with you.'

'How can you tell?' Clair asked, her brow creasing in wonder and concern. 'Does it show?'

'I see it in your eyes, the *saudade*.'

'My family. I do need to talk with them. Let them know I'm here and OK.'

'You must ease your spirit, let go of the phantoms that haunt your journey. Here,' she said, reaching up and removing her scarf, 'take this, cover your head and enter the chapel on the other side of this park. Light a candle for each of your ghosts, that their pain and yours will release in the flame and smoke.'

'But, how will I find you to return the scarf?' Clair asked, wrapping the scarf around her neck.

'The scarf is yours to keep. Pass it on if you find a reason or need. It was given to me over fifty years ago by a pilgrim. I have been waiting for you.'

The woman stood.

'I, thank you, and what is your name?' Clair called to her retreating back.

'I am called Raphael,' she said, turning around to look at Clair. 'Now go, the Camino waits.'

Clair debated with herself. Her compulsion to stay on her path, following the yellow arrows was strong, but her curiosity about Raphael's instructions and also, a sense of apprehension of not following them, made her mind up for her. She set off across the roundabout, into the park, looking for a chapel. Imagining a small structure, with perhaps a hidden door, tucked away into a narrow street, she stood awestruck before the massive and ornate Igreja de São Francisco. Easing inside, past a group of tourists being lectured by a guide, she made her way to the front of the church. Clair pulled the scarf up over her head as instructed, although she saw many women with bare heads. Kneeling before the devotional area, where over one hundred votive candles sat, some left burning by a previous penitent, she thought about whom to light a candle for. To release her ghosts, as Raphael had said. A feeling of great sadness overwhelmed her so that rational thought was impossible. Her heart felt like it would explode, so strong was the feeling.

Death at that moment was no longer a thing in the distant future but a realization of now. She was saying goodbye. Raphael had mentioned the feeling of overwhelming melancholy, or *saudade*, that the Portuguese describe as a loss of love, missing someone, and being without. It hit her all at once, this feeling. She crumpled on the red carpeted step, her head falling to her knees. Tears flowed, without resistance. She wanted to wail but knew it wasn't the place. This restrained remorse seemed to her more appropriate and then she began laughing at herself. *Who gives a good damn,* she thought? *I can wail if I damn well please.* But, concern for the others in the church, fear that the security guards might take her to the American Embassy, held her steady. *Later,* she thought, *once I'm in the woods or on a beach. Then I'll wail.*

Slowly, slowly she rose, her head coming up last. Taking a few deep breaths, she dared to look at her phone. The lines of messages were endless. Scrolling through, she saw the majority were from Adam, but also, even her parents had both texted. She lit the first candle for her mother.

After, eleven candles lit, flaming in small ways, their tender tendrils reaching up into the vastness of the cathedral, Clair stood.

Chapter 30

Adam

The flight to Biarritz was brutal, sitting in a cramped seat, for over thirteen hours, with long waits in New York and Paris. Too agitated to read or enjoy people watching as he normally would during travel, he could only pace while waiting for departures, and sit and stare during flight. Sleep came in spurts. He would jolt awake, finding his neck twisted, his head aching, mouth dry.

The taxi ride from Biarritz to Saint-Jean-Pied-de-Port was a blur, the stunning views offering no solace to his tired eyes. He had driven to Portland after meeting with Jet. The next flight out of Harbor wasn't until the next day. He couldn't wait. He caught a flight from Portland to Seattle, and from there to Biarritz. At least when moving he felt like he was doing something. And now, he was here, where it begins. In his hasty research of the Camino de Santiago, he learned that the medieval pilgrimage historically began in Saint-Jean-Pied-de-Port. *This must be where Clair is, or was, and not long ago,* he concluded. He felt this in his bones.

* * *

'Have you seen this woman, my wife, Clair?' Adam asked at every opportunity, beginning from his first stop at the pilgrim's office in Saint-Jean-Pied-de-Port, where he obtained his passport. He had told the office manager that he didn't need the passport, he wasn't walking for religious or spiritual reasons, he was only looking for his wife.

'Everyone walks for a different reason,' she had calmly told him. 'You will need your passport for accommodations, food and drink, friendship along the way. Here, your first stamp.'

And she stamped a small, folded booklet, with the characteristic scallop shell on the front. Adam held the photo of Clair in front of the booklet.

'Please, look. Do you remember this woman coming in and obtaining her own passport? It would have been about three days ago?'

Adam had rushed about, packing an old college backpack with what he considered essentials. He had googled enough information to learn he would need good smart wool socks, hiking boots, and a poncho. A warm fleece jacket, and windbreaker. Anything else would make the pack too heavy to carry across the mountains towards Santiago, in the late fall, early winter passage. A fool's game, Ben had told him over the phone, when they had finally got a chance to talk. Neither Ben nor Jodie had heard from Clair. They were as shocked, saddened, and distraught as Adam at Clair's decision to flee to Spain.

'I can catch up with her, I know,' Adam had insisted. I will walk far faster than she is able, and I won't rest until I do.'

The woman in the pilgrim's office looked at the photo. Her eyes smiled at him but her words didn't offer comfort.

'No, I have not seen this woman.'

'But, are you sure? You must see so many; how can you be sure? Is there anyone else we can ask, another person here who might have met her?'

'I am here every day and I would remember. Each face that arrives here at my door is like a work of art, holding the past in every line and shadow, and the eyes shine bright with future sights yet unseen. This woman, your wife, I heard you say? She is so lovely. I wish I had met her. I am sorry.'

It was late, the sky darkening. He was tired, hungry, disheartened. Hefting his backpack up onto his shoulders, he looked around. He was the only one left in the office, besides the manager. He looked at her name badge.

'Consuela, I apologize for taking your time. Is there a place I can stay tonight? I didn't make any reservations?'

'Yes, here is a map, with the *albergues* noted. You can call ahead, and see which ones still have beds available.'

'Beds? Do you literally mean a bed, not a room?'

She laughed, her face lighting up. 'Oh yes, and it may be a couch or rug on the floor. That is the nature of the Camino, my friend.'

Map in hand, Adam walked out, into the cold evening, street lights revealing a city settling in for the night. The Pyrenees stood sentinel in the distance. Shops and markets were closing their doors, while the cafés and bars lit up.

He entered the first café he came to, sitting down heavily in a seat by the window. People strolled through the narrow streets. Most had backpacks and walking poles. The scallop shell hanging from their packs identifying them as pilgrims. Adam marveled at this scene. *It's an entire world apart*, he thought. *Why would anyone do this unless, like me, they had to?*

A young man, dark hair and eyes, came to take his order.

Adam wasn't certain what language to use. The young man pointed to a placard where the specials of the day, as well as standing items were handwritten.

'Would you like something to drink while you decide, sir?' he asked in accented English.

'Please, red wine,' he said, 'and a plate of the fish and red bean stew,' he said, noting this on the specials. As an afterthought, he pulled Clair's photo out of his jacket pocket. Looking at it himself, seeing it as though for the first time, he felt his heart tighten at the memory of the day it had been taken.

A summer day, late August, foggy and windy as the coast gets, when heat in the valley draws cooler air off the ocean, creating the marine layer. They were sitting on a fallen tree, its roots stretching up in a wild spiral. Her hair, normally tucked into a neat bun or held back with an elastic, was escaping that day, the fog causing it to curl and frizz, like a ring of fire around her face. A face that shone with delight. They'd had their first ultrasound. A boy. She had looked at him, and he caught her, a moment when she had forgotten herself, not Dr Mercer, not Ben's sister, or her parents' daughter. Not even Adam Gage's wife. Just she, Clair, holding their son in her belly.

When the waiter returned with a large glass of deep burgundy, Adam held the photo out.

'Have you by chance seen this woman?' he asked, trying to hold his voice steady. It occurred to him that he might be taken as a creep, or predator. 'She's my wife and we got separated,' he hurriedly added.

'She is very beautiful but no, sir, I have not seen her. I would remember.'

Adam nodded his head, feeling it drop with the weight of disappointment.

'You can ask Benzozia to help you find her. There is a chapel on the side of the Church of the Assumption, a few kilometers towards the mountains. Light a candle. She will help you.'

Feeling irrationally uplifted, he left the café, his belly full and his mind relaxed after two glasses of the rich wine. He knew he needed to find a place to sleep but his heart pushed him towards the chapel. Never a person of faith, of any kind, except in a fierce negation of anything that might hold him back from making his own choices, he walked with hesitant steps towards this new experience.

'What the fuck is this?' he asked himself, as an overwhelming feeling of yearning, for what he didn't know, overcame him as he entered the nave. A deep longing for his old self and way of life, already far behind him. Nothing to do now except relinquish any final hold on the way things were and be open to surprise. He had stepped across some threshold, here where the pagan met the sacred. Benzozia, Mother Dragon, standing beside a keening Mary, Mother of God. Falling on his knees in the aisle, he held his head in his hands, gasping for breath.

A hand on his shoulder, light yet firm, started him back into breathing. Looking up, he saw an older man, wearing a thick hand-knitted sweater, jeans, and carrying a leather wallet in his hand. The man smiled, his deep blue eyes crinkling at the corners. Adam noticed a small clerical collar peeking out from the thick collar of his sweater.

'I was just heading out for a meal,' he said when Adam picked himself up, sitting gingerly on the side of the closest pew. 'Would you like to join me? Or would you prefer to remain here for a while? I don't lock the church but it will turn cold in an hour or so.'

'Yes, I would like to stay, please,' Adam replied, surprised at his own meekness. He felt like a child again, like with Jet. Was he losing his manhood, everything about himself that had made him what he was? 'Ah, I was told I would find Benzozia here.'

'Oh, the superstitions of our locals. But yes, we do have iconography for both our traditional Catholic saints, as well as some for the Basque creation stories. Benzozia, Mother Dragon, is believed to be the protector of lovers, and if you pray to her, offer a candle and some coin, she will help you find your lost lover. Are you looking for a lost love?' he asked, his face serious.

'Yes, I am,' Adam said as he stood, reaching into his pocket for the photo of Clair. 'Have you seen her, my wife, Clair?'

The priest held out his hand. 'Martin Lopez,' he said, reaching for the photo. Adam first shook the offered hand. 'Adam Gage.' He handed Father Lopez the photo.

'I have not seen her. A lovely woman. Why do you think she has come this way?'

'She is dying. And she wants to be alone.'

'I see,' Lopez said, looking up at the sculpture of Christ on the cross. 'So, why are you following her?' he asked kindly.

'I don't want to be alone,' Adam replied, just that moment accepting the hard truth. He wasn't chasing after Clair for her sake. He had to find her for his. Realizing that it took this fear of being alone, to remember how alive he had felt with her.

Father Lopez nodded. 'Stay as long as you like. I wish you a *Buen Camino*, whatever you find on your path.'

Adam sat until fatigue overcame him. Rising to his feet, he walked to the altar, lighting a candle for Benzozia, and just for good luck, one for St Jude, remembering from his own catechism during his youth, the good saint of lost causes.

Hefting his pack onto his back, he strode purposefully out through the heavy wooden doors into the late evening chill.

He called the first *albergue* marked on the map and was relieved when he was told that yes, a bunk was available. It was a two-kilometer walk. The light was less than before, and shadows played before his passage along the narrow, cobbled streets. A noise like an approaching train seemed to fill every space. As he walked, he noticed gatherings of people, in store fronts, alongside alleys, talking and gesticulating with passion, voices raised in both laughter and argument. He didn't sense anger, just the joy of conversation.

He found the hostel, was directed to a dormitory style room, with eight bunk beds, many already filled with both men and women. Finding the communal bathroom at the end of a long hallway, he washed up. The face he saw in the mirror at first seemed strange to him, then familiar. It was his original face, before all the affectations of trying so hard to be someone else created the mask he had long shown the world. It was Devon's face. The broad forehead, deep set neon blue eyes, and wide, gentle mouth. He touched his eyes, his cheeks, wiping the wetness away.

Then he returned to his bed, to rest ready to begin his own pilgrimage at daybreak, leaving behind everything he had been and walk with new steps towards his unknown future. The snoring and rustling of the other sleepers didn't keep him awake.

In the morning, cold and stiff, he followed the scent of strong coffee to a communal kitchen. Pilgrims gathered around a long, rectangular table, laden with eggs, cheese, bread, pastries, and an assortment of meats and salted fish. Helping himself, he found a seat next to a couple, sitting together in that way old friends have; a comfortable silence between them.

He showed Clair's photo, sharing his story, eager for any information. German speakers, they nodded and smiled at her photo but were unable to offer any information. Gathering his pack, he set off, following the bright yellow arrows.

* * *

'Could she have come another way? Is it possible she skipped you and went ahead, on her own?' Adam asked when he reached his resting place for the night, twenty-eight kilometers into his first day on the Camino. It had been an arduous climb, mostly uphill through the Pyrenees. His feet, back, shoulders, even his teeth ached. He had reached the *albergue* just at dusk, along with a few other pilgrims whom he had either passed or been passed by on this first day out. The manager had taken a good long look at the photo then handed it back, his face showing his concern as he told Adam that no, he had not seen this woman.

'Are there other ways?' Adam asked, stunned at this unforeseen possibility.

'Oh yes, there are seven main routes in Spain and Portugal that lead to Santiago de Compostela, and several lesser traveled paths. This one is the longest. She could have begun at any of the other routes.'

Adam cursed himself for not considering this before beginning what was starting to feel like a fool's journey. Now, he was too far into it to return, begin another route. He would have to continue on. And, he did believe, with his heart, that Clair would have come this route, only because it was the longest, hardest, and by far the most heroic of the routes. She had a lion's heart. She would not want to take an easy route.

Uplifted by these thoughts, he settled in for the night, depositing his meager belongings on a bottom bunk in a dormitory style room, with several bunks, most already taken. He wondered about leaving his gear unprotected. He took out his passport and wallet, the photo of Clair, and left the rest.

Dinner was being served at a shared table, large carafes of red and white wine being passed around. Voices were jubilant. Words in many languages. He was welcomed as he sat at the end of a long bench. A half-moon shone through an open window, casting shadows along the walls and across the floor. A large white dog lay on a rug by the fireplace, logs burning a slow blaze, casting soft illumination around the table.

He felt like the first time he had taken LSD back in college. Everything blending into one, voices, faces, stories, all part of the whole fabric of life. Like the tapestry hanging on his grandmother's wall, each thread unique and different. She had once told him that life was like the tapestry, and we can only see the hem. We have to trust that the complete design will be visible to us one day. *Was that what this was?* He asked himself. *Am I seeing the tapestry in its entirety, people coming together with purpose and vision, enjoying the simplest of acts, being human? Bodies fatigued, hearts full, minds clear of worry or lists.* He considered passing Clair's photo around but decided to wait. He didn't want anything to change this moment, when he felt his aloneness connecting with others, and it was good.

Chapter 31

Clair

The way was more difficult than she had imagined. Grateful for her good shoes, jacket, and poncho, she felt the rain fall on her head, heard it drip from the tall, sweet smelling eucalyptus and pine trees as she walked through the dense coastal forest. She had paralleled the coast for many kilometers, then veered inland. At once, captured by the rich scents of dense trees, earth, and that ethereal something that passes between all living things, she walked, looking towards the skyline, enjoying the sway and music of the limbs as they rubbed together like lovers. Catching herself stumbling over old flagstones mired in the damp path, she kept her eyes down, knowing a fall could be disastrous. Her bones were weakened by the chemotherapy and now, with metastasis, she was at higher risk for pathologic fractures. Slow, and steady, she coached herself, like the story about the tortoise and the hare Devon loved for her to read. Be the tortoise, she told herself. One step at a time.

The path wound steadily uphill, the forest growing thicker until suddenly a stream ran by, the yellow arrows pointing to an old wooden bridge. Crossing the stream, she found herself in a small village, where a local family had set up an impromptu café. They offered food, water, beer, wine, and toilet facilities in their home. Several pilgrims were sitting inside an open garage, where a fire pit glowed brightly. Coats, ponchos, even shoes and socks lined the walls of the garage. Clair sauntered through the doorway, not sure of her place. Immediately, several people waved her over, motioned to the hooks on the wall. An older man, smiling broadly, came up to her, speaking in Spanish and making hand signals towards displays of food and drink.

I must look like something the cat dragged in, she thought, *but then, so does everyone else.* Grateful to take off her wet outer garments, she dug in her backpack for a pair of fresh socks. Her feet, bright red, toenails blue, stung with heat and tingling, as she gently massaged them before putting on dry socks. The relief was sensual.

Joining a table where she recognized a couple, Bridget and Joe from Dublin, she had met on the path that morning, she helped herself to a slice of the local *tortilla*, a mix of eggs, potatoes and onion, giving herself over to the experience of being part of this confluence of beings, not needing to speak, or even listen. It was enough. For now.

As Clair sat, enjoying the sounds of laughter, talk, and strangers becoming friends, she found herself looking at the faces, seeing how each individual carried so many stories written in their expressions, lines of history etched in the eyes, along the jaw, and mouth. One face caught her attention. He was looking at her. Eyes so dark, wide set, and open, without a trace of guile or cunning. Only curiosity and kindness shone through. She quickly looked away.

'We'll be going now,' Bridget said. 'Do you want to walk with us? We're going to stay in Pontevedra tonight, in a hotel. We're too old for the *albergues*. Sharing a toilet is not my thing. And good God, snoring in six languages! Hard enough to share with this brute.' She playfully nudged Joe, who stood six five to her five two.

'How far to Pontevedra?' Clair asked. She had the pilgrim app on her smartphone but rarely used it, preferring to follow the way markers, and leave her itinerary up to chance. But it was getting late, and she didn't want to sleep on the floor, as she had at her last hostel, sharing a thick wool rug with a big furry sheepdog.

'Only eight more kilometers,' Bridget said. 'But, you know, we're in our seventies and like to settle in before dark. And looking around, in this part of the world, dark comes early this time of year.'

'I think I'll stay a bit longer, rest my feet,' Clair replied, stretching out on the bench seat Joe had just vacated, enjoying the heat from his body. 'I made a booking at an *albergue* so I'm OK for tonight. Hope to see you on the path tomorrow. *Buen Camino*.'

'*Buen Camino*,' Bridget said as she walked away, looking back over her shoulder, as Joe loped along beside her.

Clair was sipping a glass of cold Alberiño wine, looking out over a grape orchard, dotted with sheep grazing, chickens pecking, and flowers blooming all along the rows. The sky was blue now, without a hint of the dark clouds that had followed her and sometimes poured rain down upon her as she walked up through the forest. She leaned back against the side of the walled garage, allowing a deep feeling of being where she should be overtaking her doubts, guilt over leaving without telling her family, and surprisingly, thoughts of Jet bubbled up into her consciousness. Without hesitation, she opened her phone, finding Jet's contact information, opened a message and texted.

Jet, I'm OK. Don't worry. I'm doing what I have to do. I'll call once I'm settled. Don't try to reach me, wherever I am today, I won't be there tomorrow. I'm sending the same text to Adam, Ben and Jodie, so you don't have to try to call or message them. I'm well. Be well too.

And then she turned her phone off again. She didn't want to have to deal with responses, just now. Looking around again, she noticed the young man walking towards her. Tall and gangly, long dark hair pulled back into a neat bun, he looked both impossibly young and yet had a certain maturity and wisdom in his grace. He smiled as he sat down. Holding out his hand, he said, 'Hello, I'm Miguel. I've noticed you are a solo pilgrim. How far have you walked today?'

'Hi, I'm Clair,' she said. 'Today, not so far. I'm going on to Pontevedra, then I'm not sure. I sort of take it day by day.'

'Do you know about the Variante Espiritual? It is the most beautiful way, if you have the time.'

'Oh, I have all the time in the world. Please, tell me about it.'

* * *

The next day, after breakfast at the hostel in Pontevedra, she met Miguel and they set off on the road to Armenteria, the spiritual variant of the Camino de Santiago. They fell into an easy rhythm, seeing other pilgrims, sharing *Buen Caminos*. The way took them through the village of Combarro, where they decided to stay a night. There wasn't an *albergue* but a café rented rooms. There was only one available. Clair had long lost her sense of privacy and felt no hesitation at undressing down to her camisole and underwear, before climbing into a narrow, single bed. She glanced to see him remove his shirt and jeans, and looked away quickly when she realized he wasn't wearing any underwear. The other bed was angled at an L shape so that their heads almost touched.

'So, tell me, Clair Mercer, what brings you on this pilgrimage, alone?'

'I am walking to Finisterre,' she said. 'What about you?'

'No reason. Just the act of walking by itself answers many questions I have, about how to make sense of this world. It is a path through the chaos.'

'And have you found your answers?' she asked, feeling heat from the top of his head radiate to her.

'It isn't about finding, I don't think. It is about seeking.'

* * *

The next morning, they set off for Vilanova de Arousa. There was an unseasonal heatwave, temperatures climbing into the seventies. Sweaty, they stopped at a small stream running along rocks, water so clear you could see the ancient markings of centuries flowing over them. Miguel sat, stripped off his shoes, socks, and clothes, wading out into the cold water.

'Ah,' he exclaimed. 'Come in, Clair. It's refreshing.'

She stood, taking off her own clothing, and toed her way into the icy waters. She felt his eyes on her. Closing her own, she breathed in the sensation of being free, of choosing to do this, and plunged into a deep area, letting the water surround her, feeling the rocks slide across her bottom. Coming up, laughing, she saw he was standing still, watching. His eyes held a look of such deep compassion, she almost wept. Beginning to shiver, she hurried back onto the bank, her clothes warmed by the sun.

'Don't dress right away,' he called. 'Make sure you're all dry. Dampness can cause blisters and inflammation.'

'How do you know so much?' Clair asked him, once he had returned to the bank, his face turned towards the sun.

'I walk, that's what I do.'

She felt her breath catch in her heart. Those were Michael's words, almost exactly. But this man, almost a boy, isn't the Michael she met on the plane. She felt him looking at her.

'You are beautiful, Clair. Don't try to hide your beauty, or mask your suffering. We all live to suffer, and to help others heal from their suffering.'

Miguel looked long at the river, as they sat on the bank. Clair was uneasy at first, feeling like she shouldn't be doing this, he was too young. But what was she doing, really? There was nothing sexual about this encounter. They were two beings, coming together, to share moments, and that was all. But that was so much.

He waved his hand at the river, swirling, eddying, and rippling down towards the ocean.

'Life, like waves, river or ocean, moves in swells and patterns, sometimes thought to come in sets of seven. Myth or fact, no one knows for sure. The wind in storms comes in intervals, gusts and flurries. It is wind that creates swells, the more consistent winds creating the swell, not the higher impact gusts. These swells will bond together, in sets, in order to conserve energy for their vast journey over oceans. Whether sets of seven or more, that isn't scientific. What is known is that for each of us, we find our breaking point. Turbulence precedes transformation. The moment we crash onto shore or up against a rock. But the wave doesn't cease to exist, it returns to water. And so we continue on as well.

Chapter 32

Adam

Adam hadn't really thought about the distances, or the steps. He had seen the route as a driver, someone who could cross vast geographical spaces with a foot on the pedal, or better yet, sitting in a seat on an airplane. This walking, this moment by moment life, was hard. That morning at breakfast, sitting at the communal table, drinking dark, strong coffee and eating eggs fried in butter, thick bread smeared with sweet jam, cheese, and dried apricots, he had heard two men sitting next to him talking about how it was only another 500 kilometers. He was astounded. He opened his phone, downloaded a map of the area, and seeing where he was and where he had yet to go, he felt dizzy. *Good God*, he thought, *what in the name of reason have I done?* This will take over a month. It will be December, winter. And there's no way around, too late to go back. I have to keep on.

No one had seen Clair. None of the hostels he had stayed at, or cafés, tapas bars, even churches. He had stopped asking. Now, he was on this path for himself, to survive. Up and moving at dawn, he set off, finding an easy pace now, his arms swinging, modulating his breathing so that each step was a breath. Climbing was getting easier. He found a rhythm for that as well, stepping up first right, then bringing up the left. He sang, quoted entire sections of plays. He thought seldom about home, his classes, students. A sight stopped him in his tracks. A house, standing alone in a field, one tree to its side. He threw his arms up into the air, dancing around in circles singing 'La Donna È Mobile' from Verdi. A group of pilgrims walked around him, smiling and waving.

'*Buen Camino*,' they called, the chant becoming more than a saying. It was a confirmation of their sharing this road, this time, this life. He felt a cellular joy, a freedom never before experienced until a thought hit him like a strong north wind. What if Clair was already dead?

Walk, he thought, *just keep walking. The next town, the next hostel, I'll get there. If she is going to Santiago, I'll find her there. I would know if she was no longer on this earth, a part of the fabric of humanity. I would, wouldn't I?*

And so, he did, over hills, through villages, snow, rain, sunshine. Meeting people who knew him only by his first name, Adam. Welcomed and accepted, sleeping on a couch with a total stranger, a woman who like him, arrived too late for a bed. They slept end to end and the comfort of her warm body soothed him to sleep.

Chapter 33

Clair

The cathedral spires were visible from the bridge, over a causeway entering into Santiago. By now, the numbers of pilgrims had picked up, even at this time of year. The energy and excitement were palpable. Several were gathered at a crossroads, where two signs pointed in a different direction, leading towards Santiago. They clustered together, speaking and gesticulating in multiple languages, asking which way to go. Clair made her best guess, and walked away from the group, keeping the sight of the spires in her mind's eye, even as she entered another dense forest.

Without warning, the forest ended, and she was on a busy, commercial road, with large vehicles thundering past. It had been so long since she had been in a city, she was momentarily disoriented. One bright yellow arrow pointed the way across a six-lane highway. Once across, she stepped into a café for a bathroom break. After buying a bottle of water, she sat and watched as the world sped by. She felt OK. Pain had become her constant companion, and she didn't know if it was the cancer or just wear and tear. She lived on ibuprofen and paracetamol. The local wines and strong pastries helped, she thought. She couldn't tolerate beer or ale, a great sadness to her. She walked on, slowly now, not wanting this part of the journey to end. After Santiago would be Finisterre. That would be the end.

The sounds of voices began as a soft hum, like her bowing in the early movements of Pachelbel's Canon. Then, as in a symphony, gaining momentum until she was there, carried along by the sounds to the entrance of the Cathedral de Compostela, home of St James, center of her universe for now. The Pilgrim's Mass was about to begin. She walked in, genuflecting as she settled into a pew towards the back. This was the place to leave all of her suffering behind. A door to a small confessional was open to her right. She knelt in front, speaking in halting Spanish. The priest recited his prayer, taking her face in his large, rough hands and wiped her tears away. He blessed her. Eyes tearing still, she sat again in her pew, then followed the procession up to the altar to take communion. *This is all I needed,* she thought. *Now I'm ready.*

Bright lights shone against the winter darkness when she walked out of the church. The square still held gatherings of pilgrims, many overwhelmed with emotion at having arrived at their long-sought destination. A bagpipe was sounding a plaintive anthem somewhere in the near distance. Clair walked through the winding, narrow avenues, realizing she was starving and exhausted. She sat down outside a tapas bar, relishing a moment of stillness. The café was quiet this time of evening, the transition between day and night. A waiter, dark hair combed back, dressed in black pants and white shirt, offered her a plate of cheese, nuts, and potato chips. A bottle of water, still, was placed on the table. She ordered a glass of Alberiño, *ensalada* and *tortilla*. She had come to crave this simple and filling meal, which left her satiated and without the frequent digestive distress other foods often caused. Music played down the avenues, floated out of windows, cracked open to let in the cool November night air. Smoke from pipes, cigarettes, and wood stoves mixed with the sounds, creating a mixture that took her back, way back to earlier days, when her family acted like one, taking vacations in the Redwood Forest and Yosemite National Park. Her father smoked a pipe, its resonant scent lingering in the air outside the cabin door, where her mother made him go to smoke. She would stand with him, as they watched the night sky open like a crystal box full of jewels. Her mother's radio played songs from the local station, ballads of love, loss, and the mercy at the bottom of a bottle. Clair felt her breath catch as she had a vivid flashback of Adam, smoking a cigarette. 'The last one,' he had said, smiling. 'I'm quitting, for our baby.'

* * *

The walk to Finisterre was less arduous than the walk to Santiago. The path rambled through villages, over Roman bridges, and down roads running side by side with modern highways. Fewer pilgrims took this path, choosing to stay in Santiago or return to their homes having accomplished their goal. Clair enjoyed the solace. She had treated herself to a hotel room in Santiago, with her own private toilet. She had hesitated at first, worrying about the Visa card. Surely Adam was watching for its use. At this point, she decided, she didn't care. It was almost over.

Chapter 34

Clair

The rock sat lonely among the cliffs, historian to all that had gone before and would come after. The cold, gray north Atlantic Ocean churned, casting foam onto the large flat surfaces where wild goats pranced. She had passed the zero-kilometer mark, where a few hardy souls were taking pictures, capturing the moment on film, thinking this feeling of triumph would last for ever. How little they knew, she thought, smiling inwardly. Nothing is for ever in this material world, but if we open ourselves, we can find a way through to the place where everything meets. She was here now. Devon's end of the world. She sat down, laying her pack beside her. How good it felt to take it off. She rolled her aching shoulders, feeling the ever-constant prickle of nerves regenerating in her severed breasts. *How funny,* she thought. *Even as I am dying, my individual cells are continuing to act as though this body of theirs will live for ever.* She held in her hand the small red truck. Carried all these miles, days, through every chemo session, under her pillow at night. This truck, holding his tiny handprint, had been her token. Kept her going. Now it can go too. *We are here together my love. But not right now. Now, I need a meal and sleep.* Walking towards the village, she saw a small café, and heard children's voices. Entering she found it mostly empty, two women behind the counter, three children riding tricycles, around and around the middle of the room.

Smiling as she entered, she sat, enjoying the sounds of children. The youngest of the two women came over.

'What would you like? I am sorry for the noise, my children,' she said, but she smiled broadly.

'Not a problem for me,' Clair replied. 'I enjoy seeing and hearing them. I'll have an *ensalada* and *tortilla. Gracias.*'

The meal was fresh. She could see an older woman cooking behind the short counter. After finishing her simple meal, she walked along the marine boardwalk, until she came to a small building, in which she heard strains of strings, violin, cello, and maybe a viola or perhaps an indigenous instrument. Looking through a window, she saw a middle-aged man, dressed in a black suit, white shirt, and dark gray tie, holding lessons for a class of young people, between the ages of six and maybe fourteen, she thought. She wandered in. On the wall, a sign advertising for a part-time music instructor caught her attention.

'Hello, I'm Clair Mercer,' she said to the music tutor after his class had dispersed. 'I see you're advertising for help?'

'Dr Martin De Los Santos,' he said, bowing from the waist. 'I am, yes,' he said in clear accented English. 'Do you play?'

'Yes, I play cello. And I know other strings – violin, viola, guitar – well enough to mentor.'

'Estupendo! How soon can you start?'

* * *

She found a small room to rent monthly, and began her new job. Each morning at eleven, she walked the three kilometers

260

to the music school. First the very young ones, three to five, brought in by grandmothers, dressed in black. Then in the afternoons, the older children, sullen and unwilling. It became her mission in life to inspire them to love music. She found popular sheet music for strings. She played Bob Dylan's *Desire* CD so they could hear the electric violin. And it began to work.

Chapter 35

Adam

The cathedral wasn't what he had been expecting. Something more akin to the great Oz. The square in front was buzzing with youth protesting for a free Galiza. Amazed at this transformation from forests, farms, villages, miles and miles of step by lonely step, he was blinded by the light of so much activity. A hotel stood off to the left. He wanted to spend one night in a bed, luxuriate in a long hot bath. He could snore as much as he needed to without being shushed by a strange voice. Over six weeks on the road, he felt fit. His body taut from the daily walking, his mind calm. People flooded into the cathedral. He held back. *What would I have to offer?* he wondered. *What would I give? Maybe just a look inside. To see the art, the architecture.* Remembering his experience in Saint-Jean-Pied-de-Port, he was afraid he had set the gods against him.

It was mass. People gathered in pews, in aisles, standing, kneeling, sitting. A sight he had never imagined captured his vision. The Botafumeiro came swinging across the divide between altar and penitents, casting a thick, pungent scent with its fog of incense. The feeling of being caught up in something far outside of his control overcame him, his legs folding, bringing him down to the kneeler. For the first time, he understood all that Clair had been railing against, and why she wouldn't give up. And he knew, in his heart, like Clair had always known, that his son still lived, in this moment, here in this place, ringing out through these voices, captured in the incense carrying centuries of human longing, and holding and letting go. He was ready. He just had to find Clair and hold her one more time.

He would keep walking, to the end. If she wasn't there, at least he would know he had done all he could. And, he had become addicted to this walking. Each day new, opening with possibilities. To keep on had become the purpose. Not to finish.

Chapter 36

Clair

After work one day, she returned to her rock. It was January. Cold, dark. She didn't feel alone, and she didn't feel like dying. She sat out on the edge, looking north, towards the Costa da Morte. She fingered the red metal truck in her pocket. A dense fog bank was rolling in, blurring the mussel fishermen's traps, the boats moored in the harbor. She felt a presence behind her. It didn't alarm her. Pilgrims came here throughout the year, and locals were here always. This was a place to sit and look out, connect with something so much more than the moments of the day. She felt the person coming closer, recognized the energy. Heat radiated up through her belly, her heart began racing. Stunned, she turned and saw Adam. Silhouetted against the setting sun, his hair, long and unkempt, blowing away from his face, alert with recognition.

'Clair, I found you.'

He sat next to her. His shoes were duct taped together. She laughed so hard, it hurt.

'For God's sake, Adam, what have you done?'

They sat together as darkness settled in and lights came up in the village.

'Do you have a home here, Clair?' he asked. 'I could use a hot shower and, well, a good night's sleep.'

* * *

The next morning, as Clair was getting ready to leave for work, she could feel Adam watching her from his place on the bed. They had lain together, close enough to feel each other's heat, but not touching. She didn't have a couch. The only other furniture was a single chair, a small table by the window looking out to sea, and a few large pillows scattered about on the floor. She had listened to his quiet snoring, more like snuffling, as a small creature might do rooting around in the dark. She found it oddly comforting.

'You look wonderful, Clair. Where are you off to?' he asked, rolling to his side, leaning on an elbow.

Her hair had grown out, curly and fine like a baby's. Still dark brown but with streaks of gold and red, as though burnished in the Galician sun. Thin but fit, she felt stronger than she had in years. She didn't think about the cancer. Finding a way to live with it instead of being at war, Clair felt she had made peace with it all. Looking at each day fresh and clear, she found joy in her students and music.

'Work. I teach music at the primary school. Strings, you know.'

'Yeah?' he said, sitting up, the sheet falling to his waist. 'Do you think they need a theater teacher?'

Clair looked at him, at his wiry frame, his face covered by a beard, mostly gray. This was a different Adam.

'I'll ask,' she said, smiling. 'Let's see how it goes.'

Chapter 37

Clair and Adam

'I need a long walk,' Clair said, as they sat at the window, overlooking the beach at Langosteira. Warmer now, the new season's sun bringing more and more people, both pilgrims and locals. 'I have Semana Santa, or our spring break, free. What about you? Can you get away for a few days?'

Adam looked out at the mussel boats, thinking about his work now, farming and harvesting the shellfish. At first, he worried about their suffering, but then, talking with locals and his workmates, he was told that they were not able to escape pain so then, it stood to reason, that they couldn't feel pain. He accepted this and found joy in the simple manual labor. There hadn't been work for him at Clair's school and, thinking back, he was thankful it had worked out this way. Being out on the water, spending time with these good people, bringing in a harvest that benefitted so many, felt right. His body was tired at night. His mind clear.

He and Clair would eat a simple meal, drink the local wine, walk down to the lighthouse, sit on the large, flat rocks and watch the waves move against currents and wind. It had taken them a while to feel at ease with each other. Wanting and needing, immediate. After that first awkward night together, they began to touch. At first, just a hand, finding the other's in the dark, early hours before dawn. Hands touching became legs and feet entangling, until bodies turned to one another. Gently, his hands explored her chest, running tender fingers over the scars.

'When did you have the port removed?' he had asked one morning, as they lay together in the first light of day. He rubbed a hardened area over her right clavicle, where the chemotherapy infusion port had sat, creating a callous in her skin.

'I found a clinic here that took it out. After about a week. I knew I wouldn't go back on chemo, so why keep it in? It itched, and was a constant reminder. A foreign object that didn't belong.'

'And you're OK? I mean, how do you know what the cancer is doing?' he asked, rolling over onto his side, looking at her. A tattoo of Celtic knots chained together crossed her entire upper body, from one shoulder to the other. He could feel the scar tissue beneath but the wounds were no longer visible.

'We have found a way to live together. I don't try to kill it, and it doesn't try to kill me,' she said, throwing her long legs over the side of the bed. 'I'm off to work.'

When Clair had returned home that day, Adam had the table spread with food, wine, and flowers.

'I have a job,' he had said, throwing his arms in the air.

Clair wasn't sure how to react. She had loved her time alone now for the past two months. Did she want to share? Used to be, she would come home, drink her tea, eat whatever she had left over from lunch. Watch the horizon until dark. This was new. Required energy. Did she have it?

'And so, what do you think this means?' she asked, looking at the spread on her small table, which before held a single bud vase with whatever wild flower she found on her walk home from the music school.

'I think it means that I'm staying for now. And it's OK if you don't want me staying with you, Clair. I understand. But I'll be near. Close, you know.'

'Why, Adam? Why would you do this? All of this? Walking the Camino? Being here? I don't understand,' Clair asked, sitting cross-legged on a pillow, under the window, looking out to sea. There was no room to pace.

'Because I love you, Clair Mercer. And I want to be with you. Now, and for ever.' He had sat clumsily down on the floor in front of her, taking her hands in his. 'I'm not asking that you love me back. Or that you even want to be with me, spend time with me. It will be enough that I know I am close to you. Is that OK?'

Clair had looked at him for a long time, into his eyes, clearer now than before.

'It's OK, for now,' she had said, feeling the warmth of his hands, the heat radiating from his body. Smiling, she stood, one fluid motion. 'I'm starving. Let's eat.'

And the days, weeks, and months passed. They found a larger house to rent, on a monthly basis. Clair played and taught music. Adam worked long, physically demanding days on the mussel boats, finding peace in the labor and community. Becoming part of the fabric of the place, their presence known to local markets, cafés, and events. They learned about the history of Galicia, it's Celtic roots, and pride. Both being without strong family ties, except for Ben and Jodie, this ancient belonging captured their hearts and spirits. Spring brought rebirth, music festivals, protests against ruling Spain, and Clair felt the need to move.

'Where to? And how far?' he asked, sipping his strong black coffee.

'Costa da Morte,' she said dramatically. 'Death Coast. To Muxía. It's around twenty kilometers. A good day's walk.'

'OK, let me tell Joachim I'll be gone for a few days and we can head out. You do want to stay overnight, yes?'

'Yes, but let's not plan on anything. We might want to continue on to the Camariñas. And who knows, we might just keep walking. We both have our pensions. And our jobs are, well, dispensable. My kids enjoy our music together but they can certainly take a break for a while. And I'm sure your mussels would enjoy a break too. So, let's be pilgrims again and take it day by day.'

Adam stared at his wife, so different from the Clair he had known before. That Clair would have each step of the way planned, down to where they would stop to eat, have coffee breaks, sleep. This Clair, with her hair, now long, streaks of sunlight creating sparks of fire in the deep brown waves, was transformed.

'So, let's begin this new path,' he said, standing. 'I'll run down to the boat to tell Joachim. Maybe you can load our packs?'

She was an expert at packing now. Just the bare essentials. Dry socks, a few toiletries, light sandals for after the walk, one change of clothing, and for her, a light dress and shawl, for evening and to sleep in, in case they did stay in an *albergue*. At the last moment, she took the red toy truck from its place on her bedside table, and tucked it into the inside pocket of her pack.

Their walk began at the north end of Finisterre, by the Baixar Cross, looking over and beyond the long Langosteira beach. For most of their walk, the Atlantic Ocean was visible. Long known to sailors as the Death Coast due to the number of shipwrecks throughout history. But the scenery dispelled any sense of dread or remorse for what had been lost before.

When they left the curtain of ocean to their left, they encountered gentle forest paths and rural country roads, walking through farms and villages. At the Lires estuary, they walked along the waterline, laughing and splashing each other. They discovered a rhythm to their walking, their steps synchronizing. Thinking back to their first walk together, returning to her house from the party, she remembered this about them. Time, distance, and regret had severed that connection until their steps had diverged, bifurcating their lives and leaving Devon alone, on the beach, vulnerable and defenseless. Inwardly shuddering at the recollection, she faltered. Adam felt it, reached out and took her hand. She held his, feeling the warmth and strength.

The path narrowed and he eased behind her, giving her hand a last squeeze before letting go. They stopped often, marveling at the waterfall as they crossed the Castro river. During a sudden shower, they stopped in the lee of one of the ancient *hórreos*, paying silent homage to both the Christian and Pagan practices that they embodied. A wayside offering water, fruit, sundry snacks and juices welcomed them. A sign, HELP YOURSELF carried the message that they had both found representative of the Camino. They walked on until, coming out of a forested area, the ocean was once again in their sights.

Muxía, the westernmost point on the European mainland, was quiet when they arrived. Locals were enjoying a long siesta time, and the flood of pilgrims had not yet reached its maximum flow. They walked through town, out towards the zero-kilometer marking, to Land's End. The monument to the Prestige Tanker, known as the Split, stood sentinel over all. The large flat smooth rocks invited sitting. They found a spot, down close to the water's edge. The ocean was quiet, waves rolling in, unfurling below them. This place, long a landing for endings, and a haven for the broken. Clair felt a connection with all the troubled souls who had sat here before her, and was grateful for Adam's solid warmth. She leaned into him.

'Are you cold?' he asked, wrapping his arm around her, pulling her into him.

'Yes, but it's OK. I like the feeling. It reminds me I'm alive.'

They watched the waves for a while longer until a fog, so dense they felt each drop of moisture on their faces, rolled in.

'I'm hungry,' Adam said. 'Thirsty, tired, stinking, and happier than I have been in a long time. How about you?'

Clair looked up at him, his eyes shining with joy.

'Yes, to all of it,' she answered, taking his arm as they walked towards the village. A cluster of young women stood talking, several small children gathered at their feet. A boy, around two years old, was playing with pebbles, lining them up in a circle around himself. He was dressed in a pair of blue shorts, and a red top. His hair was light brown, with wispy curls falling in front of his eyes. When he looked up, he smiled, two teeth showing through rosebud lips.

Clair stopped; her breath suspended. She felt a jolt of recognition, so strong, she wanted to grab him and hold him to her heart. A moment so dense with spirit, import, and substance collided with the past. Here he is, she knew.

Adam had begun walking away, heading towards a tapas bar just ahead on the left.

'Wait,' she called to him.

He turned and watched as she slipped her pack off. Her face was a portrait of wonder, as though she had discovered the secret of the universe and it was here, on this path, right now. He moved to stand closer to her.

Digging in her backpack, she pulled out the red truck. Walking up to his mother she asked her if it would be OK if she gave the boy this toy truck. She had learned enough Galician Spanish and Portuguese to be able to communicate well with locals.

'Oh yes, *gracias*,' the woman said, smiling down at her son.

Clair reached down, and laid the truck on the ground, in front of the boy.

He jumped up on his legs, clapping his hands together. Sitting back down, he began rolling the tiny truck around his pebble circle, making roaring noises. The mother smiled at Clair and Adam.

'Clair, are you sure?' Adam asked as they walked away, towards a café with a sign out offering tapas and *queimada*.

'Oh yes, I am sure. Adam, did you see him?' she asked, stopping and holding his arms. 'I mean, did you really see him?'

Adam looked into her eyes, then back at the boy. He took her hands from his arms, holding them to his heart.

'I do, Clair. I see him.'

About the Author

The Wave is Kristen's first novel. She studied dance and literature, and spent her early career as a dance teacher, performer, and choreographer before becoming a nurse. She obtained a Master's degree in nursing, working in psychiatry and palliative care. *The Wave* was inspired by her own pilgrimage on the Camino de Santiago. She has taken several writing courses through Faber Academy, Curtis Brown Creative, and Professional Writing Academy. Kristen lives on the Oregon Coast with her family.

Coming Soon...

The Bluff

Prologue

Body.

That was his first thought. The way the shape was lying, limbs reaching up into the air, tangled in long, slivery ropes of kelp, strands of seaweed like hair draping over the edges. A cold January morning, silver disk of waning moon floating above the horizon. The surfer drew in a deep breath as he stood looking over the fence at the vehicle pull-out, relieved to be the first to arrive. Word would spread fast through the mostly telepathic communication system, and he had been hoping to beat the locals out to Simpson's Reef. Surfable only about half the year, he didn't want to share this prized spot with anyone. The wind was light, offshore, at mid-tide.

He paused, looked again. Just a log. Not realizing how tense he had been, he exhaled, laughed at himself. The barking of the harbor seals covering the small, rocky haul-out off shore about five hundred yards, mixed with the waves and wind, seagulls cries, pulled his thoughts back towards the ocean and anticipation of his plunge into the water. Timing was everything here.

A fine marine layer covered the horizon. This cove, only

accessible at low tide, was quickly being submerged by the incoming tide. Just the right place, the right time for that clean break all the way to shore. Visualizing his long ride, he pictured himself cutting back early, so as not to crash. Scanning the cove and rocky shoreline, he planned exactly where he would enter the water.

Other debris from last night's low tide, driftwood, sections of crab traps, and bright colored floats littered the beach. Taking care climbing down the bluff carrying his surfboard, he felt every one of his forty-eight years. As he edged closer, he caught the glint of something bright and shiny, emanating from the center of the form.

Once his feet were on firmer ground, he laid his surfboard on a flat rock. A sense of dread gripped his insides. Not wanting to admit to himself what his hammering heart was telling him, he climbed down to the cove, small white birds fleeing at his approach. Looking closer, he could see clearly. The surfer fell to his knees, doubled over. He stayed that way for moments, frozen in a state of uncertainty. A form, female, arms wrapped around the log, as in a final embrace. Long, dark hair, encrusted with shells covered her face. A round, silver medallion, like the moon, dangled from her neck.

It was up to him, he realized. Everything that happened now. He wanted to stay with her, to bring comfort, and at the same time, knew he had to go for help. His cell was up at the top of the bluff, in his truck. Not wanting to leave her alone, exposed, he laid his surfboard against the log, covering her form as best he could. Saying a promise to her that he would bring help, he climbed back up the steep, rocky incline, to the top of the bluff. Finding his phone, he dialed 911. Standing at the fence, looking down onto the cove, he could see her, still and silent, waiting for someone to take her home.

Chapter 1

Sirens sliced through the Sunday morning quiet. Crows cawed in response, setting off a flurry of raucous calling back and forth. Geese waking up on the river bank below joined in, sounding alarm as their wings flapped in takeoff. *Somebody's having a rough start to a new day.*

This thought danced through Sawyer's mind as she and Rhys sat at their kitchen table, enjoying a relaxed, Sunday morning breakfast. Looking across the table at Rhys, she felt a deep sense of contentment, that they had been through so much these past few years, and now could enjoy the rewards that love and patience brought. Carli was fine and would continue to be fine. She had been so strong, teaching them, her parents, how to accept and support her.

'Did Carli make it back home?' Rhys asked, taking a long, last sip of his coffee. The remnants of an omelet pushed aside as he leaned forward, elbows resting on a bright yellow place mat. His hair, once a rich brown, now flecked with gray and silver, fell boyishly over his forehead. He flicked it back with his free hand.

Feeling suddenly uneasy, the sirens, remembering, Sawyer stood up, jostling the table.

'She said she was coming home but I don't know for sure.

She might have stayed in town at Meredith's. I'll check.'

Their daughter's room was at the top of a flight of steep, narrow stairs. This old river house, built at the turn of the century, was impossible to heat in winter. Sawyer shivered and pulled her fleece robe tighter around her as she navigated the dim stairway and then the hall, to Carli's room. Light filtered in through the skylight, revealing an empty, made up bed. Hesitating a moment, taking in the feminine patterns and colors, lilacs and yellows, fluffy pillows, taking up space along with stuffed animals, Sawyer felt a first tinge of concern. Brushing it away, she hurried back down the stairs.

'I think she must be in town, not wanting to drive all the way out here after the party. She said it would be a late night, some kind of club initiation, you know, the dancers and their theatrics.'

She shrugged her shoulders as she said this, acting lighthearted, but inside she felt a burning sensation, like acid. She began busying herself with wiping down the long granite counter top with a sponge.

'Did she call, text?' Rhys asked, as he scrolled through his own phone, looking for any messages or missed calls.

'No, but, that's not too odd, she knows we go to bed early and she wouldn't want to wake us.' Her answer ended on a lilt, as though asking a question rather than giving a fact.

Needing to keep moving, Sawyer began picking up their dishes from the table, carrying them to the sink. She turned and leaned against the counter, her face showing her growing concern. She crossed her arms across her chest. The morning sunlight was beginning to shine through the white lace curtains, warming her back.

'Even though we've told her over and over that we don't

mind. I'll just wait a bit, too early to call her. I'm sure she's sleeping. These kids she's with now, they're good kids. I don't worry about them. Nothing like the ones from before,' she said, turning around and looking out over the river, high now with the winter rains.

She didn't want to alarm Rhys. Maybe he was doing the same for her? she considered. That was how it had been before, both of them pretending until it was too late. Or, almost too late. Carli had survived and so had they, as a family.

'Sawyer, do these kids know about Carli?' Rhys asked.

Sawyer turned her head, looking at him. Seeing fear displayed in his eyes, his mouth, a tight line, and shoulders, reaching up towards his ears, she trembled.

'I don't think so, but Carli's so private. She doesn't talk about it much to me, just seems to be happy and enjoying her life here. That's all I care about.' Sawyer replied, picking up a red checked towel from the dish drain beside the sink, and twisting it around and around in her hands.

'I guess. I still worry about it. Kids can be so cruel,' Rhys said, pushing away from the table. He walked over to the counter, standing next to Sawyer, looking out the window. 'She's OK, I would know it if she wasn't, in here you know,' he said, pointing to his heart.

The grassy bank leading down to the river was frosty. Leaves shimmered with dripping ice, creating a prism of rainbows as the sun crested the coastal range mountains to the east.

More sirens, different ones now. Their house was only a few miles from the beach, where accidents happened frequently, especially this time of year. Drownings as people underestimated the strength of the surf; sneaker waves washing sightseers off rocks, into the ocean; wrecks as people partied, smoked, drank and then tried to drive. The narrow, twisting roads, called the Seven Devils for good reason, could be treacherous.

They turned towards each other, bodies leaning together, as they had been doing for over twenty years. Sawyer looked up, smiled at him with a look of relief, that the sirens weren't for them.

'Yes, I know,' she said, snuggling into his chest, wrapping her arms tighter around his body, enjoying his heat.

The sound of the Coast Guard helicopter's big rotary blades captured their attention, their gazes returning to the window. Looking west, towards the ocean, they could see it making wide circles, over the shoreline.

'Must be doing some training,' Rhys said, gently releasing his arms from around Sawyer. 'I'm going to get dressed, maybe get in some golf today. It's supposed to warm up later. Want to come?'

'No, I'll stay here, wait for Carli. I want to hear all about her night. I'll run into town, get something special for dinner. It's her last free evening before school starts again,' Sawyer answered, pushing her curly auburn hair back from her face. 'Maybe I'll go for a swim at the club. You go ahead, I'll finish up here.'

As she began to rinse their dishes, her phone, laying on the counter, beeped a notification. Rhys's echoed, the incessant noise shattering the morning's peace, and their world.